Long Time Walk on Water

Joan Barbara Simon

Published in 2009 by New Generation Publishing

Copyright © 2009 Joan Barbara Simon
www.joanbarbarasimon.com

First Edition

The author asserts the moral right under the Copyright, Designs and Patents Act 1988 to be identified as the author of this work.

All Rights reserved. No part of this publication may be reproduced, stored in a retrieval system or transmitted, in any form or by any means without the prior consent of the author, nor be otherwise circulated in any form of binding or cover other than that which it is published and without a similar condition being imposed on the subsequent purchaser.

A CIP catalogue for this title is available from the British Library

Also by Joan Barbara Simon:

The Red Room

Voicing those questions, those desires which convention has tamed out of the 'good' female, Joan Barbara Simon and her chorus of eloquent, critical protagonists dare to sidestep propriety in their search for sincere personal fulfilment and a redefinition of the intimate experience.

'Surprising literary maturity.' *WASAFIRI*

Mut@tus

Miss Virginia Mendes stumbles from the bourgeois bliss of her brittle marriage into the world of virtual romance, convinced that He must be out there, somewhere. Discovering instead... a woman who learns to know her mind and sheds her qualms about giving the world a piece of it. Of her sensuality, her philosophy, her triumphs and her pitfalls... all the Woman she is.

'This is quite simply one of the most extraordinary and brilliant books I have ever read (…) Its prose, like its subject matter, leaps to life off the page. Dark, disturbing, and forensically brilliant at dissecting twenty-first century sexuality. It has everything Anais Nin and Brett Easton Ellis have, wrapped up in the same incredible package.'
Online reviewer, Amazon UK

'Sexy, funny, thoughtful read... Approach with an open mind and be prepared to be entertained. This is that great thing: a life-affirming book.'
A. S., Isle of Skye, Scotland

Introduction

Joan Barbara Simon is the author of *Mut@tus*, which she herself describes as 'intellectual erotica'. She is also the author of *The Red Room*, a collection of poetry and short prose pieces of the most exquisite sensitivity and sensuality. Unlike the other works, her novel, *Long Time Walk on Water*, is much more in line with the post-colonial tradition of writers such as Andrea Levy and Caryl Phillips. By thus moving Janus-like in and out of the post-colonial tradition, Simon has become adept at crossing all sorts of borders, from linguistic and narrative to racial and sexual ones.

In *Long Time Walk on Water*, Simon also crosses generic borders between fiction and autobiography on the one hand and between realism and fairy tale on the other. While some episodes could be read as at least partly autobiographical, the author warns her readers not to 'go in search of strict adherence to the facts or chronology of life, least of all vis-à-vis my own, for the protagonists slip in and out of names like garments, and Time shifts the plates of the earth.' The true-to-life side of her fiction is reinforced by short sections providing factual details about Jamaican emigration to the United Kingdom, Enoch Powell and British politics of the 1960s, racial categorizations of black slaves, etc. At the same time, she introduces a fairy-tale framework that questions the assumptions of realistic novel-writing. Thus the novel is subtitled a 'family fairytale' and most of the episodes are given richer interpretive potential by being intertextually linked with particular nursery rhymes.

The style of the novel is marked by frequent shifts from Standard English to Jamaican English and vice-versa, as in the following passage:

> He snorted even more –
> > him a pig man, Cato thought
>
> then Walter continued on his way.
> She could smell him before she could even see him. Mek me feel sick.

As the point of view shifts from Cato to his mother, it is marked both by graphological deviations and by the shift to Jamaican English at the very end. The perspective is often that of a child and hence amusingly defamiliarizing. Here, for instance, is Mandy musing on the Sikh boys in her neighbourhood: 'And they're not allowed to cut their hair. And the boys wear it in a bun on the top of their head under a hanky.' Moreover, Simon's language is studded with richly evocative metaphors, of which the following are just two – though interconnected – examples:

> Ruby closed her eyes and sang. And when she sang, the music unbuttoned her pain with its gentle fingers and stood aside to watch it chiffon to the floor.

> Gertrude, for the first time in her life, found that she was singing. There were no words, and it was not really even a song, but it was something beyond her control; the secret language, and it wafted over to the midwife in dolorous clouds to smoke a dance before her eyes. It danced of pain. Of shame. Of broken pride. It circled the room in search of promises. Stroked the panes in need of visions. Rose from the girl on the bed who could not have her baby.

Both Ruby and Gertrude had a baby forcibly taken away from them, and it may be that such metaphorical humanizing of the mother's pain is the only way of making it bearable. The song, even when wordless, is the 'secret language' that binds the women together and gives them strength. By thus emphasizing the pain and hardships borne by women, Simon takes her place in a long line of brilliant Black British and Caribbean women writers including Louise Bennett, Jean 'Binta' Breeze, Michelle Cliff, Merle Collins, Lorna Goodison, Merle Hodge, Jamaica Kincaid, Andrea Levy, Grace Nichols, Marlene Nourbese Philip and Joan Riley, among others. As Nichols puts it in her poem, 'We the Women':

> Yet we the women

who praises go unsung
who voices go unheard
who deaths they sweep
aside
as easy as dead leaves
(*i is a long memoried woman*, Karnak, 1983/1990, p. 12)

What these writers have in common is a desire to fill the historical gap or silence by making the women's voices heard and telling their stories – both the good and the bad sides of the stories.

Other major themes of the novel include sexual awakening, the beauty and brutality of human relationships, racism and discrimination, as well as the traumatic experiences of young children at the hands of frequently callous parents. Indeed, the long line of inadequate mother- and father-figures is somewhat reminiscent of similar characters in James Joyce's *Dubliners*. One of the most memorable moments in Joyce's collection of stories is the terrible scene at the end of 'Counterparts', where Farrington, after a series of frustrating experiences both at work and in the pub, vents his pent-up anger on his little son when he eventually gets home. Because the boy let the fire go out, his drunken father grabs a stick and 'viciously' strikes the boy who in his fright and pain cries out:

> Don't beat me, pa! And I'll ... I'll say a *Hail Mary* for you ... I'll say a *Hail Mary* for you, pa, if you don't beat me ... I'll say a *Hail Mary* ... (*Dubliners*, Penguin, 1914/1992, p. 94)

In *Long Time Walk on Water*, there is an even more traumatic episode: this is the haunting story of young Cato, who grows up in Jamaica with Miss May, until his parents arrange for him to join them in England. Cato now finds himself living 'in a world filled with strangers ... whom he could neither love nor understand'. In this state of utter loneliness and lovelessness, he withdraws more and more into his own world, dreaming about Jamaica and wetting his bed. The violence of the subsequent toilet scene is almost unbearable: the father thrusts Cato's head into the toilet bowl while flushing it repeatedly and nearly choking him. Finally, with his hand and feet tied, he is locked up in the dark cellar:

> Cato whimpered in the dark, doubled back like an abnormal foetus. His hands, his eyes burned; burned like the sun in Jamaica, the sun in the back yard of the house where Miss May lived. His eyes burned like the sun, only now he could see no orange; he could see no orange and red. He could only see black.

Another tragic episode is the story of Joy's punishment and exclusion from all family meals, as a result of which she becomes, like Cato, a stranger in her own house, and is eventually reduced to a state of near starvation. As in so much of Caribbean women's writing, it is the grandmother who tries to feed Joy and restore her to health, at the same time turning on the inadequate mother who 'mash up her own chile'. In this way, the strong grandmother figure links *Long Time Walk on Water* to such archetypal Caribbean figures as Nanny, the Maroon freedom fighter, or Christophine in Jean Rhys' *Wide Sargasso Sea*.

Moreover, there is the disturbing absence from the novel – after a brief appearance in the very first chapter – of Rose's children, Marlene and Leroy. She left them in the care of her friend Junie when she (Rose) journeyed to England in search of work and a better life. In one of her letters to Junie, she writes that she 'would work 24 hours a day, walk a long long time on water if it mean my children can come over and get a good start in life.' This by the way is also the explanation for the title of the novel. Yet what happens is that Rose embarks upon a relationship with a white Englishman, spends her money on an expensive bedspread, new clothes, hairdo and make-up, and seemingly forgets her children more and more. At the same time, however, the novel remains ambiguous about Rose's change: she feels guilty about buying some of the things she does, and her relationship with Jack is aborted before it can develop into a full love-affair.

The similarities between *Long Time Walk on Water* and *Dubliners* are not limited to thematic parallels but there are also obvious structural parallels: though *Long Time Walk on Water* is not divided into separate short stories, it has a loose episodic structure recounting – sometimes comic and sometimes tragic – slices of the lives of various characters. In this Introduction, I have focused on the children, because their experiences are often the most traumatic ones, but the adult characters are no less memorable, whether it is Sally, the unmarried mother who confronted her daughter prejudiced teacher, or Uncle Roy, who proves to be a source of inspiration for the narrator, 'opening the wardrobe so that I may feel the fabric of his life brush my soul'. Together, this almost Dickensian cast of characters produces a dazzling literary work which deserves a place not only in the tradition of post-colonial writing but more generally in the tradition of the English novel. Like Joyce, Simon is a consummate verbal artist: just as the former uses a style of 'scrupulous meanness' to convey the deadness of modernist life, the latter uses rapid and delicate shifts in point of view and sensuous, metaphorical prose to capture the harshness of the post-colonial experience in late 60s – early 70s London.

Professor Jean-Jacques Weber
University of Luxembourg, Luxembourg

From the author

The summer of '89, I remember it well. Public transport strikes in London. Having to walk from my grandmother's in Brixton to the language school in Bayswater where I was teaching. Losing my way through the London parks and arriving unforgivably late, only to discover that most of the students had spared themselves the battle so there was no one to teach, anyway. Heatwaves rippling up from the tarmac. The scorching sun sapping your energy and dehydrating your nerves. That auspicious summer was instrumental in re-shaping my entire attitude to the spoken word. My head filled with still vaguely understood terminologies which had nonetheless heightened my sensitivity to the two dialectal strains of my own childhood (the one, gritty, guttural, with its echoes of African tongues, the other, chewy, nasal, learnt in the playgrounds and down the alleys of London), I would fall into a sofa at my grandmother's hot, crowded council house where the telly was almost always on, and marvel at the effortless beauty of her speech; at its colours and sequins, its fine stitches and imagery. To my amazement, I discovered that my grandmother, *my* grandmother, was a singer, a warrior and a heroine. Yes, a heroine. How poorly we understand the sacrifices she was prepared to make; rending herself from her children and crossing the Atlantic, ignorant of what awaited her, more than a little frightened and certain only of her faith in God. How new life in England would be. With what relish letters sent "back home" would be read. The jealousies, prejudice and impatience one could expect to encounter in the Motherland, but also the gifts of companionship, joy and love...

A big thank you, granma. One big big thank you from you grand-daughter.

A word or two on my language. My rendition of Jamaican English is governed by two factors. Phonetically oriented, it is partly modelled on the melodies of the language acquired at home, thus the experience gained by ear, buttressed by the Dictionary of Jamaican English (1985), edited by F. G. Cassidy and R. B. Le Page. At the same time, and recognizing the need to make it accessible to the untrained ear, I have 'smoothed out' Jamaican English in places, choosing instead standard English spelling whilst attempting to retain the Jamaican syntax. My intention, first and foremost, is not to deliver a sociolinguistic masterpiece, for which feat, in any case, I regard myself as being ill-equipped. Rather, I seek to transmit something of the vigour of this wonderful dialect. Pardon, therefore the occasional inaccuracies, which, no doubt, have nested themselves in these lines.

Long Time Walk on Water is a family fairytale, thus suspend your disbelief; do not go in search of strict adherence to the facts or chronology of life, least of all vis-à-vis my own, for the protagonists slip in and out of names, like garments, and Time shifts like the plates of the earth.

JBS. July, 2009

For my family, past, present and future.

And for Inès, who taught me how to love.

Foreword

To one who bears the sweetest name
And adds a lustre to the same
Who shares my joys
Who cheers when sad
The greatests friend I ever had
Long life to her for there's no other
Can take the place of my dear mother
(Anon.)

(poem on a tea-towel pinned to the wall in grandma's kitchen)

The facts:

Jamaica

The name Jamaica is derived from the aboriginal, Xaymaca, meaning 'land of wood and water'. The capital city, Kingston, was founded in 1693. With a surface area of approximately 11,000km² divided into 14 parishes, and the largest island in the Britsh West Indies, Jamaica lies 145 kilometers south of Cuba in the Caribbean Sea. Discovered by Columbus in 1494, it remained in Spanish hands until conquered by the British in 1655. From the C18th negro slaves were imported to work the plantations as the aboriginal people had died out under the hard labour imposed upon them by the Spaniards. Jamaicans - 80% black population, 80% Protestants - speak English, and their patois consists of a colourful mixture of English, old and new, as well as Spanish, French and African tongues. A member of the Commonwealth, Jamaica gained independence on August 6th, 1962.

The Jamaican flag was officially hoisted on 6th August, 1962. It consists of a golden diagonal cross separating triangles of green above and below, and ones of black to the left and to the right. The colour gold stands as a symbol for sunshine and natural treasures, whilst green is an allusion to hope and to agriculture. Black, finally, represents the problems of the past, but is also a symbol of the present.

The Jamaican coat of arms, conferred upon the then British colony in 1661, underwent a slight variation in 1957. The silver shield, decorated with a red cross studded with five pineapples, has on its top a crocodile, and is supported to the left and right by a pair of Arawak Indians on a ribbon with its well-known saying: 'out of many, one people'.

Great Britain

Great Britain is the official name used for England, Scotland and Wales since 1603, when the English and Scottish crowns were united in the person of King James VI of Scotland, who then became King James I of England. With Northern Ireland, it forms the United Kingdom, the capital city of which is London. The United Kingdom of Great Britian and Northern Ireland, with a surface area of approximately 244,000km², is divided into 49 counties and 6 Metropolitan counties in the case of England, 8 counties in the case of Wales, 26 districts in Northern Ireland, and 12 regions in Scotland. Inhabited by the Celts from C7th BC, and occupied by the Romans until 407 AD, Great Britain was then invaded by various Germanic tribes and finally conquered by the Normans in 1066. The first parliament came into existence in 1246. From the C16th onwards one witnessed the expansion of the British Empire, out of which the Commonwealth of Nations was created after the Second World War.

The British national flag is popularly known as the *Union Jack*, although this term is in fact correct only when the flag is flown on the jackstaff of a warship. The Union Jack was officially hoisted in its current form on 1 January 1801, and is a combination of the crosses of the patron saints; the thick red cross of St George (England), the white diagonal cross of St Andrew (Scotland) and the red diagonal cross of St Patrick (Ireland), inserted into the cross of St Andrew. The national colour of Scotland - blue - forms the background of the Union Jack.

The royal coat of arms in its current form came into use upon the coronation of Queen Victoria in 1837, with a slightly varied version in use in Scotland from 1910. The heart-shaped shield unites the emblems of England, Scotland and Ireland; the three leopards of England occupy the first and last quarters, whilst the second is occupied by the lion of Scotland and the third by the harp of Ireland. Around the shield is the saying: 'the shame be his who thinks ill of it'. Below the shield, the famous: 'God and my right'. Supporting the shield to the left is the British lion, and to the right, a unicorn (formerly the Welsh dragon). The whole is crowned with a royal crown guarded by the British lion.

The fiction:

1

The plane landed with a bump. Rose squeezed herself against the seat, her fingers clasped around the cold armrests. When she opened her eyes the plane was still racing along the runway so she dug her forefingers into the rectangular metal ashtrays and closed her eyes once more. She had tried to learn the national anthem in case anyone asked her, after all, how could she just pick up herself and go all that way and not know a thing. Nobody she knew had learnt the British national anthem; they had better things to worry about. United Kingdom. Rose could think of nothing. Two addresses ensconced in a pocket of her handbag, that was it. United Kingdom. Great Britain. The Motherland. *Hinglan…*

This was it, that moment that had been beckoning her as she stood over the grave of her starved child, for whom the corn she had planted in desperation had not grown quickly enough, despite good J.A. sunshine and her nightly prayers. That moment was now real and rapping at her door. The plane had not crashed, even as it had swooped down over the island, pecking like a famished crow at a crumb. She had not been sucked out of the emergency exit, nor had her food got up of its own accord to float around when the stewardess had brought the passengers their dinner. And there was air enough for everyone, like in a train, really, only you could not open the windows.

The captain spoke a few words. It was a chilly day in London, they could expect repeated drizzly spells. One or two moans on board, one or two jovial remarks that the captain should take them back.

"Yu can unfasten yu seatbelt now. We reach." The Jamaican stewardess spoke in a gruff, warlike manner, not bothering to smooth out her Jamaican accent as she had done for the other, white, passengers.
"Neh figget seh yu a two pitni a huome fi feed..."[1]
"Wat me have at home to do is none a your business."

Junie and One-foot had accompanied Rose, Leroy and Marlene to the airport, each in their Sunday best. One-foot had been talking about nothing else for weeks, over dominoes, summoning up indifference as he told how he would be going to Kingston to see someone off at the airport. The Jamaican check-in assistant was quick to pick up the whiff of these country people. She saved Rose for last.
"Name."
"Emily Thompson."
She flicked through the passport.
"How long yu gwine stay in Hinglan?"
"Fi good."
"Who yu madda?"
"Hortence Thompson."
"An yu farda?"
"Herbert Granger."
She put the obligatory tag on the old, worn suitcase and shoved it back across to Rose.
"So dem nat married? How old yu is?"
"Nineteen."
"Chilren?"
"Marlene an Leroy. Marlene's five and Leroy's tree."
"Dem full name."
"Marlene Hortence Thompson. Leroy Steven Thompson."
One-foot: Kuya![2] Is wat dis whole heap a questioning? Wat mek yu nevva question di other passenga? Yu only look at dem ticket

---

[1] neh *figget...* = don't forget that you have two children at home to feed
[2] k*uya* = look here!

an weigh dem loggage. Rose, no answer no more question, yaa[3]. Is nosey di black bitch nosey.

Check-in assistant: You quashie[4] don't know notting! Yu tink seh because yu gat a likkle money can fly yu can ignore di rules an regulation? You tink dem gwine let anybody off di street march in a Hinglan widdout dem want to know is who yu is?

One-foot: Is who live on di street? Gyal, yu betta *watch* yu mouth fore me *buss* yu lip! T'raated![5]

Check-in assistant: Is *ignorant* people like you give black people a bad name.

She resumed the interrogation. "Married?"

"No, me nat married."

"Is who dem farda?"

"Tek it easy now, yu hear Rose? No worry 'bout di pitni dem. Me look after dem fine fine till yu can send fi dem."

"Me know yu gwine treat dem good, Junie."

"An you watch di white man dem. No have notting to do wid dem. Notting! Dem act like dem nice an den they tek yu chop off yu head, yu hear me?"

"Gu weh, One-foot, yu too styupid. Nobaddy gwine chop off me head!"

"Yu styupid fi true!" scoffed Junie, her tone mellow, her eyes yolky with adoration.

"Mammi, me no want yu fi go![6]" in her Sunday dress, her hair neatly plaited and her skin oiled till it shone, Marlene made one last desperate attempt to keep her mummy. "Dem deh seh me madda run weh leff[7] me." Tears.

"Behave yusself, Marlene! No tek no notice. You know seh me woulda nevva run weh leff unnu[8]. Me deh go because me no have no choice. Me gat no *choice*, yu hear me? You tell dem

---

[3] *yaa* = you hear (me)
[4] *quashie* = country bumpkin
[5] *t'raated* = Jamaican swear word
[6] *no want yu fi go* = don't want you to go
[7] *dem de seh me madda run weh leff me* = they're saying that my mother has run away and left me
[8] *unnu* = you (pl)

from me! An when dem deh carry on, tell dem is jealous dem jealous dat yu madda gwine give unnu di chance to be someting in dis world, yu hear me?"

"Lord, mek she arrive safe an well," Junie prayed.

"Thank you for travelling with us. I hope you had a pleasant journey," the English stewardess speak like a book.

"Very. Tank yu." Rose stepped out of the aircraft. Into the Motherland.

2

The door slammed after a quick "Thank you!", after the taxi-driver had been paid and had winked at her as he drove off. From the corner of her eye she spied the cab-man wheel his vehicle round in a seamless U-turn further down the road. In his rear-view mirror, he had her framed, still standing where he had left her, looking up at the houses.

So, this was Beswick Road. An infantry of redbrick and glass, shoulder to shoulder; the house number painted on the pane above every front door demuring half a dozen steps in from the pavement, past the small, kempt front gardens which watched without comment. Not many people on the street. Not like back home. Pale, lonely-looking, dreary herds had wandered, morosely, past her cab window as cab-man insisted through the London streets to her new home, *Hinglan*, where the sun seemed to have changed its mind. Rose wondered how on earth it might have come about that such a cold, miserable place be praised melodiously in parishes far and wide for its green and pleasant lands. It began drizzling. Again. Light flakes of water you don't even notice at first, playing with you, meaning no real harm, but Rose had had her hair done especially, plus her clothes were new, so she picked up her suitcase, pushed open the garden gate and mounted the steps to the front door. A three-storey house with further rooms, it seemed, in the basement.

"Lord have mercy! Dem live undergrown like some sort of animal!"

When she pushed the bell marked *Brown*, it screeched, alarmed, as though Rose had unexpectedly, maliciously, dug her fingernails into its side. No-one came at once.

"If yu tink me ringing dat bell one more time!" she cursed through her bottom lip, taking a step back to crane her neck up at the house. Her new home. She wondered how long for. Another step back and she caught a young black girl sweep the curtains back from a ground floor window, report over her shoulder what she saw, then disappear before she had had the time to catch Rose smooth her skirt out as she went to wait at the bottom of the stairs, her handbag swinging from the crook of her arm, her posture studiously polite and 'educated'.

"Juss hopen dat blaasted door before me drench, yaa," and whilst the cussing came naturally, she had to will her toes down hard against the sole of her shoe to stop her right foot from tapping impatiently that way. Inside the house a door opened. Was closed. A key laboured in the lock to keep whatever out of sight. The floorboards creaked all the way to the front door, which inched open just enough to reveal half of a slender young West Indian girl.

"Yes?"

Mrs Brown, who had had to go to work despite the new arrival, had instructed her daughter, Carmen, to let the woman in and show her the room. Rose followed Carmen up the stairs. Someone had been cooking. Curried mutton. The radio was on behind a door on the first landing. Sounded like the news. Maybe she should try to speak proper English. It might get her a better job, Rose thought, but then, everyone had understood her well enough so far. She wondered what sort of a person her boss would be. She had never been inside a factory before (*im betta not tell me him have someone else fi di jab when me go there tomorro*)... The banister sleeked across the palm of her hand. The stairs creaked ignominiously beneath the carpet. Carmen felt she ought to say something. Asked Rose if she reach over safely. Yes, Rose said and considered telling her the story about the passport but changed her mind. Later, if they became friends. Carmen was younger than her and didn't much look as though she knew anything about anything. Did she like England, Carmen asked. So far so good, Rose said, noticing that Carmen did not speak Jamaican English.

"Tell me someting. Yu born here?"

"Hm-hm, I was."

"So how long yu madda here already?"

"About twenty years, I reckon. Somefing like that."

"An how old yu is?"

"I'm nearly fifteen."

"Yu gat any children?"

Carmen laughed, "Me? You gotta be joking! My mum'd *kill* me!" And then Carmen ran out of things to say so she continued up the stairs in silence.

Someone had tried to pretty up the second landing with a bushy busy-lizzy in a plastic mesh flowerpot next to their door. The bright pink flowers stretched out in the direction of sunlight from stems as thick as rhubarb. The occasional petal had fallen onto the doormat calling Welcome To My Home. All the doors were painted brown. Two or three doors on each landing. Dark brown carpet with autumn leaves wafting up the stairs. Later, Rose would ease out of her shoes. Run her toes along the carpet. *Yes, man. Rich man country, dis.* Let me wait an see what di other people dem here is like, she was thinking when Carmen said, shyly, "That's your room," handing over the key she had been playing with in her pocket the whole time.

A miniscule room at the very top of the house, but at least she did not have to share it with anyone. One small window, looking out onto the backs of the houses in the street running parallel to Beswick Road. Little poky patches of green with junk lying around; rusting pieces of she knew not what, bicycle wheels, car parts, clothes hung out to dry but getting wet again. One or two gardens had been done up rather nicely, though, with rose bushes and other pretty flowers just dying to come out. One or two trees already in bloom. Pretty, thought Rose, looking down on the well-tended gardens. Real pretty. A woman ran out in her slippers to pluck her washing from the line. Workmen busy on a roof further along. She heard a crash every now and then as old tiles were tossed down the front side of a house she could not see but was pretty sure looked just like hers.

Mrs Brown's house had a garden too. Not that you were able to see it from so high up. Not that this bothered her. Rose could not imagine she would have much time to sit in the garden, anyway. Share such a small patch of green with a house full of strangers? And who wanted to sit outside in that everlasting cold anyway? Wrap up wrap up like an Eskimo and can't enjoy yourself? She had her own room. That would have to do. There, nobody could pester her with questions she would rather not answer. She had not come to England to make friends, she had come to work, she told herself as she walked away from the window, trying to establish some sort of feeling for the room that was now hers.

The walls were papered brown. Brown bordering on red with small orange flowers between a network of green diamonds. The paper was loosening in places, peeling back to reveal a cream-coloured underside, and in others, it rose away from the wall in small, blistery bubbles. The carpet, unlike the one in the hallway, a murky blue and reasonably new although it had already started to fray around the door. Like the flowers, the pipework was orange. A wheel-around paraffin heater, stationed in a corner, with enough paraffin left in it for a week or so till she had sorted herself out. So this was to be her home. Once again, she wondered how long for, wondered if her children were missing her already and if she would miss them enough, it was so new; leaving Jamaica, flying over, riding in a taxi, her hair, her clothes; she sincerely hoped she would miss her children enough. In that tiny room, dominated by the double bed, her landlady had found precious little yet just enough space to squeeze in a table, a chair, a small wardrobe and a bedside table. The stains on the mattress, to Rose's mind, highly suspicious. The cigarette burns... Carmen watched her face from the doorway, relieved when Rose made no comment.

"It'll be a really nice room once you doll it up a bit," Carmen encouraged. On the middle floor was a shared kitchen, she went on. You needed your own pots and pans. To punch gas, you put your coins in the slot on the side of the gas metre, then you turned the knob. Toilet's outside, Carmen spoke to her feet.

"Tell me someting. Is how many people deh live here?"

Eighteen, said Carmen, on her way down the stairs. Money matters Rose should talk over with Mrs Brown when she got back from work, Carmen threw over her shoulder.

Too tired to unpack, yet in great need of sleep, Rose forced herself to open her suitcase to take out the essentials:
her blanket
her nightdress
an old school cardigan she always wore to bed
and the picture. Her long fingers carefully undid the bow she had made out of a length of string, then smoothed back the layers of old newspaper. (Smile). Walking over to the bedside table, she let her fingers brail over the glass frame.

... yu madda thief, she run weh leff unnu!
Behave yusself, Marlene! No tek no notice. You know seh me woulda nevva run weh leff unnu. Me deh go because me no have no choice. Me gat no choice, yu hear me? You tell dem fram me! An wen dem deh carry on, tell dem is jealous dem jealous dat yu madda gwine give unnu di chance to be someting in dis world, yu hear me? ...

She moved her handbag aside to make a little space. Set the picture down, carefully, like an egg. Quick, quick, out of her clothes, her shoulders clenched against the unaccustomed cold. Rose folded her new orange suit, placing it reverently over the back of the chair before she wriggled into her nightie and buttoned up her school cardigan. Cold and dark was this place, man, but she would worry about that later. Wrapped up in the blanket, she thanked the Lord for bringing her over safely.

Shut eye.

3

London, April --, 19--

Dear Junie,

How are you? I'm sure you are fine and One-foot is fine. I hope Marlene is fine and Leroy is fine. Give them my love.
I cross over safely. England is very cold. It's raining all the time and there's no good sunshine. With weather like this the people bound to be miserable. I already miss Jamaica. The address I had is correct when I get to England. The houses are really small and squash up together. Never mind. A roof is a roof. I am so tired after the journey, but I think, let me sit down and let you know I reach safe. Tomorow I must go and look work. London is so big there must be work for everyone. As you know I have a job promised to me. I hope him don't forget. You know how them say the streets of London are paved with gold, well, there's not one word of truth in it. But I hope all the same that things work out how I planned and that I don't come here for nothing.
Hear this. I get off the plane go to customs or immigrations or something like that. Him ask me, is this your passport? What a stupid question! Me say, of course is me passport. Whose passport it suppose to be? Hear him; it could belong to anybody for all he know, we all look the same. I glad One-foot wasn't there or him would box off him facety head. Generally the white people friendly enough. So many of them stop and ask me if they can help me at the airport. I didn't know what to do. All I had was the slip of paper with the address. Some of them look at me a bit funny but is ignorant them ignorant. One woman take me to the taxi and tell the taxi driver me is a friend so him not to drive no long route but take me direct. Me nearly die laughing! The

English taxi them peculiar you see! Big and black like a bug and you got room for a whole heap a luggage in the back with you. Them even got one clapdown seat if is more people. We drive a long long time before we get to London. Them got one big red bus them call double-decker. Take you everywhere you want to go, the taxi driver tell me. The taxi driver nosey you see! Him want to know where me come from and how long me going to stay. I just smile and tell him little bit. You can't be unfriendly. Tell One-foot I still got my head.

I am very tired and I'm going to sleep a little bit. I will write you soon. I'm surprised, I see quite a few black faces here in London. Say hello to everybody for me and let them know I reach safe.

Junie, Marlene, Leroy, One-foot, goodbye and God bless.

Yours,

Rose.

4

Tell the truth and run -

*Run, as fast as you can
You can't catch me I'm the -*

Little teapot short and stout,

Here's my handle...

Here's my spout

Cato was a quiet little boy. Large, doe eyes. Fleshy nostrils. Luscious lips. Cute in his own way. Vulnerable-looking to a point. In any case the type of face, the skinny legs, the crusty knees that will tug at a woman's protective sentiments. A helmet of tight curly hair shielded his head from the intense heat of the Jamaican sun, and glistened bronze as he sat playing with some twig clamped in his excited hand. This weapon proved to be just the thing for crushing the ants he had recently unearthed. So he jabbed. Twisted. He pasted the black spots to the ground and put an end to their haste. His free hand, disinterested in such one-sided combat, went in search of other pleasures, namely in the nasal and aural orifices. Now, here was adventure indeed! Wily digits circled, plunged, scooped, always bringing their find forward for inspection, gaining varying degrees of silent approval before happily trotting off in search of more buried treasure.

"Yaakshi! Y*aaa*aksh*iii*! But stap! Is where di 'h', 'e' an two sticks[9] is dis blasted likkle pitni! Cato Octavius Marrison!" Miss May filled the yard with his name. "Yaakshi kwittabag! Is where him deh?[10]"

The familiar voice boomed sonorously, and would have motivated every other little boy to brush off his pants before scuttling over, his face tinged with the hue of an apology. Cato, impervious, squatted right on there in the dusty hide-out, adamant in his desire to terminate his minute enemy. If others might only detect an aggressive note in these castigations, velvet-voiced, then good luck to them. Both Miss May and her Yaakshi knew how to honour, wordlessly, the conspiracy of their mutual affection. She might rant, shove and swipe. Still, not a soul ever walked God's earth who could box his head as hard as his Miss May, box him literally off his feet or singe his ears with a well-placed lick, yet convey more more more than any other female with her lingering touch or the moist pressure of her lips upon responding skin.

"Dat likkle pitni you see, man! Me gwine cut him likkle black behind!"

"Him giving you any trouble, Miss May?"

Cato's ears seized the question, the voice attributed in an instant. The stick, discarded, rattled to the ground. Clouds of brown-grey dust faithfully followed his coated soles as they ran off into the bush.

Goneril was her rightful name; the name on her school reports and on the church scroll. She used it seldom. And heard it seldom. To call her Goneril was to identify oneself as an outsider. Uninvited to share those moments of authenticity; a thick slice of slitty-eyed bitching, the dawn-dewed sighting of the girl with her hair uncombed and her night-rags crumpled. The unabashed scratching of some body part, or the fingernailing of dirt from one hand into the palm of the other. None of these did Goneril Morrison perform. The originality of the rightful name was a

---

[9] i.e. hell (the 'two sticks' being double 'l')
[10] *is where him deh?* = where is he?

fierce point of combat in the female community. Many a church scroll that had testified to the aspirations of young mothers for whom Biblical names had lost their appeal. Many a vicar wincing inwardly as he placed his hand upon the head of Princess, Duke, Admiral and Count, who would later be found scratching around the back yard as Tété, Dar-dar, One-son and Pinkie, or even under some perfectly normal appellation; Sarah, John, June. Having decided upon a sufficiently elevated name for her daughter, Goneril's mother promptly kipped the distinction overboard and proceeded to call the child Vechie,

who now stood, a dark, slender, reed of a girl, in the middle of Miss May's kitchen, small eyes inspecting, silently approving of the cleanliness where her son lived. She sported a new hairstyle, dutifully checked in the broken mirror clinging to the wall in the passage. Reasonably attractive is what most would say, her face enhanced by her unusual dark brown eyes with their blue, outer ring. If only she had been a few shades lighter, she might even have been what many would call pretty. Goneril pulled herself up to her full height, wishing her behind were not so 'well-formed', shall we say, nevertheless feeling this to have been amply compensated for by her thin lips and her widely commended intelligence,

which had not, alas, provided the necessary armour to stop her from waking up very ill in the mornings when still only a young girl of fifteen. And once again when she was in her eighteenth year. On both occasions she had borne the attacks nobly, her eyes firing poison-blue darts of scorn at all who dared to glance below her shoulders.

"Top in di class and on top in di bed! Yes me dear, is so it go."

"Wat? Dat blacka chaaka-chaaka gyal buck up already? Wid a name sound like some disease s'mady me know pick fram one small-island woman, she can count herself lucky, but you know, is every hoe got im stick a bush..."

Work had been difficult to find, with the little there was usually reserved for the soft-haired, light-skinned girls who took the places in the banks, offices and shops irrespective of any want of skill, intelligence or interest. Of this gossamer hierarchy Goneril was perfectly aware. At school, along with many others, she had suffered the taunts of the brown-skinned girls, of the mixed girls and of the Indian girls who would let loose their hair as a sign of superiority and bask in the tangible envy of their ugly step-sisters. Another Indian playmate might be privileged to brush out the shiny, blue-black mass, silking it through fingers, weighing and assessing it like an experienced merchant. Ugly step-sisters stood at a distance. And gawped. If evva me did have a pair of scissors, yu see! Goneril's hair barely covered her ears. Yes, they were all black, but there was black, and there was *black*. No slipping through that boundary for Goneril Morrison, for all that she had blue rings around her soft brown eyes.

The children, an encumbrance, had to go. The eldest, a girl, went to stay with a woman from the district with grown-up children, willing to raise another, glad for a little company along with the prospect of some helping hands. The boy, Cato, went to stay with Miss May. It was known that some 'aunties' had a tendency to be cruel; beating the children, starving them, working them hard, but if Goneril were to have a chance, if she were to attack and vanquish the impregnable fortress, the children simply had to go.

She stood for a moment outside the bank where she had heard of a vacancy for a clerk. Smoothed down her dress before she walked in. Men in white shirts sat at their desks, working gratefully. Industriously. Their hair shone and their clean, clipped nails drummed, drum drum, impatiently on the table for the next invoice. Brown-man bank clerk everywhere you eye turn till them fall upon one, whose dark, smooth skin looked oddly out of place. Brown-woman bank clerk everywhere you eye turn. Slim, brown, pretty things with real gold earrings. Dark man look up from his work. See Goneril. Smile. Goneril, nod him a welcome. Brown-skin girl walk with a furious pace up to all this blackness.

"Is what you want?"

Her tone said everything.

"I've come about the job."

"What job?" She surveyed the other's clothes, her hair, her skin with a twist of the lip like seh she sure she have scurvy.

"The job for a clerk."

"There's no job for a clerk here."

Goneril had been through this time and time again.

"May I speak to the manager, please?"

"He's not here at the moment. I tell you, there's no job... I got that job. We don't need a clerk here anymore."

What was the point. Goneril turned to leave.

One day. You wait an see. Him who laugh last laugh best. One day. You just wait an see...

5

Miss May dragged the resisting Cato into the kitchen.

"Dyam foolish likkle bwoy. Nevva see a bwoy so likkle an stupid. Inside!"

Cato hid himself in the folds of Miss May's skirt. Burnt copper brown, rotund, his belly, unlike Cato, was more than ready to show itself, could always be seen between the tight little T-shirt and the baggy, wear-an-leff shorts.

"Yu not gwine say hello to me, Yaakshi?"

He said nothing.

Goneril tried her best to appear amused but hurt pinch up her lip. The child simply refused to speak to her, to show her any affection whatsoever. Maybe she should take him away, he was far too fond of Miss May for her liking.

"So me hear yu gwine go a Hinglan?"

"Yes, Miss May. Me can't fine no work out here. Me madda say is not too bad out there an yu caan easy easy find a jab."

"Mm-hmmmn. Is so me hear. What about im farda?" She nodded over her shoulder at Cato.

"Im gwine come, too."

"Is when you two gwine go?"

"Next month."

"Hm-mmmn. Yu gwine dead wi cold! Yes me dear! So yu see, yu not gwine see yu madda dis lang lang time, so say g'bye, nuh? Yaakshi! Me tarkin to yu!"

The boy pushed himself up into the fold which was Miss May's behind, the better to conceal himself. He understood that his mother was to leave for a long time and that he would not have to see her again. He fidgeted.

"Bye."

The obediently muffled farewell made its way from deep within the folds of Miss May's skirt, not to mention the folds of her skin, reached the ears for whom it was intended and fled through the other door leading to the back yard.

    Miss May stood the boy in front of her. Looked at him long, looked at him hard. He averted his eyes, looking to the left, to the right, over this shoulder, beyond that foot. His knees pressed together for moral support. She caught his face, holding him firmly under the chin. Forced him to look at her. Old, soft eyes met large, bright eyes. A smile worked its way, involuntarily, over Cato's face, illuminating his entire countenance, spreading wider until it became a full, toothy grin. Miss May could not suppress a laugh. Succumbed even to a teeth-sucking *styoops* of foolish affection. What could he do but laugh in return, then, taking permission from her lenient eyes, Cato ran back to the yard to retrieve his stick.

    From the kitchen, Miss May surveyed without comment the boy murdering his foe. She readjusted the scarf on her head, wiped her hands clean on her apron and continued with her work. Metal pots clinked against each other in the cold, soapy water. Fat, ringless fingers swirled, dipped, shook with dexterous speed. Shiny pots and fat-encrusted pots, pots with dents and handleless pots to be steered from the stove by work-my-entire-life hands wrapped up in cotton rags. What a shame shame shame that bwoy dislike him madda so much. She was a mother, too. She felt for Goneril. Im angry? Tink she run weh leff him? His sister was only a name. And is when him last see him father? Silently condemning this getting of children only to scatter them around the country, Miss May could also understand how the little Cato must feel.

    "Poor likkle ting," she thought, "yu can't demand what yu nay even give..."

6

Goneril and Walter had been living in England for some time. They had gone to London. Other blacks had gone to Birmingham, Manchester, Sheffield, Bristol, Liverpool; to the big industrial towns where the work was plenty. True, the jobs on offer were not of the best kind. Dat don't bother nobaddy. Work is work and work would suffice for the aspirants to carry out their long-term plans of sending money home, getting the children over and giving them a better start. Who knows; you might even be able to save enough money to own a nice house. The dreams knew no bounds.

Goneril's mother had singled out south-west London and was living in Brixton which was fast becoming a colourful and boisterous West Indian community. Yam, ackee, saltfish, hotcombs, afro wigs and reggae music all began to make an appearance in the market. People bumped into others from back home, 'Is you dat?', stood chatting, comparing experiences of the journey, accommodation, employment and British sermons, parting after an exchange of addresses, a 'Go good!', a 'Tek it easy!', each looking forward to seeing the other again, both walking off in satisfaction, feeling that bit less isolated and away from home.

Walter had found a job as a non-skilled labourer in a car factory. Goneril suffered herself to work as a washerwoman in a laundry. As a start. Both were industrious and managed to start saving money. The relationship was working well; everything still so fresh, exciting, with the children out of the way. Before long, Walter found an opportunity in America. They discussed it. It was agreed that he should go. Within a few weeks, he was all set. Eighteen months he planned to stay, not more than two years. He would save hard to send money back to England, for he had more responsibilities now; Goneril was expecting her third child and they would get married when he came back. Yes, life was definitely looking up.

Walter. Who them call John. *Jahn*. Short, dark, slim, handsome, he came from a large family of twelve surviving children, continually changing in their collaboration with and against each other, like the silvery pearlings curling on the inner ear to the hushings of a sea-shell bouncing off tropical light. Force-ripe, sinewy, scarry-shinned and chalky-jointed pitnis every one of them, hardened by the exigencies of poverty in paradise. Peace was a word they had heard in a history lesson. Once. And Quiet you could have when praying silently on a Sunday morning. Walter's mama and papa could not read; they had radio and word of mouth. Walter himself had not been the most regular attendant at school, more often down by the river than behind the school-desk. More at ease with a stone than with a satchel in his hand. He could speak. He could hawk dollar bills. Him no waste him time on algebra and trigo him don't know what him ever gwine wear a shirt and tie go a work?

The ruler of the house was a broad, brown, leather belt fastened to a large, metal buckle. When not being used to hold up Papa's trousers, it was liberally, forcefully applied to the behinds of the children who ran, yelped, laughed cried in their fear as, like so many chickens, they were chased around the yard, the cabin, before finally being pinned down and whipped good and proper, however trivial the offence.

"Who don't hear must - "

"*Feel!!*" the others finished off, in timing with the lashings.
And from a safe distance. Tomorrow it could be their turn, for all that some were in the meantime big, strapping men able to box Papa down. Grown up girls with that roll of the hip, cooking his food and wishing they could get their hands on a good dose of arsenic…

Young man Walter had seen the proud Goneril, who them call Vechie, walking around town.

Dat one tink her shit can fry…
He, too, had been quick to taunt when she had first fallen pregnant, choosing quietly to ignore the fact that one of his sisters

had slipped low low down the ladder by having her first child at the tender age of thirteen. Along with everyone else in the family, he had beaten her severely, only to mete out forgiveness in the same measure as wrath when the girl produced her almost-white offspring, the darling of its illiterate grandmother, who would not have anyone scold him, the one *bakra*, that is to say *white*, in the family. Thus Sonia, who them call Tweetie, was miraculously transformed from the pariah to the pride of the family, and if she never lift a finger do a stroke of work since, she already do better than most with that there likkle pitni.

Walter knew of Goneril's daughter. Out there. Somewhere. He, too, had a son. Look like. Is what the mother say and by all accounts the child favour him as a shame. Walter's mother took an instant dislike to Goneril; the gyal too black. Nearly as black as herself.

Goneril was seventeen.

"Hss...hss."

She chose to ignore the call, walking straight with her head high.

"Hssss...hsss."

"Is who yu deh hiss at? Tink me is dog?"

"Wat mek yu nay answer?"

"Me answer when s'mady speak to me, nat when s'mady hiss, yaa."

"Kuya! Is wat mek yu so himportant?"

Goneril sporting the duet of a peach blouse tucked into a light, floral skirt which complimented her dark complexion. Walter's eyes running over her body. He strutted nonchalantly. A good-looker and well he knew it. It mattered not that he had nothing else going for him; never having had a job, being practically illiterate himself, a young man in his twenties with a lifetime of idleness to look forward to, though always the possibility of a woman who would feed his appetite. Both of them.

"Is where yu pitni?"

"Nevva you mind bout my pitni."

He crossed over to her right side as she had turned away so as not to look at him, so as not to let him see that she was, albeit against her will and despite the frown of her better judgement, smiling. Walter put his arms casually around her waist.

"Warnt annadda one?"

"Jahn, yu moss tink me can't do betta dan dat."

"An yu moss tink yu can find s'mady who can do betta dan me!" He laughed at his own good wit.

Goneril pouted as she continued on her way.

"Joss yu gu weh, yaa!"

"Yu no want nobaddy see yu new bwoyfren?"

"Bwoyfren?" she scoffed.

"Spit in di sky, fall in yu eye."

In silence they walked a little way. He eyed her.

"Vechie..."

"Is who tell yu fi call me name?"

"Ganeril Marrison. Yes man, wat a mouthful..." he sidled up to her, "tink yu can get yu mouth round someting bigga...?"

Before long, Cato was on the way. Walter acknowledged himself as the father but felt no onus upon him to assist in the child's upbringing, harbouring instead a secret pleasure that he had put a spoke in the wheel of Goneril's bright future, for it was not without some discomfort that he felt, as she would always make him feel, her superiority over him. Now they were more on a par.

Push had come to shove and Goneril wanted to go to England, where her mother had gone a few years previously, sending back after her favourable reports. Her mother would even pay her fare, though she kept this fact to herself. This was Walter's opportunity, too. Sure. Why not? He didn't have to go with her, but he saw visions of a second-hand car, saw himself rising above his brothers and sisters, saw the prospect of steady employment with sick pay and bonuses, he saw a sound welfare system, he saw commodities; he saw money and comfort. As the father of Goneril's son, he could not let her go without him. He got the money together. For himself.

America. What a place! Money, opportunities and women. Ah! The women! What a time Walter had had! Some of his sisters, not to be outdone by him, had promptly scrounged the money together and had gone off to America themselves. Vechie, a washerwoman! That tickled them very much. Further explanation was impatiently batted aside, what did they care that it was an industrial laundry? As far as they were concerned, she was up to her elbows in other people's shitty drawers, with jaze eating away at her skin. Malice brightened their eyes every time they asked after her, though they jiggled around the question as to what exactly *their* work entailed, nimble of tongue as they had been of foot when hopping just out of reach of Papa's brown leather belt. You think Walter bother? His sisters only knew America. Its sweaty industrial buildings. Its basement flats. He knew America *and* England, that cold place on the other side of the ocean. He milked their awe.

Now he had a little girl. What a beauty she was! Everyone in Jamaica was delighted with the pictures Goneril had sent; she had been to a real photographer and had pictures taken of his little girl, look at her! What a beauty! Look at all that hair! Look at the new white dress and those new white shoes! Everything new! Everything new and white!

"Mm-hmmmn. A nice nice baby."

There could be no contradiction. Goneril going up in the world, man. The young mothers held onto the photographs a little longer, fondling the paper, staring at the child's clothes, at Happiness, through heavy, sad eyes.

Walter had been dutifully sending money back to England. Goneril, meanwhile, had set about getting his residency papers. The Home Office sent this and this and this paper to sign here and here and here, good Lord! With a resolute tilt of the chin, she hauled the day towards her. Fish might a wriggle but fish gwine fry.

Needless to say, Cato would have to take a back seat.

"Yaakshi! com look pan yu likkle sista."

"Gee! Gee!" He bounded up the stairs, leaving his luggage at the bottom. As he came through the front door, the door on Goneril's floor opened, closed quickly, hasty footsteps making their way up to a higher floor.

"Gee! Gee!"

She came to the doorway to meet him, in her dressing gown, her eyes alert. She suffered herself to smile.

"So, Jahn, yu come back."

He held her tightly and kissed her.

Her arms hung lifelessly at her side.

He could tell she had no clothes on underneath that dressing-gown. Slid his hand inside to touch her.

She closed her eyes and waited for it to be over.

He pulled her to the other side of the door, smirking.

Footsteps... tentatively... down the stairs, hesitated... as they reached her floor... listened:

to her faint protests...

to the first howl of the bedsprings...

then quickened down the remaining stairs and fled through the front door.

A muffled weeping rose from the woman stretched out on the floor, sniffing as her nose ran watery mucus and blood. She wiped it with her sleeve. The baby hollered from a corner of the room. Agitated feet paced up and down in front of the window; up and down. What the hell was he to do now? The bitch. He could not stay with her. Bitch! *Bitch*! Stay in England? No, he'd go to America. No! His sisters would laugh him to scorn. Dat dyam bitch, yu see! His hand swept quickly over his head. He looked her way. Away in disgust, what was he to do? What was he to do now? She had the effrontery to tell him that he had to marry her. She had her mother in England and could stay regardless. Now she even had an English daughter. *His* English daughter, she dared to toss at him over her swollen lip. He, Walter, could only stay if he married her. If not, the Home Office would promptly send him back to Jamaica. First class, she goaded. The disgrace! He couldn't! The bitch! They could always say it was premature... People would talk. His sisters! Oh my god! His mother! Leave the bitch! Why the hell not? Simply go back to Jamaica and leave the bitch! No! His pride; *it would not.* What the hell was he to *do*? Storm over to her, pack her by the hair and belt her with the full force of his strength. Goneril's head crashed to the floor. Grabbing her head again, again, he pounded the floor with her face. "You bitch! Yu dyam bitch! Bitch! Bitch! Bitch!"

They were married. She wore a brilliant white dress, fitted closely at the waist and tailored by a woman who had charged her more than she was worth. Anyone needing her dress that quickly must have her reason, the woman scented the dilemma and cashed in on it, though she did offer to add a few inches to the waistline, just in case. Goneril's stomach still nice and flat; look as long, look as hard as you like. She smiled at all the guests as she played with her gold ring. He had bought her a nice one after all. She was a married woman. A *Mrs* at last.

A daughter, born seven months later, was registered in Walter's name. Faces darkened, brows knitted together in black, thunderous clouds. Eyes narrowed, shooting sparks of lightning in suspicious thought. Walter stood defensively by his wife's side as the noise brewed, as the tramp, tramp, tramp of the army could be heard marching, marching nearer and nearer. Walter and Goneril fled for the cover of their room, busied themselves with being happy; their peace offering to the gods of Malice and Gossip. Their canon against attack. The gods were eventually appeased. The impending storm blew over. The white flag of surrender fluttering in the sigh of relief issued by the newly betrothed, who were both glad to see the army retreat, disband and return to civilian life.

Mr & Mrs became the proud owners of a three-bedroom terraced house. Moved from SW9 to E7 and even had enough left over for a second-hand Ford. The girls began to go to school. Sandringham infant and junior school, round the block. The children in Jamaica were to be sent for now that Mr & Mrs could claim a position of relative comfort; were having a bathroom built onto the house and there was even talk of having a telephone installed. The eldest girl would look after the family whilst Goneril went to work. So the girl, being more useful, was sent for first. She and Walter did not get on. He poured even more affection on his little girl, as if in spite. At least his son would be arriving soon.

7

"Yaakshi! Y*aaa*ksh*iii*! Dat pitni yu see man!"
Cato came running.

"Miss May?" He stood in the doorway, panting slightly, his everlasting dusty toes playing with the cool, hard floor.

Try as she might, Miss May could not get him to wear the shoes sent to him from England. He would persistently sneak off and toss them away somewhere until, forced by a few brisk clips to his head, he would retrieve them, clean off the dirt, then place them beneath his bed.

Miss May looked at his feet.

"Dem in di bedroom," he said in his defence. His eye caught the blue envelope with its red stripes in her one hand; saw the two thin sheets of blue paper in the other. He looked from hand to hand, from paper, to face, inquiringly, fearing the worst.

"Fram yu madda. Say moss send yu come."

Cato hung his head, which was growing hot, a sure sign that he was about to cry.

"Miss -"

"Me know yu no want-" she interrupted, her voice faltering as she watched the tears rollicking down Cato's cheeks, happy in their escape, their freedom; they were staying here, in Jamaica with Miss May. "But stap! Wat is dis?" Arms akimbo, she confronted the young boy for whom her affection, she willingly confessed, was without rhyme or reason. "Yu mean fi tell me dis big grey-back bwoy who gwine haffi go all di way a Hinglan pan him own gwine stannup ya[11] an bawl like a pitni? Get out a mi kitchen 'fore me lose me patience!!" With that she gave him a shove in the back which sent him careering out into the back yard.

---

[11] *Stannup ya* = stand (up) here

Dat poor likkle pitni bawl, you hear! Him roar like a bleeding lion! Bitter, bitter, bitter, what a strange sensation for him, to cry without having been the victim of an act of aggression. But then, he had... He threw himself around in the yard, knocking himself against the trees, against bushes, bruising himself wilfully before he collapsed in the dirt.

Miss May don't pay him no mind. Busied herself, locked up her ears, drew up her face. Nearly eight years this boy had been with her. She pressed her lips together, worked furiously, attempting, in vain, to prepare herself emotionally to give the boy up.

Why did everyone say that England was such a wonderful place? Why tell him that he was so very lucky and that he should love and respect his parents for all that they had done for him? What had they done for him? They had taken him away from Miss May and forced him to live in this cold country full of white people. They had forced him to wear shoes and to live in a house with five strangers whom he could neither love nor understand.

"Me no want to hear seh yu carrying on wid any of dis foolishniss, yu hear wat me saying to yu, Yaakshi!" Miss May's last blessing rang in his head as the woman, who could not bring herself to accompany him any further than to the frame of her kitchen door, receded from sight. Grateful! Be grateful... love... respect... work hard for you... big sacrifice... proud... The pesky words chased him like a wasp. He felt the weight of a great responsibility. Bowed under the pressure of it, confused, feeling himself to be ungrateful, yet not quite knowing what to be grateful for. The pressure of it! Head bowed, eyes down, thus he went along, quiet and solitary, among these strangers, in a world filled with strangers.

8

    Goneril never ceased to be irritated by the boy. She had resigned herself to the fact that he was not a loving child. Him is a narsty, sneaking… That Miss May had a lot to answer for. She had once caught him hobbling into the room.
    "Is wat di matta wid yu foot?"
    "Notting."
    "Me say - " and she popped her eyes, accentuating each word to show that she meant business, "is *wat* di *ma*tta wid-yu-*foot*?"
    "Nothing!" Cato pleaded, only wanting to be allowed to go on his way.
    She sucked her teeth, "Bwoy, come here!"
Reluctantly, the boy moved in her direction.
Goneril bent down to look at his foot.
He stood rooted to the spot.
    "Liff yu foot!" Dis bwoy soft in di head or wat? Wat mek me haffi tell him ten time? She dug her knuckles into her hips, popped her eyes at the floor in front of her, and waited.
He lifted. Cato's soles were cracked, were filthy; the bottom of his shoes had completely worn away.
Only now did it strike Goneril that he had had those shoes for rather a long time. It hadn't occurred to her to buy some new ones for he had never complained. She softened for her apology,
    "Go an wash yu foot dem."

    Walter was disappointed in his son. Him is a narsty, dutty[12]… and his hair was never combed. Walter beat him viciously for everything and anything. Holding the boy by the

---

[12] *dutty* = dirty

neck, his fingers pressing tightly, he would drag the fine-toothed comb through the boy's thick, unruly hair. Cato screamed, pink palms and gums flashing. Walter's eyes shone wildly and his nostrils flared. Again the comb was forced through the hair, teeth snapping in the event. Again... again... and again...

Cato was a bright boy, but enthusiasm is prone to die in the absence of encouragement. His parents dismissed him as a simpleton. His eldest sister was a bright one, too, though often too busy to study. After school she would have to cook, clean, wash the children before: up, to bed! She would rub her siblings with a bitter vigour, spinning them around brusquely, mishandling them until their soapy, glistening limbs moaned. A secret pleasure she derived from pushing them behind the knees under the pretext of washing them well, there in the crack where the dirt was hiding; a shove they would get and a tut they would hear as their slippery bodies tottered and collapsed. The youngest sister would instinctively reach out for the supporting hands of her two older sisters only to be spurned by them both. Cato washed himself separately under his sister's supervision.

"Wash it, an wash it good!" she ordered, pointing at his sex.

He turned his back to her, stealthily, and splashed a little water over it.
For some reason, it always annoyed her that he turned his back to her. If only she could grow up, get a job and be rid of the whole lot of them, she thought, resenting the fact that she had been brought all this way just to be someone else's maid.

Goneril worked from early afternoon to night. Walter often took the night shift for the extra money. The children rarely saw him. He frightened them. They kept out of his way. All except his little girl, who had not taken long to work out that, according to some unarticulated yet visible rule, she was Number One. Her coronation undisputed, she delighted in nothing more than in provoking her siblings, though, truth be told, she did have a hard time provoking Cato, tortoised in himself as he was all the time. When remunerated for her endeavours with a well-earned slap, she would fling herself against some item of furniture, bawl theatrically, then run off to her father. To Daddy. Who would normally be snoring in the foetal position. Burrowed under the blankets. Down the stairs he would thunder, cursing, belt in hand, and lash the culprit until he had drawn blood. Spitting abuse, and satiated, he would return to his hollow. Throughout all this, there she would stand, Number One; spluttering now and then for good measure, although her lips never failed to curl, just that little bit, at the sides.

Cato made a friend in his youngest sister, though words were rarely exchanged. Outsiders both, their souls held hands for comfort.
Cato came home one Saturday morning after a game of football. Ding dong! Goneril opened the door, for he was not trusted with his own key.
"Well, you win dis time?" his mother asked aggressively as she continued sweeping the floor, such hard, fast strokes, as if she hated the floor or hated the broom or something.
Cato shook his head.
"Ten nil."
Goneril's laugh was vulgar and derisive.
"Bwoy, you useless."
He shrugged. He was the goalkeeper. Cato headed for the stairs, his favourite sister at his heels.
His mother resumed her work. She sorted the clothes for washing, filled the big, metal bath with hot water, knelt over it and began to scrub. She scrubbed skirts and she scrubbed shirts. She scrubbed socks and she scrubbed trousers. Scrubbed them as clean as they would ever be. She began to wring the clothes. Her hands burned. She could hear movement in the bedroom. Walter was getting up. She snorted corrosively, wringing harder.
Walter whistled as he dressed. Applied some new aftershave liberally to his face then retrieved a small gift from its hiding place and slipped it into his trouser pocket. Pat pat. Smile.
Talking could be heard in the room next door. Two young voices. Walter came out to stand in the doorway. Cato and his youngest sister, sitting on the floor, knees drawn up beneath the chin, were jabbering away. Suddenly they sensed a presence, looked up, and fell silent. Walter grunted at them as he made his

way down the stairs. The chatter recommenced. He stopped halfway down the stairs. The step creaked under him. Again, from upstairs, silence. He snorted even more –
    Him a pig man, Cato thought
then Walter continued on his way.
She could smell him before she could even see him. Mek me feel sick. Dressed up in a way he hadn't dressed up for her in a long while.
    "Me nat here." He jiggled the car keys.
    "Is when yu coming back?"
Their eyes skirted around each other's periphery.
    "When me come back." Answer enough. He man-stepped out the front door.
Goneril lifted the heavy bath to the back door. Removed the cover from the outside drain and tipped the water, glug glug gug glug into the hole. Something clinked, clink clink against the metal pan, shone, before disappearing down the drain. A button? It had shone in the grey murky water like a goldfish. Yes, just like a goldfish. A gold-
A spasm of cold draught sucked its way through her. She forced herself to look at her hands. At her left, ringless hand... then birthed an interminable sigh, which hauled itself over her shoulder to sit on her curved spine, like a bundle. Shoulders sagging, she carried the tin bath, listlessly, back into the house.

9

The sun beat down on his back. He lay there in the grass, eyes closed, safe in the friendly world of his own mind inhabited by the multitude of friends he had never known in reality. The grass crackled in the heat. A thousand noises assaulted his ears. He could hear the birds' chirping medley, he could hear the insects and he could hear the trees. Yes, and there, in the distance, he could hear Miss May cursing in the kitchen. Yes, Miss May, there she was and he; at home, at home.

Behind his lids, he saw red, saw orange. He squeezed them tight. He could see black, too, and the rings which were his eyes; green and blue and light. His opened his eyes ever so slightly, mingled the orange of the insides with the bright light of the outsides, filtering in through a thousand minute black feathers... A winged insect settled on his nose. He brushed it away with a giggle. The river whispered, calling him, inviting; *Come on, come on, Yaakshi, come to me, touch me... put your hand in me... feel how wet I am... mmmnn!! Isn't that nice...? Come on, come on then...*

Come...

He pressed himself into the grass, pressed hard as his body tingled, his back prickled and his groin responded to the invitation.

Come to me... let's be together... are you wet, too? Yaakshi... I want you to...

Something was happening to his body he grew hot he found himself needing the toilet. He resisted, forcing his muscles to contract, to push the feeling, the need away. It came back
and he pushed,
it came back
and he pushed.
Come to me... come to me...

He could no longer withhold. He got up, walked down to the river, dropped his shorts by the bank and sat himself in the cool water. Together at last.

Cato woke up slowly. Like a deep-sea diver, his mind rose to the surface, sad to leave the comforting darkness behind. He saw the curtain which divided his section of the room off from that of his sisters. A prickly shiver raced down his spine, like the grains of rice they had put in a tube to make an instrument, a rain slushing, sea-shore splashing... He turned to face the wall... and shrank: warm and moist. The sheets beneath him were warm and moist... His heart sank. Why? Why did it always happen? He fought so hard against it, he fought so hard, willing himself to wake up in time. Why did it always happen? He felt his head growing hot, hotter and hotter. The pressure built up behind his eyes, oh no! What is this? Again? He sprang up from the bed, dashed downstairs to the toilet, praying, praying... but Walter was in there. He could hear the soft, deep moaning from the other side of the door.

Get out! Get out! I want the toilet! I want -
He wasn't going to hold out he flew up the stairs, eyes searching ravenously. Spied an empty flower pot, grabbed it just in time and relieved himself,
aaaaaaahhh....
letting his water out, slowly, so that his sisters wouldn't hear, hoping there would not be more than the pot could bear...
He hushed the pot back beneath the bed. Confused, angry and ashamed, he slid between the sheets, his body crying out against the cold clamouring wet, his mind, his heart wishing themselves back, wishing themselves back, back to the night before...

Walter was in a bad mood. His little gifts were no longer appreciated. Walter was in a foul mood today. He stormed around the house like a tempest so that even the furniture seemed to shy out of his way. Goneril don't pay him no mind and go long upstairs check the children bedroom.

The children sat in front of the television set. The youngest barricaded behind a book. Cato, withdrawn into his innermost centre, waiting (waiting, waiting)...

"Dat *narsty* likkle pitni! Dat *blasted narsty likkle*... Jahn!... *Jahn!*"

Her husband grimaced.

Goneril strode into the room with a small pot in her outstretched hand and her head kipped back in disgust. The pot only half full for she had kicked it over, unaware.

Walter guessed in a flash what had happened and charged over to the boy. Punch. Punch. Spit, cuss, kick, cuss.

"You narsty likkle wretch!" him box the boy down to the floor. Snatched the pot from Goneril and as he did so the contents splished over their fingers and sprinkled the floor.

"Shut up! Me say *shut up!*" He punched into Cato harder to stop him from crying.

The little girls screamed and ran away.

Goneril, sensing the wrath she had unleashed, scurried to the kitchen, closing the door behind her.

"Drink it! Drink it you narsty likkle wretch yu!" he thrust the pot at Cato's head.

The boy's eyes and mouth clamped shut. The yellow water splashed over his face. His eyes stung.

Walter raged, screamed, ranted. He thumped. He booted.

The kitchen door flew open. Standing, falling to his knees, hauled up by his hair, Cato was dragged through to the toilet.

"Dear God!" the words spurted out without her consent but Goneril didn't dare to interfere.

Walter forced Cato to his knees, grabbed the boy's neck and thrust his head into the bowl. He flung the remaining urine over the boy's head, and flushed, pinning his son down with his knees. Cato, choking, gasped "Daddy! Daddy!" through his teeth-torn lips,

"Me sarry! Me sarry Daddy!"

The boy too big, but Walter pinned him against the bowl, sat his whole weight upon his son's bucked shoulders. And flushed again. Seizing Cato by the hair, Walter dragged him back through the kitchen to the cellar under the stairs.

As soon as he got some air can breathe him plead,
"Mummy!"
Silence...
"Mummy?"
working his way, in between blows, over to his mother, who hastily dried her eyes and busied herself, refusing to look at her son.
"Mummy?"
Pig man hand grab big bwoy by the neck.
"Miss May! Miss May, help me! Miss May! Miss May!"
The plate jumped out of her hand and sprang to the floor, shattering. The jagged pieces danced devilishly around the kitchen. She turned on her son and hissed,
"Get out! Just *get out*!"
Walter blasts the cellar door open with his foot. Lunges for a six-foot length of flex, ties Cato's hands behind him, tight, until the flex bites into the boy's wrists, ties his feet to his hands so that the boy is forced to double back.
"Shut up!"
He smacks the bulb out of the socket, propels Cato into the black cellar with a kick, locks the door, rages around the house, daring anyone to confront him, then him storm out.

The girls cried and snivelled in their fear. No-one dared to release Cato. Goneril, frightened, angry, forced her hands to continue with their duties. Sick, she felt sick; sick because of what she had just witnessed, and sick because she was, once again, with child. She looked at her replacement wedding ring. Octagonal, each face engraved with a cross; not the holy cross of our Lord, but an *x*, as on the page of some badly-done homework. Tears spread over the surface of her hands, say Howdi but me can't stay, and leap off down the spaces in between her fingers, blip, blip. Her youngest sat outside the cellar, crying, trying to push her fingers through the crack at the bottom of the door and not succeeding. Cato whimpered in the darkness, doubled back like an abnormal foetus. His hands, his eyes burned; burned like the sun in Jamaica, the sun in the back yard of the house where Miss May lived. His eyes burned like the sun, only now he could see no orange; he could see no orange and red. He could only see black.

Walter did not return for the whole day.

      He heard footsteps outside the cellar door. Irritated. Impatient. The lock was fumbled with. The door was opened. Would he smell it?
      "Come out!"
He resurrected from the cellar, was cut free, stood up, big bwoy a whole head taller than his father, but with his eyes to the ground. Could he smell it?
      "Smile!"
Cato would not look at him.
      "Me say *smile!*"
His lips moved a little at the sides. His eyes, blank.
      "Now gettout a mi sight!"
He slithered up the stairs, like a fog, ignoring his sister who had sentinelled, whose gaze was following his hand on the banister whilst hers squeezed tight around the railings and strangled

One little two little
Three little Indians

Four five
Once I caught a fish alive

Mary had a little lamb...
Dumper truck

Tip me up and pour me

Out

10

"Emily, yu still deh sleep? Wen yu ready me cook a likkle dinna. Tek yu time an unpack yu tings. Me no in a no horry." Mrs Brown's person filled in the doorway, her eyes only and the smell of her talcum powder ventured into the room.

"Tank yu, Mrs Brown. Me will come down in a minute."
In spite of her exhaustion, Rose had not slept at all at all at all well in that lumpy bed in that gloomy room in the lap of the Motherland. She sat up with a groan, her head cocked, her eyes screwed up against the harsh light of the naked bulb suspended from the ceiling and prodding its dirty finger into the open wound of her semi-consciousness. It had stopped raining, at least – praise be! She hadn't a clue what time it was. Dark enough to be ten o'clock at night. She stretched over for her –
but it had stopped long ago, halfway across the ocean.

"Tek yu time." The door closed, leaving the smell of talc behind to keep an eye.
Rose swung her feet, deliberately, down to the floor, where they waited for her mind to catch up. Then she began to unpack:
    another blanket
    two pillow cases
    three carefully ironed and folded blouses (for work)
    two old school blouses (for home/ bed)
    two smart blouses
    one knee-length skirt (work)
    one less presentable one (home)
    one pair of hand-made, bell-bottomed trousers (with an
    elasticated waist and two patch pockets at the back. Her
    pride and joy. The material had come from Canada
    together with a picture from a magazine her aunt had sent
    her for her eighteenth birthday. When she got bored with

them, she could cut them into hot-pants and save the
surplus material for something else)
    one halter-neck (if it ever got warm enough and she saw
other girls walking around dressed like that; she was *not*
going to make a poppy-show of herself).

She to and fro from the suitcase to the wardrobe:
    a bundle of underwear
    two pairs of shoes
    another nightdress

She came to the household goods:
    an old, clean-scoured dutch pot of her mother's (received
along with some other things before she was turned out
when she fell pregnant)
    another pot (one pot not enough)
    two plates, wrapped in old newspaper
    a couple of spoons, knives and forks
    two mugs
    one can-opener

and, in a plastic bag:
    her chamber pot.

She found her tin containing a few tastes from home:
    cocoa
    a piece of baked breadfruit
    hot peppers
    nutmeg
    some loaves of bulla
    coconut dosey
    two sticks of sugar cane

and put the lot in the lower compartment of the bedside table
along with:
    her hot-comb
    a tub of Dixie Peach hair oil

and, finally:
    her black, well-thumbed, leather-bound Bible.

The envelope with half of the money she had, rolled into a tight ball secured by an elastic band, went into the left cup of her bra. The chamber pot, under the bed. Rose slithered back into her clothes. She can't tarry. Mrs Brown was waiting.

"Come an sit down. Me know yu must want a likkle food fi eat."

"Tank yu."

Chicken, boiled green bananas and potatoes. It was lovely and warm down here. Rose picked up her knife and fork.

"So, yu mek di journey safe."

"Yes. Me was fraid yu see! But me mek it safe."

Mrs Brown let her eat for a while. "Is who deh look after yu two chilren dem?"

Silence.

"Yu no haffi look at me like dat. Me know wat yu tinking: is wa she know 'bout Jahn Smarl an im 'ave monni?"

Smile.

"Me know a ting or two becars me is Richard gadmadda... yu nevva know?"

Rose cut another ring of boiled green banana and pushed it around on her plate to leave her time to think.

"Wat dem name?"

She did not answer right away. How much did Mrs Brown know, how much would she want to know? "Marlene... Marlene an Leroy."

"Oh yes. Me remember now. Dem deh stay in a yu distrik?"

"Wid mi fren, Junie." The food tasted good. She wiped a potato around in the gravy then lifted it to her mouth.

"Junie... she di brown skin girl who madda deh live in America and got one jailbird bwoyfren?"

"Me don't know 'bout no jailbird bwoyfren but her madda deh live in America fi true."

"Hm-hm." A long silence pursued Mrs Brown's reflections.

Rose concentrated stubbornly on her food, chewing slowly, fastidiously, English style.

"But look!" exclaimed Mrs Brown, "Me put down dis ya big plate a food, and don't even bring yu a drink! Let me get some orange squash. Yu drink orange squash?" she was already on her feet and halfway to the kitchen.

"Tank yu," said Rose, as Mrs Brown placed a plastic mat under the glass.

"Is wen yu last see Richard?"

"Dis long time now." The young woman grew subdued. She hadn't seen him since her second pregnancy. He hadn't sent her a penny. It had taken her a long, long time to swallow her pride and write to his family.

"Wotless good-fi-notting. Him disappoint me, yu see. Him was soch a nice young man. Me no know is wat mek im turn bad..." Richard's god-mother picked up a chicken bone from her plate and sucked it clean. "Me don't hear notting from him dis long time. Last me hear he go to America."

The room was crammed with furniture; crotcheted doilies, pink and yellow seat covers almost everywhere, family pictures on the sideboard, a tea-towel with *Bless This Home* pinned on the wall and next to the door, a mirror with the island of Jamaica and its celebrities: Robert Nesta Marley, Marcus Garvey, Sam Sharpe, Alexander Bustamante, Paul Bogle, George William Gordon, Nanny. A tea-towel in praise of motherhood. Rose wondered which one of Mrs Brown's children had given her that, or if Leroy or Marlene would give her something like that one day. She wondered how the verse for the fathers went. There probably wasn't one. And Mr Brown? What sort of a man might he be, married to Mrs Brown? Rose found it hard to imagine, but right then her eyes fell upon a picture of the Browns on their wedding day, one of those black-and-white mirrored pictures which had been coloured in. Mr Brown wore his hair parted on the side. His white-gloved hands ceremoniously around his bride.

"Yu look tired. Yu nay sleep good?"

Rose shook her head apologetically.

"Nevva mine. Me gwine gi yu a likkle rum warm yu up and mek yu sleep." Mrs Brown laboured over the back of her chair, opened a sideboard door, dug right to the back of it, retrieved a small bottle of Wray & Nephew, hooked a small glass (wedding present) from the top of the sideboard with her forefinger, set it down, poured. "Here, drink it." She studied Rose who, in many ways, reminded her of herself at that age. Nice young gyal.

They sat a while longer, exchanging information about Jamaica, about England. Mrs Brown told her where the buses went, where to change, how to get about and who the people were who were living in the house. She told her which shops to shop in and where she could get soul food. Another half an hour elapsed before Rose felt she could safely excuse herself.

"Me got to be going now. Tank yu for the dinner, Mrs Brown."

"Is arlright. An yu can call me Miss Brown. Di white people dem say Mrs but me no like it."

Rose reached for the doorknob.

"One minute! Me gwine give yu someting." Miss Brown heaved herself to her feet, retreated behind a door… re-emerged with a lampshade. And a picture of Jesus. "Dem was in yu room, but me nay sure if me wudda like yu or if we wudda get on, so me tek dem down. But yu is a nice girl, nice and mannersable. Yu meet Carmen? I glad she born here… Is one a me favourite picture this, you know. Tek it hang it up in a you room. Is one nice white lady from work bring me back this lampshade from Spain." She could have gone on but she looked into Rose's face and take pity on the girl. "Me can see yu is tired and need a bit more shut-eye, so go upstairs an lie down. See yu in di morning. Just remember one ting: it gwine get much better from now on."

11

London, June --, 19--

Dear Junie,

How are you? I'm sure you are fine. Give my love to Marlene and Leroy and say hello to One-foot for me.

I settle down more or less in London now and got a job can earn a little money. Here is a little something for you and the children. It's not much but I know it will help. I got my own room which I'm slowly slowly making nice. I know one or two girls from work and we go to the same church. I feel less lonely in London now I got my work and must do something but I miss Jamaica and my children. I write to my auntie in Canada to say thank you for the money and everything but I don't hear no word from her. If she send a letter to J.A. can you send it to England? I going to write her again because I don't want her to think I'm ungrateful.

I never know you could get so much soul food in England! Them got quite a few cooly shops here you can buy yam, saltfish, green banana, ackee. My landlady Miss Brown tell me a sweet joke the other day. She say when she come to England how the English people was primitive and nasty and how is black people come to England make them know them must peel the skin off orange and banana before them eat it! Did you know the English also used to walk about barefoot over here in this cold? Is so Miss Brown tell me. So you see, not much difference between the two a we after all. This double-decker I told you about, I ride with it every day, you know! I go upstairs and sit at the front can see all of London! But they don't play no music in the bus like back home. Everybody just sit there like a long drink of water and don't say nothing.

I see a nice wig I going to save up and buy for you. It's the fashion in England, you know. I want to give you something nice let you know I appreciate how you look after my children for me. So him come to England? Last I hear, him wanted to go to America. I hope I don't set eyes on him. I got nothing to say to him.

Give my love to everybody and you and the children stay in good health. Goodbye and God bless.

Your Rose.

One more thing before I finish for this time. When you go to the post office count the money good don't let them cheat you. I want you to open an account for the children and put the money I send you for them in don't leave it in the house. People know them mother in England and will think you got money in the house.

Yours,

Rose.

12

    Rose slipped the letter into the postbox as she turned the corner to the multi-storey office block where she was employed as an early morning cleaner, a little sideline she had found without help from anyone. Six weeks on, after reading the ad in the local paper - cleaners always wanted. Good rates! - after pulling open that heavy red door to the public callbox, stepping into it for the first time, explaining who she was and being offered the job there and then, six weeks on, and Rose had slowly fallen into the routine of rising early. The voice on the phone informed her she had to be on the premises by a quarter to six, would earn an hour and a half's pay, for which she would have a specified number of floors to clean. Rose nodded her consent. Miss Brown then explained how to get there, and because Rose had a good head, she nodded once again to everything without needing to write any of it down.
    She had got up at four-thirty, moaning. "Dem sleep underground, wear wig pan dem head even wen dem got a head full of hair, an dem get up go work inna di middle a di night. Bwoy, is wat a race a people dis is..."
    During the twenty-minute bus ride she would treat herself to a little kip, waking up after the bus had taken a sharp turn left, the next stop being where she would have to get off. A brisk walk down the main road followed; left at the traffic lights, then the second on the right. From there she could already see the main gates of the ten-storey office block. Rose had no intention of getting over-friendly with the other cleaners; Clementine, a Trinidadian, Betti, an African, Mary, a middle-aged Irish woman with telling yellow fingers to match that chronic cough she had resigned to. Marjory and Lou were both English, and as the supervisor, Lou was the only one with keys to the main gates, though all had keys to their own cleaning cupboards, Rose's

being on the third floor. Rose was the youngest in the team. Mary the oldest. Lou the entertainer, who sometimes did not turn up until half past six.

"Sorry, girls!" she would say in a breathless hurry as she came rushing up to the main entrance, outing her fag, accepting, without rancour, the stern regard of her grumbling, frost-bitten workmates. "We'll 'ave to give it a bit of elbow grease this time, won't we?"

The managerials started turning up around eight. A cleaner or two, whoever wasn't in a hurry, might still be indulging in a chat in the tea-room over a mug of tea and a custard cream, though on a late day, the women would still be dashing around wiping away dust and setting files with a brisk irreverence back on their shelves.

"Another night on the town, Lou?" one of the managerials would always end up joking as he walked in with a newspaper folded under his armpit, or removed a tie from his jacket pocket to hang it up on the coat stand for later.

"Wish it were, wish it were..." came the standard reply as Lou propped a buttock on an item of office furniture. "But my old man, you see, he likes it so much he won't let me go on a morning." She pouts. "I can't help it if he finds me so irresistible! He does, you know! "Come on, Lou," he says, and he got such a nice way o' saying it, "Come on, Lou," he says, "I got something better than money..." Well," Lou had a remarkable way of being loquacious with her body; you didn't even have to listen to her, but on she went. "I'm a woman wiv a big 'eart, ain't I?" And on. And on. "Cheerio! Cheerio girls, see you in the morning!"

Rose stood at the bus-stop, her hour and a half done, her mind running through the things she had to do before her main job in the pie factory started. She could do a quick bit of shopping and have a look in at Pollard's to see if their children's underwear had come down in price. Oh, and the rent had to be paid. Miss Brown, though friendly, was strict, and sent Carmen to each of the tenants on a Thursday evening to remind them that the rent was due the following day, wanting it as soon as her tenants came in, and before they had the chance to squander it over the weekend. Four or five people, waiting at the bus-stop. Always the same faces, engaged in small talk about the weather. About the prices. One particular man had smiled at Rose a couple of times before, had said "Good morning!" to her once. Rose just look him up and down, is what im tink im doing?

"Bet it's not half as nice here as it is where you come from, is it?"

"I *beg* yu pardon?" She span round, irritated by the sudden voice so close to her ear.

"Said it's probably much nicer where you come from, ain't it?"

No answer.

"Sunshine all the year round, white beaches, warm sea, lazy days... That's wot we fink anyway, but if it was such a bed a roses, you lot wouldn't all be here in the first place, right?" he winked at her. "Where you from, the West Indies?"

"Yes, if yu must know," she said, giving him no encouragement, unused to people - to white men - just marching up and making conversation with her like that.

"Yes, I must know. Gotta be careful wot I say, don't I? Africans and West Indians don't like to be mixed up, do they?"

A man of about forty, or so she guessed, she could never tell. Roughly her height, fair-haired, slightly ginger, he had those watery blue eyes and that pale skin. Rose could see the veins in his head, thumping greeny-blue. He looked like a fish.

"You from Jamaica?"

She eyed him critically, "That's right."

"That's important to know too, you see. I can't well talk about 'small island people' if I ain't sure you're not one of them." Rose had to laugh in spite of herself.

"Oh yes. I know a bit or two about John Small and him got money. That's wot you say, innit?"

Kuya! Rose nearly dead laughing.

Other people in the queue turn round. Turn back.

Good Lord, this long long time she never laugh like that! Not since she leave home. A deep, deep-from-the-belly laugh, petering out against her will, leaving behind the embers of a smile to flick at the corners of her young, cupid lips, too tender, too pretty to harbour the hardship they had grown to know.

"Kuya! Lord have mercy!"

"Oh yes! I've gotta few Jamaican friends down at the docks where I work. Nicest bunch, they are, really nice bunch. Livened up the place no end, if you ask me." He smiled into her bright, moist eyes.

"Yu work in the docks?"

"That's right. Used to be a taxi-driver. Know London like the back o' me hand, I do, but, well," he sniffed, "that's anovva story. Hated it in the docks at first but as I said, oh, here's me bus," he shuffled forward with the others, "anyhow, my name's Jack. See you again sometime, I hope." He got on, took a seat near the window, nodded to her as the bus pulled away with a hiss, then a purr.

13

    Several blocks of council houses lined up beside one another, like a row of indifferent criminals being led out for their daily roll call. Tiny windows pressed into slabs of grey concrete spy out connivingly at the youths hanging around in groups in doorways, around corners. Youths smoking cigarettes they could ill afford. Youths with spray cans shoved resentfully into back pockets, inside bomber jackets. 'Wogs out!' 'NF'. Once you get off that bus that puts you down before the council estate, it's the daunting anonymity of fifteen-storey, twenty-storey monsters jutting out between the multitude of low-rise blocks connected to each other by a dizzy web of bridges, stairs and alleyways. After a battle of more than two years, the residents had finally managed to persuade the local council to paint the doors to each 'house' a different colour, since not only relatives but the residents themselves were forever losing their way. Consequently, Lyndon House doors had all been painted a dark green, Havelock House a light blue, Clarence House an optimistic yellow. A placard at the top of the main road leading into the estate read: Welcome to spaghetti alley, otherwise known as the hall of mirrors. Please leave your faces in the foyer. Thank you. Management.

    "Someone reckons he's a real clever dick," mutters Jack as he winds his way through the estate; past the first two low-rise blocks, past the newsagent's, the fish-n-chip shop, the launderette, the post office, the betting office and the off licence. A short queue had formed in the chippy, and through the fluttering multicoloured strips of a plastic curtain hanging in the entrance to the betting office, men's voices joke, shout, hope, swear. Post office being next to the betting office and the off licence, a fair amount of welfare probably never made it to a man's front door, thought Jack, such if life. He turns another corner: Where do the fucking architects live, eh, some urban artist wanted to know. And underneath: In a house like you do you ungrateful bastard. Workers of the World Unite had been crossed out and replaced by: All you need is Love, the universal imperative embellished by crudely sprayed peace-flowers.

A couple of houses in the block are boarded up. Amazing, how quickly a place can run down. It hadn't been that bad when they had moved in, Jack remembers. If everyone were to plant a few flowers on their balcony in the summer and make sure their kids went to school, he didn't want his kids turning teenagers in this environment but what could he do? His feet smack the concrete floor. The sound carries far, far enough for gangs lurking behind pillars yards ahead to know you were on your way but he lives there and isn't afraid. Boys trying to be men. He'd smack their bloody heads together if they ever tried to mug him or anyone in his family. In a parallel house an old lady is sitting by her window, her curtains pushed aside. She looks out over her mug of tea. Further along, rock music blasts from a bedroom window. Elsewhere, a mother, fraught, fed up; "Daniel! Come 'ere before I give you one! Come 'ere right now... you fink I'm joking?" Silence for a while, then, "Daniel!" Jack can hear the impatience brewing in her voice. "Right that's it, you've had ya warning." Whack! A toddler screams out that wet, gargling scream. Father storms into the room, starts effing and blinding, but Daniel's mum gives as good as she gets. Maybe it will come to blows. The old woman shakes her head as she withdraws from the window. From the profanity. Jack takes a shortcut past the playground; two car-tyre swings mope from the branches like carcinogenic fruit, a metal slide, a see-saw and a sandpit, or at least it had been, before the sand had been pinched. Another left turn, and Jack is home. Lift's not working again. He begins to climb the stairs to the seventh floor.

"S'at you, Jack?" She was in the kitchen.

"No, it's Father bloody Christmas."

"Daddy! Daddy!"

"Hello, my darlings," he cooes, bending down, ruffling their hair, letting his children clamber all over him, impulsive as cubs.

Giggles.

He makes his way down the hall through to the kitchen, two kids clinging from his neck.

"Hello, love."

A peck on the cheek, "Nice day?" She wipes her hands on her apron. Pushes her hair into place. She had been beautiful once.

"Same as usual."

Jack sits down at the kitchen table in the hot, small, cluttered place so hard to air on cold days such as these. The paint blistered on the wall around the cooker.

"What's for dinner, love?" He picks up a crayon. Colours, absent-mindedly, with daughter, Nina.

Jack's wife stands over the sink peeling potatoes. "Police were round. Door-to-door questioning. Some old lady in Havelock was mugged coming back from the post office this morning, I dunno... Ben got a gold star for a story he wrote at school, didn'tya, darling? Go'n show daddy your gold star..." she dunks the peeled potato into the sink of cold water then plops it into the pot on the cooker. Leaning against the cupboard, she begins to clean the juice and mud of the potatoes from her fingernails, looking, every now and then, out of the window. Nothing ever happened out there, but you look out of the window just the same, like a fish in its bowl doing the rounds.

Jack looks at his wife. How many times had he told her it drove him up the wall the way she kept fiddling around with her fingernails like that.

"What's for dinner, love?" he asked once more.

"Oh! Sausage n mash. Got a little baked beans left over from yesterday. You can 'ave those. Don't much fancy going to work tonight. I Just don't feel like it..."

"Oh, it's not so bad, love, let's face it, it's easy money."

"Treat me like muck, they do. I'm just the ice-cream seller, nobody, ain't I?" She said she was gonna start looking for something else.

The potato skin fell in dirty ringlets onto the draining-board.

"Just don't you give it up before you've found another one, that's all. I don't earn that much, Monica, and you know it."

"Whose fault's that?" she retorts, the corners of her mouth turned to stone.

"Don't start, love, I've had a hard day."

"And d'you fink I sit around on my bleedin' backside all day? What do you fink I do all day?" she snatches another potato and goes to work on it.

"Come on, love…"

But she wouldn't hear of it.

"Don't you *love* me! If you'd kept away from the bloody bottle you'd still 'ave your licence and'd be making some decent money instead of rubbing shoulders with all those coons down in the docks! Talk about taking a step down! First you were the organ-grinder, n now you're the *fucking* monkey!"

"Go n colour in your bedroom, Nina, there's my darling. Tell Ben I'll be up in a minute to have a look at 'is gold star. I promise."

Nina didn't take much telling. She is up and off in a shot.

Jack, holds his breath, for a second, presses his fingers into his tired eyes, but he can still see her; her greasy hair, her stony grimace. Then it just happened; he darted from his chair and lunged in her direction.

"Can't-you-con-trol-your-self-in-front-of-the-chil-dren-for *Christ's* sake?" and he pounded the sink with his fist.

Monica jumped. She held onto that potato as though it had the power to shield her from harm, but he grabbed her by the blouse, his fingers swiping her braless breasts lollopping around on her ribcage.

Monica yanked herself free.

"Don't *you* tell me how to behave wivva children! I know them a fat lot better'n *you* bloody do! Come home, give them a kiss and that's it. Fink your duty's done, duntya?" She peeled away furiously. "Bet you haven't even noticed that Ben needs a new pair a shoes. You don't have to hear im crying cos he can't have a pair o football boots, *do* ya?" she spat, flicking the knife in front of his face. "Three years in school, he is. When the hell've you ever been to an open evening tell me that, go on, tell me!" She sniffed hard. "Nina starts school at the end of the summer. Fink I'm gonna send her to school looking like that? Sometimes

I'm ashamed to take her out a the house, she's got nothing decent to wear. When was the last time she got somefing which ain't second hand? When's the last time *I* got somefing new, for that matter?"

"I'm off!"

"That's right, piss off to your cronies down the pub! What the hell do *you* know about bringing up children?" she shouted after him, grabbed a handful of peelings and slammed them into the green floral pedal-bin at her feet.

Jack slid his jacket on.

"Daddy, you gonna come up and see my gold star?" Ben whispered from the landing.

"Later, darling, later. Daddy's just out to get a bit a fresh air, okay?"

"Morning Jack, ow's ya back?"

"Morning, Pete."

Ping! Ping! The two men clock in then head for the locker room. When he pushes the door open, Jack is greeted by the habitual sight of men sitting around tables in the smoky atmosphere of the basement. Some of them are reading the morning paper as they slurp from their flasks. Most of the white men sit together, all the black men at another table, drinking, reading, playing cards. One has just slapped his winning domino down on the formica table with a tremendous thud, which earns him a round of appreciative pats on the back from the cluster of men behind him. One or two white men are over with the black ones.

"Morning, boys!"

"Jack!" They like him. His natural way. Didn't care much for the others, but Jack, he was okay.

Pornographic pictures splayed across the walls. A busty blonde on a chair in her high-heel shoes, she is holding a whip up to her face and bites into it ravenously, her breasts hanging down like two enormous party balloons. A woman, dressed up as a schoolgirl in her blouse, tie and hat. She is naked from the waist down, bending over in front of a mirror, pulling her buttocks apart to show dark pink flesh circled by wisps of light ginger hair.

Looked like tinned mushrooms to Jack, who had seen such pictures so often, they weren't even exciting anymore. He is sitting on the bench, flicking his way through *The Sun* when another black docker walks in and hangs his tweed jacket up in the adjoining locker.

"Morning, Bob. Bet you didn't bring that jacket over with you, did you?"

"Is how many time me haffi tell yu. Me name Robert, not Bob. Me is no Englishman."

"Wot? You're kidding? And there was I thinking you'd just come back from a long holiday in Tenerife! You mean to tell me that tan's natural? You wouldn't be trying to pull my leg, now would you, Bob?"

"Me name Robert. Me name not Bob."

"Aw, come on, you like it anyway, don't ya?"

Robert sits down next to him for a moment to change his shoes.

"So, Bob, how's it going?"

"Yes, it deh gwarn[13] alright."

"That's wot we like to hear, innit!" Bob gets a slap on the back. Jack stretches his legs, then saunters off.

"Jyack, man! Come here a minute, nuh?"

He goes back to the domino table. "What's up, Linford?"

"Me got a fren outside deh look a job. Every where im go dem turn im down. Tink yu kyan do someting get im inna here?"

"Well, you know I'm not a foreman..." he stands there thoughtfully, "but you know wot, I'll pop out n'ave a look at im. Can't do any harm, can it?"

As he gets to the door, a fat white man, Jack doesn't know him personally, is fooling around, licking the breasts of the woman in the picture on the chair.

"If my old woman had tits like these, I'd never get to work I tell you that much, lads!"

Guffaw.

"Lads, lads..." Jack laughs out of a sense of solidarity, yet he is shaking his head, "wot is this world coming to, eh?"

---

[13] *gwarn* = either a) go on, or b) go and, according to the context

A young black man standing around at the top of the stairs; not quite knowing what to do with himself, afraid someone might come and grab him by the collar to throw him off the premises. He jumps as soon as Jack appears.

"Hello, mate. You looking for a job?"

He is.

"Wot's your name, then?"

"Richard."

"Richard, is it? By the way you talk I'd say you're from the West Indies."

"Me from di West Indies fi true!" the handsome young man's face erupts into a smile.

"Yeah, thought so... you from Jamaica as well, ain't ya?" With a finger to his nose, "I know, I know... Anyhow, I'll give you a tip, Rich. Roll your sleeves down. It don't give a good impression, know wot I mean? And button your shirt up. Got a tie?"

"Me a tree tie a doors[14]!"

"Well, they're no good to you there, son, you need one round your bloody neck!" Jack's eyes show he means no harm. "Button your shirt up as I said, put a tie on and come back in a day or two, see wot difference that makes, eh?"

"You the manager?"

"Nope, but I know wot I'm talking about." He winks. "Gotta go. Good luck, Rich." He heads off back down the stairs. "Don't forget now. See ya, mate!"

"Jyack! Jyack! Is wa yu say to him?" Linford is at the bottom of the stairs, waiting.

"Calm down, calm down, flippin' ek!" Jack brushes past him, gets his flask, takes a slurp. Takes his time.

"We just had a chat, that's all. Noffing for you to get your hair all curly about."

---

[14] *a doors* = at home

14

London, August --, 19--

Dear Junie,

I hope this letter find you in health and strength. I glad to hear Leroy feeling better now. Kiss the children for me and say hello to One-foot and everyone.

The weather begin to warm up a little bit now it's the beginning of August. You want to see the people them how them strip off and walk around half naked and how them freckle up freckle up like a ripe banana! Foolish you see! Me no have no time for them!

Fashion is different here. The women them wear one boogooyagga[15] shoe on them foot when you see it you nearly die laughing. Them call it platform shoes. If you don't watch you step, I tell you you going to break you foot in no time!

And them got one skirt call a mini skirt. Some women so disgraceful and wear it so short, them batty just hang out a doors[16].

Them also got one fashion where them crochet clothes with a crochet needle. Ask me if the woman them don't wear no bra and don't even crochet it fine to cover themself up! You know what them cover up? Them eyes with sunglasses! Even shorts them crochet and me see more than one woman already wear it with no drawers underneath. Flinging them raw fish in everybody face because nobody want it!

Marlene don't have to remind me it's her birthday in September. Is how she think I could ever forget? But I not only going to send a little extra something for her, me going to send a little

---

[15] *boogooyagga* = big and ugly
[16] *batty just hang out a doors* = their backside is hanging out in the open air

something for Leroy too or else them going to fight like puss and dog.

The girls them here young you see! When I think what I do with my 19 years and what they do. Them practically still suck lollipop. One or two nice English girls where I work. They always say - Emily, you are so secretive, why don't you talk more about yourself. Me don't tell nobody my business. Nosey them nosey. Them always go out for a drink and ask me to come. I always say I'm tired or I got something planned. Think me going to drink away my hard earn money? One African woman where I work call Betty. Face broad like a frying pan and she ugly ugly gone to bed[17] but me and her get on all right.

I don't see him yet and as far as I'm concern I hope it stay that way. Don't write me no rubbish about boyfriend. Me already get two presents from one and the presents them nice as a shame, me would never give them back. But, is who have to pay the bill? And you tell One-foot to shut up with him foolishness before me send somebody come chop off him other foot!

Always your loving friend,

Rose

---

[17] *gone to bed* = as a shame; like nobody's business

The facts:

Pigmentocracy

The rule of the pigment, people of African descent most approximating European ideals à propos skin, hair and facial structure, and having the most European blood being attributed a higher status than pure Africans. Africans of European influence were not only regarded as congenitally superior, but, more importantly, were also treated as such.

These 'superior' blacks (pigmentally speaking) were often manumitted and frequently the inheritants of handsome property from their slave-owning fathers. This practice was of such significance that, according to an enquiry of the House of Assembly in Jamaica in 1761, coloured offspring and freedmen were the owners of land valued between £200,000 and £300,000. Swift legislation soon prohibited whites from bequeathing real or personal property worth more than £1,200 sterling to any coloured or black.

Pigmentocracy of the British colonies:

Negro	=	child of negro + negro
Sambo	=	child of mulatto + negro
Mulatto	=	child of white man + negress
Quadroon		child of mulatto woman + white man
Mustee	=	child of quadroon (or pure Amerindian) + white man
Mustiphini	=	child of mustee + white man
Quintroon	=	child of mustiphini + white man
Octoroon	=	child of quintroon + white man

In the British Caribbean - with the exception of Barbados - one was designated as legally being white after the category of mustee, which of course meant that one automatically became free...

The fiction:

15

"Rose? Is how yu deh fly up di stairs like a phantom an can't even say howdi?"

"Marnin Miss Brown! Me never know yu was at home."
The minute she had walked into the house, she could tell that someone was in the kitchen pressing hair. It had, however, never occured to her that this person might be Miss Brown. Firstly, because she thought Miss Brown to be on day-shift. Secondly, because Miss Brown had her own kitchen, yet here she was, in her dressing-gown, a cap full of curlers on her lap, and stinking up the whole house.

"Yu don't have day-shift this week, Miss Brown? Me did tink yu was an day-shift."

"Me got a wedding to go to on Saturday so me change it round can get a few bits an pieces done, know wat I mean? This is me fren Gwendoline. This is Rose, one a me tenant."

"Marnin."

"Marnin."
Gwendoline parted Miss Brown's hair, rubbed in a carefully measured forefinger of Dixie Peach hair oil, then combed it through briskly as smoke curled up from the metal hot-comb on a front ring of the gas cooker, swirling its way towards the opened window. In a practised movement, Gwendoline swept the comb up from the cooker and swung it through the air, flicking the thick smoke from it, deftly. She whisked up some of Miss Brown's hair, held it tightly, then applied the hot-comb with a sizzling 'Hsss!'

Miss Brown: Yes, daughter of one woman me know deh get married, and send me a invitation. Nice young girl find herself a nice young man settle down and do tings proper.

Gwendoline: Well. (*blows on the comb*) Me don't know how s'maddy so black manage find such a nice young man. She better keep an eye on him.

Miss Brown (*in strong objection, turning round and glaring up*): Is wha black got to do wid it?

Gwendoline: Black got everyting to do wid it, yu know dat as well as me know it. Me no know no nice young man find a black woman stay wid her yet!

Miss Brown: You too stupid an prejudice, yaa Gwen. Is dis ignorant backward attitude stop black people from get anywhere. Back home no matter how yu got brain, if yu black, di teacha dem give yu bad grade write letter tell yu parents is dunce yu dunce. Yu want to know how many beating me get bicars a dem blasted lie teacha dem? And wen yu well an truly black, yu lucky if yu toe even 'llow fi grace di classroom! And if yu brown, no matter how yu dunce, yu find a good job can earn monni.

Gwendoline: My dear! (*slams the comb down on the metal ring so that the short black hairs caught between its teeth curl a bitter-smelling brown in the light blue flame.*) But if a woman too black me don't like her, yu know. Me just don't. And if her head too tough, me like her even less.

Miss Brown (yanking round yet again): Is wha yu trying fi say?

Gwendoline: Me not trying to say notting! If me nevva like yu, me wudda use up me time deh press yu hair?

Miss Brown sits back, sceptically.

Gwendoline: Arlright!

Miss Brown: Black people dem is dem own worse enemy, yu hear me? Shortly fore me come over here, me did stop off at Maas Richaad to buy some bread.

Gwendoline: Him where dem say donkey did kick him tree time?

Miss Brown: Who seh dat?

Gwendoline: Me no r'memba!

Miss Brown: Yu gwine let me tell di story or not?

Gwendoline's lips screw up in offence. She pulls the damp hair tighter than need be.

Miss Brown (noticing the gratuitous tugs but choosing to say nothing): Anyhow, him close around seven an me just manage get in in time. Whole heapa people stan up deh did want to buy a likkle bread fi di evening. Ask me if dat dutty good-fi-notting big-lip nigga no pick out him best bread fi di light-skin one dem an chase all we black one out say him close shop! Pick up him broom an want to sweep we out a im shop like seh we is a piece a rubbish!

Gwendoline: Yu mek dat deh hugly twis-up-face nigga sweep yu out a im shop?

Miss Brown: Me! Is who yu tink yu talkin 'bout? Me snatch him broom out him hand an gi' im one raated lick pan him head, yu see, 'bout im did want to sweep me out a im shop! Got one likkle poky shap, tink im is s'maddy. And me, who dem say was dunce an can't learn notting, come a Hinglan, turn nurse and got me big house right here in London. (*sits up, as straight as proud*) Tink me ever going back?

Gwendoline: Yu no want fi go back? (*slices the hot, greasy mass with the tip end of the comb and wraps carefully portioned strips around a curler.*)

Miss Brown: Me? Yu too styupid! Me will go back for a holiday now an then, but tink me gwine go back live wid dem ignorant people? Me plan fi go back next year or di year after, if life spare, and me gwine bring two special someting fi dat deh Maas Richaad put it right down pan him counter fore im face and march out.

Gwendoline: Yessah!

Miss Brown: Me not saying di white people dem can't be just as bad. Dem equally ignorant an malicious wen dem feel like it (*handing up a curler, mischief in her voice*). One nasty ole lady in me ward name Mrs Walker, yu see. Mess up herself in di bed sit down smile at me when me haffi scrape dat shit from her behind. Last week I give her a dose of her own medicine. She shit up herself and wait fi me fi come on duty. Hear her;

    "Nurse Brown! Come and change me!"

Di woman deh order me about like a likkle Hitla. Me just ignore her. Di whole time she deh call out;

    "Nurse Brown! Nurse Brown! Come and change me!"

Me just go 'bout me business like me no hear a word (*hands up another curler*).

Gwendoline (flopping Miss Brown's ear out of the way): But stop! Wha mek she no call someone else? You is di only person haffi look after dat cantankarras ol' witch? Kuya! Did anybaddy ever see me trial! All di white nurse dem on tea break or wat?
Miss Brown: Is get me she out to get me, innit? Anyhow, me do me nine-hour shift march out put on me coat an go home, yaa. Next day she lie dere in di bed on her side. Her batty break out in a rash wid all dat shit pan it.

"Marnin Mrs Walter, how are you today?" me ask her.
Gwendoline (pressing her opulent stomach against Miss Brown's shoulder, infusing the latter with warmth as with the smell of one of her many buy-a-market fragrances...): Gu weh! Yu too wicked!
Miss Brown: She call me a black bitch, innit. "Well," me say, "sticks an stones might break my bones, but *cuss-cuss no bore no hole in a me 'kin*[18], no sah, and if yu tink seh me gwine scrape weh any more shit fram dat shrivel up batty, yu just try me." Fram dat day to dis, she no mess up herself again.
Gwendoline: Yessah!
Rose, still waiting patiently in the doorway throughout the repartee, allowed Gwendoline to finish a whole row of curlers before she ventured, "Miss Brown, I got to be going now."

"Hm?" Miss Brown turned to look in the direction of that voice, surprised to find Rose still standing there as though waiting for a command. "Oh yes, child. Yes child, arlright. Go good. See yu tomarro. Anytime yu deh go somewhere special and want yu hair done Gwen glad fi do it."
Rose glanced at the said person, who confirmed her consent with a nod and a smile.

"Go good," repeated Miss Brown, pulling her dressing-gown across her thighs. "See yu tumarro."

> *One man went to mow, went to mow a meadow*
> *One man and his Spanish girl turn around*
> *Spanish girl...*

---

[18] *cuss cuss...* = cussing won't harm me (won't bore any holes in my skin)

16

Touch –

The soft, warm glow of the incipient day seeped in through the window, fondling the sparse furnishings of the room. Not much to look at, let it be said, yet clean. More than clean; immaculate. Sally prided herself on the spotlessness of her cabin, cleanliness being next to godliness, as she wholeheartedly believed. She sat in front of her breakfast, praying ardently. Sat at a rickety table which stood precariously in one corner, flanked by benches of equally dubious stability. Home-made clothes covered her sinewy body. Many long, dark skirts brushed the floor around her. Her strong, muscular arms rested underneath the shawl which hugged her shoulders. Her fingers, dry and old-looking, the nails hard and brown. Hands that could have belonged to a woman in her fifties. Hands that could even have belonged to a man. Thick-skinned, working hands. Instead, they belonged to a young woman in her twenties who had stopped counting her years. Light ricocheted off the furniture, off Sally's body. Patches of colour swam across the surface of the table, over Sally's hands as she broke pieces of bread to put in her mouth. Another long morning. Another long day at the house cooking for Mrs Williams who, although white, was a nice progressive lady who treated her workers well. She was particularly fond of Sally, whom she allowed much liberty and a few small favours, for Mrs Williams was not totally insensitive to the problems of a poverty-stricken black woman who had a young child to add to her troubles. She had generously donated much of what was to be seen in this two-roomed cabin and permitted Sally to return home at the end of each long day. After eating, Sally laid out her daughter's breakfast, then made her way soundlessly into the child's room.

Room? A length of cloth held up by tired-looking rusty nails was all that had been needed; one in the wall and one in a wedge of wood used to fill a sizeable hole in the roof. The cabin's only window hid shyly behind the fabric wall in Tété's corner. As Sally had acquired enough curtain (Mrs Williams), she allowed herself the indulgence of gathering them into lush folds, there to keep out prying eyes, although not a neighbour far and wide. The material cornering off Tété's section of the room had not, alas, been in such plentiful supply, hence stretched drum-tight, its hem barely kissing the floor. As compensation, the two wooden walls had, long ago, been given a lick of light blue paint which, here and there, ruffled open like a chrysanthemum. Yes, it was a snug little room and room enough. No use giving a child more than it needed. Only make it turn out bad.

The child slept, mouth open wide, with a look of contentment. A look that belied the shock of a sound thrashing in the middle of the night occasioned by one of her mother's spot checks on the cleanliness of the child's feet. Tété had taken the risk of going to bed without washing her feet in the basin in the yard. After all, Sally had stealthily lifted the bedsheets only the night before; she had felt the light breeze up her legs and in her nightgown. Surely mama wouldn't check again so soon. Sally smiled to herself as she recalled the child's startled look as she felt the first whack of the beating-stick across the soles of her feet.

"Look how you - foot - dem - black!"

Whack, whack, whack. Sally had a good ear for rhythm.

"Go - an - wash - you - nar - sty - dut - ty - foot - dem!"

Even as the child jumped up, screaming, jigging around the room to avoid the beating-stick, so Sally followed, bending low and aiming at the feet, every now and then catching her on the calf, which sent both child and jannimatta[19] even higher into the air.

The child now lay almost horizontally in the bed, having arrived at this comfortable position after much tossing and turning. Not bought, but made, the bed consisted of a wooden door balanced on four large stones. Blankets, old clothing, made

---

[19] *jannimatta* = deposits in the corner of the eyes after sleeping

a mattress with which the young body wrestled every night beneath a multicoloured quilt like a tortoiseshell atop her. This latter, a luxury, and well the child knew it. Other children simply had to wrap themselves up in the cloths which made the mattress. Not good enough for Sally, and certainly not good enough for her one-and-only child, so she had accepted, grudgingly, the quilt from Mrs Williams, muttering to herself "wat bag no want him give shatova."[20]

On her way out of the dark room, Sally took something out of her pocket, slyly, and hid it in one of the deep pockets on the child's school pinafore (Mrs Williams) draped over the back of a chair. She tied her head. Checked her face in the mirror (no jannimatta? Check. No whitey-whitey round the mouth? Check. Ears clean? Check. Hair o.k.? Check). Quietly, she left the house to barefoot the hour-and-a-half stretch to Mrs Williams'.

A smacking of the lips and a rubbing of the eyes to remove the green, crusty deposits heralded Tété's return to consciousness. She lay in bed, enjoying its warmth to the last minute. Her day was as regimented as a trooper's. Up, make bed, put on house dress, fetch water (the river was two miles away), breakfast, wash up, wash self, put on school clothes, check school things, remove headscarf (kept on till the last minute to keep hair neat) - *school*!! The drill was finely tuned, thus Tété knew precisely how much time she would need for its execution. The unexpected assault in the night had interrupted her sleep to the effect that she had slept longer to recover the lost time. When she woke up, she felt immediately that it was later in the day than either herself, her mother or the schoolmistress would have liked. In a word, Tété was late.

She performed her drill in record time (jannimatta? Check. Whitey-whitey? Check), grabbed her schoolhat (Mrs Williams) and sped through the door. A passer-by would have been intrigued to know what invisible hand yanked Tété back as she ran to school. For she was as surely yanked as a petulant puppy is by its new, young owner. Tété appeared to suddenly

---

[20] you only give away what you no longer consider good enough for yourself

jump back, then proceed at a dignified pace. The invisible 'lead'? Sally's stern face together with her firm hand which had both, in their inimitable way, reminded Tété on not infrequent occasions that she, that is to say Tété, was no dog, and that, furthermore, up the road, there was no bone. This was understood to mean that she should walk slowly, and like a 's'mady'. Awareness that she was late for school and that walking like a 'somebody' would make her even later forced Tété's knees, every now and then, to bend deeply as if wishing to break into a trot; caught between not wanting to disobey her mother (her running to school would, by some miracle, always reach her mother's ears) and not wanting to be at the receiving end of schoolmistress' sarcastic remarks. Worse still, she might even be at the receiving end of some freshly snapped twig which she could at this very moment picture in schoolmistress' hand as she stood at the entrance of the school, making a big show of looking at her watch. Tété's stride became longer, kicking out her long skirt in front of her. Stride, stride, bend, dip, quick quick - yank! – stride… stride… (Me is a s'mady...), her hands in her pockets as she concentrated on walking as quickly as possible whilst still being a 'somebody', but no, you kyan't walk good wid you hands inna yu pockit, but what is dis? Her fingers had fastened onto an unusual shape. Unusual in as much as it wasn't usually to be found there. Usual in as much as Tété immediately recognised the hard object, its hairy shell with its firm, grained interior. The discovery brought a twinkle to her dark eyes.

17

Teacher Johnston stood on the threshold, eager to display her authority. She savoured it as one does the sweet syrup of a mango rolling down one's chin as the tongue, vainly, slides over the teeth to remove the slithers of mango flesh which have lodged themselves there. What a joy it was to have power, to be looked up to in the community when all around seemed to be bowing and scraping to the Powers that Be! Teacher Johnston had education, could speak English 'fine'. Not satisfied with having made something of herself, she would have given anything to be light-skinned, soft-haired and a good deal less strapping. Her disappointment at not being able to actively obtain these ideals had hardened her into a bitter woman whose hatred she reserved for the unsuspecting and undeserving darker-skinned children placed in her tutelage.

Tété she hated with a vengeance. Not only was she black, she had unnerving grey eyes and she was damned intelligent into the bargain. The child, dirt poor, would ordinarily have become adept at field work by now had it not been for the pig-headedness of her mother who, unfortunately, also had the support of her employers (Mrs Williams). What an eyesore, that pickaninny; running around barefoot in her cutdowns. Never mind that none of the other children were wearing shoes. At least they owned a pair and had them on on Sundays. Tété's fatherlessness was frowned upon by all. Not her illegitimacy, no, but her fatherlessness, for although they called themselves Mr and Mrs, few were the legitimate marriage certificates to be found in the community. Tété had no father, no, or at least no-one had publicly acknowledged her, an omission which delighted Teacher Johnston, oh yes, who never missed an opportunity to speak of 'your father' or 'your parents'. She herself had never married, alas. By some quirk of Fortune, her ideal man had always failed to see in her the ideal woman. Her complexion proved quite a source of consternation for the men of the island. Nor was she ever allowed to forget her unforgivably unfeminine size of shoe, which haunted her every time she dressed, undressed, looked down, or attempted to cross her legs. It became a reflex action of hers to glance quickly over a woman's left hand, to steal a look at the hem of the skirt, but rarely did she encounter such recalcitrant feet as her own, may the skirts be ever so long. It was a private joke that Teacher Johnston should thank her lucky stars for long skirts. Was even rumoured she wore men's shoes. And as she glanced down at the hem of a skirt, there was always a wicked light in the other woman's eye which Teacher Johnston never failed to see, curling her toes uncomfortably, seeking solace in the fact that she, at least, was literate, had education. The same could not be said for everyone, no, may the skin be ever so light, the hair ever so soft, or the feet ever so small. Teacher Johnston pictured Tété at her desk, working solemnly, rubbing her small dirty feet against one another, and she set her mouth as the bitter thoughts drove in. Never would she ask Tété for the answer unless convinced that the child could not deliver a satisfactory response. When Tété calmly, correctly, replied, sniff would go Teacher Johnston, sniff at the air, then pull her head back and proceed, leaving the rest of the class in a mild state of confusion.

"So. What's the answer? Brown!"
Brown solemnly gets to his feet to risk repeating Tété's answer. Bwoy dunce as a shame but teacha no beat her so im tek a chance.

"Very good, Brown. That's correct. Sit down."

Tété approached the school. Schoolmistress stood swishing her stick.

"Late again, Morley. Did your *parents* forget to wake you up?"

"Marning Teacha Jahnstan. Sarry, Teacha Jahnstan," she hurried into the school.

Whack!! Tété caught a swish on her thigh.

"Stan still wen me talkin to you, you facety[21] likkle pitni!" Teacher Johnston could never carry off an outburst in fine English.

Tété stood still, looking at the teacher inquiringly.

"Is what you deh stan up wait for? Hin di classroom an si' down!" Whack!

Snigger snigger went the children as Tété took her seat. Her slate and chalk she removed from her pocket. Let them snigger; she was a somebody and she had something in her pocket. Nothing could spoil her day.

Resourceful as ever, the children amused themselves in the 'recreation area', and this in spite of the dirt patch assigned to them on which to live out their fantasies. No swings, no ropes, no tyres to throw oneself onto. No. But knowing nothing different, and having their privileged position impressed upon them daily, the children happily played in the dirt yard.

Groups of boys, emulating their fathers, bragged about what they had and what they could do. Each strove to outdo the others, to earn the admiration of his peers. They all wanted to be like father; bold, intrepid, taking stick from no-one. Two young boys, kicking around in the dust, warmed up for today's bout.

"Yu ever smoke ganja[22]?"

"Yeah man. Di stuff wikked like a bitch, eee?"

"Gu weh, yu too lie!! Yu too likkle an lie!!"

"Is who yu deh caal liar? Look pan yu head, how it favour[23] button hole!!"

The onlookers jig around, jig jig, laughing, slapping their fingers together, egging them on.

"Look pan fi yu head. Dry and roll up like a peppercorn! Tink me no see yu yestiday wen yu ask yu madda bout someting an she tell how "yu too kitty lite up. Yu kitty too lite up to much![24]" he imitates his rival's mother, pushing up his chest,

---

[21] cheeky, rude
[22] marijuana
[23] *favour* = looks like
[24] you want to be too involved in everything and are just too plain nosey for your own good

sticking out his behind and opening his eyes wide, all the while scolding in a high-pitched voice. "Den she leggo one bitch lick pan yu big old peppercorn horse-head." Thump! He clouts the boy.

The onlookers roll around in the dust, kicking their legs, screeching, howling. It was clear who was the victor today.

Angry, embarrassed, peppercorn horse-head turns on the onlookers.

"Is who unnu deh skin unnu teet[25] at? Damn piss-bed likkle pitni unnu!!" Off he struts, man-like, proud, as he had often seen his father do after 'words' with his mother.

Time, however, would sooner or later take him gently by the hand, reveal to him that father could be looked at from more than one angle: she would show him how to walk a full circle around father, viewing him from the side, from the back, from angles father was at pains not to disclose to son. "Look!" she would say, "look how he squirms when you look at him from behind. Look how he is bold when you are smaller. Look how he brags when you are his equal. Look, how he licks his lips and rubs himself when you are female, young and ripe. And look, watch his posture slink as he comes into contact with his betters and now how his pride swells like a puff-adder the minute they are out of earshot." This patient, self-effacing teacher; you begin to understand why she is always chuckling to herself, unmasking the hero to expose the vulnerable man. Time, the best playmate one could ever have.

Tété, having found herself a quiet little space, stood nibbling at her piece of coconut. She felt the very strong desire to sit down. This would however mean dirtying her skirt, for which crime she would surely receive a beating. So she stood. It was a glorious day. Movement had slowed down to a minimum. Even the birds seemed to be doing slow motion, or so she thought. Last night's whipping and her lateness were worlds away.

"Is wat yu got there?"

Tété jumped, a thief caught in the act.

"Hello, Mary-Jane."

---

[25] grinning, smirking so that the skin of the teeth can be seen

"Me say is wat yu got deh deh nyam[26]?"
Tété was not overfond of Mary-Jane; a show-off and the teacher's pet.

"A piece a coc'nat."

"Gimme likkle bit, nuh?" It was not a question.

Tété's arm refused to extend itself in the direction of one greedy-eyed, big-mouthed Mary-Jane.

"Bwoy! Di pitni craven[27], eee?" Mary-Jane said in sham astonishment as she made signs of going off in another direction. Suddenly, her arm lashed out like a snake's tongue at the coconut in Tété's fist.

Tété, by this point on full alert, managed to swing her arm back a fraction of a second before Mary-Jane had made a swipe at her prized possession.

"Yu craven papaless pitni yu! Keep yu dutty likkle piece a coc'nat. Me nay even did want it." Off she went, swinging her hips and tossing her head as it was her mother's wont to do in open defiance of her husband's belligerence.

In the classroom, try as she might to resist, Tété could not refrain from looking at Mary-Jane, who in turn threw dagger looks back at her. Teacher Johnston? Writing sums on the board, her back to the class, her ample behind rocking in time with her arm, ever so much like someone vigorously waving goodbye to a friend at a station.

"Please, Teacha Jahnstan, Morley eating a piece a coc'nat..." Mary-Jane whined, then, with a smirk, gave Tété her *got you* look.

Tété's heart jumped. Why! It simply wasn't true!

Schoolmistress span round in an instant.

"Morley! March yourself here this minute!"

Tété stood up, resigned, the thought never having crossed her mind that she could take anything more than a minute to transport herself from her chair to be face-to-face, or rather face-to-waist, with schoolmistress.

---

[26] eating greedily
[27] greedy

"Show me the coconut!" Teacher Johnston forced the words out between tightened lips.

"I wasn't eating it."

The classroom hushed at Tété's audacity.

"Me say *show* me di coc'nat!"

The child dug deep into her pocket to produce the said offensive item. It lay, pathetically, in the palm of her hand with teeth marks decorating the circumference now considerably smaller than it had been at dawn.

Schoolmistress glared.

"Eat it!"

"I wasn't eating it."

"Me say heat di coc'nat!!"

"I was not eating the coconat, Teacha Jahnstan."

Schoolmistress grabbed the piece of coconut from the child's hand, scratching her in the process, forcing the coconut to the child's mouth.

Tété was an easy-going girl who, up to this point, felt her honesty to be sufficient to free her from this misunderstanding. When she gleaned, however, that Teacher Johnston was bent on humiliating her, her Morley pride shot to the surface. Her teeth clenched tight, not to be opened by the fingers forcing themselves into the small, pink cavity. Maliciously, schoolmistress scratched the child's gum as the whole class looked on, greedily. In an instinctive reaction of self-defence, Tété's strong teeth clamped down on the intruding digit, sending Teacher Johnston springing back with a howl. The point of no return, we could say, had been reached. Steaming with rage, schoolmistress seized the long, wooden ruler from her desk. All the other pupils squeezed their buttocks together, barely daring to breathe. The pain sliced through Tété's palm, the force of the blow knocking her hand down towards her waist. At the back of the classroom, someone sucked in his breath. Ruthlessly, Teacher Johnston beat the child. Neither did she limit herself to the child's palm. There was a loud *Crack!* as the wooden ruler made contact with the child's shoulder. Tété, biting her lip, refused to cry, refused to give in.

Crack! Smack! Lash!

Teacher Johnston, exhausted, flung the piece of coconut into the straw bin and shoved Tété into the corner of the room. Weakened by anger, by pain, the child stood facing the wall, undefeated. Considerable time it took before schoolmistress sufficiently regained her composure to proceed with the day's learning. Home-time came. The children, subdued, filed out of the classroom, each casting a glance at the little girl in the corner, the little girl who had been standing there for the best part of five hours. Schoolmistress gathered her pedagogic equipment, namely two sticks of chalk, her face mirror and her handbag, then marched imperiously out of the classroom.

"Child, is wat yu still deh do deh[28]?"

"Teacha Jahnstan put me in di corner."

The old caretaker shook his head from side to side. He hadn't had any learning and could often be seen, balancing on his broom, beaming with pride at the children in the yard. He himself had grandchildren. Proud he was of them, too. They could read and write, look forward to a bright future, as he often told them, for with education, nobody, but nobody, could take advantage of you. He had his own reasons for being particularly fond of Tété, whom he now looked at through sad, paternal eyes.

"Pitni, is time fi yu go home, yaa." The authority of giving the child the permission to go home sweet on his lips, similar to but stronger than whenever he would tell that he worked in the town and not on the land. He felt like a somebody.

"*Me* tellin yu yu kyan go home. Go long, now." Sweet! Besides, he had the right to tell this child what to do, all adults having the right to tell children what to do. Nor could he bear that batty deh jillap like a calabash[29] Johnston, who delighted in making him feel inch high. Why, he was old enough to be her father and knew a damn sight more about the things that counted. He relished thwarting her authority, albeit in her absence. And

---

[28] 'Deh' in Jamaican English has several meanings: a) the present continuous, placed before the verb. Thus, *deh do* = doing. Compare with Mary Jane's *deh nyam* = eating. b) meaning *there*, thus *deh deh nyam* means there eating and *deh deh bawl* means there bawling, i.e. crying. c) meaning *they*.

[29] bottom galloping, jumping up and down like something being tossed in a calabash

why should this child get a thrashing, which she was certainly in store for, on account of her? Tété was a bright one. Just about as bright as can be. He thought of Sally, then sighed, his mind on the past.

Tété went home, late.

18

Sally sat on her double bed, sewing, ruining her eyes, apparently not aware of the child lingering in the doorway. This bedroom, her pride and joy, was meticulously kept. It consisted of a double bed, such as didn't grace the house of the other villagers, a wooden chair, a mirror. No-one was allowed to sit on the bed, a ready-made-bought-from-town (Mrs Williams) bed, with solid wooden legs, to even breathe on it should they disturb the layers upon layers of lacy frills. After a minute or two, without looking up from her work, she said in a voice affecting indifference, "Is what time yu call dis?" Mrs Williams had had other plans for the evening and had let Sally off early which accounted for why she was at home before the child, and that even though the child was hours late.

"Teacha Jahnstan keep me late."

"And why?"

"Mary-Jane tell lie pon me. She tell Teacha Jahnstan dat me deh eat di coc'nat," she paused, "tank you for di coc'nat... dat me deh eat di coc'nat in class. An me never!"

"So is wat happ'n?"

"So she -"

"*Shee!!* Is who yu deh caal *she*?" She is the cat's mother. As much as she disliked schoolmistress, Sally would never tolerate 'facetiness' and 'disrispek' from any child to any adult.

"So Teacha Jahnstan tell me fi eat di coc'nat, an me wouldn't."

"Yu wouldn't?"

"No. Sh– " Tété quickly corrected herself, "Teacha Jahnstan 'cratch me in a me mouth, an me bite her."

"Yu *wat*?"

"Mc bite er. An she beat me."

The (not altogether unexpected) news of the beating snuffed the glow of pride which had infused Sally's face. She jumped off the bed and moved menacingly towards the doorway.

"An yu stan up deh deh bawl like a pitni!"

Tété was a mere nine years old. How could she be anything but a pitni.

"Me nay bawl. Is dat mek Teacha Jahnstan beat me bad an nevva mek me eat no lunch!"

"*Waat*?" Sally's every exclamation louder than a fog horn.

"Me nay eat no lunch, an is just now Maas Bill tell me fi go long home." Tété's courage could no longer stand the strain of being so valiant. Hot tears quivered from her eyes via her cheeks to her toes. "Look." She showed her mother the wealed skin on her arms and shoulders where the ruler had struck.

"Maas Bill tell yu fi go home?" Sally's voice softened.

Tété nodded, no longer able to speak.

"Come, eat yu dinner."

"An she dash weh[30] me piece a coc'nat!"

---

[30] throw away

19

A strange sight it was indeed that greeted Tété as she woke up the following morning. So strange, it took a good few minutes to burrow its way inside her head. There was her mother, Sally, sitting on the bench. Doing nothing. Just sitting. Waiting. Fear instantly leapt into the child's heart, is wat happ'n? Sally waiting to beat her? Why? Something to do with Mrs Williams, perhaps? Mrs Williams, whom Tété had never seen, but automatically, naturally feared. So flustered was the child by the sight that she completely forgot her drill and, mustering up her courage, she tiptoed out of the bed, gingerly into the room, her heart fluttering.

"Come eat yu brekfaas." Unthreatening. Mild even, at least as mild as Sally would ever allow herself to be. They ate in silence. Sally cleared away the dishes and washed up in a bowl of water, but stop, wat in heaven's name... Tété could hardly believe her eyes or peel them away from the extraordinary sight, but recollecting, she jumped up and scurried off to make the bed.

"Is where di bone? Drink some more tea."
Completely, utterly bewildered by now, Tété returned to the table to drink another mug of tea, slowly, not only because she did not really want it (not being accustomed to having tea for breakfast), but also because it dawned upon her that, this morning, she had no need to hurry, her mother apparently wanting her to be late for school, what in heaven's name... She tried out a phrase in the privacy of her own mind, one her mother exercised daily; Lard in heaven have mercy. Did god have a beating-stick, she wondered. It was then that she noticed the mug; a china teacup which her mother had rescued from Mrs Williams' dustbin and from which her infrequent guests were invited to enjoy a cup of tea. Being within breathing distance was usually good enough grounds for a beating. Here it was in Tété's hand. She almost dropped it. It had

a gold-painted rim. Delicate blue birds were chasing each other all over it. A dainty little handle it had too, fussing down from the golden rim and causing you bother so you were sure not to ask for another serving and overstay your welcome. A tiny piece of gold paint was missing, but not so as you would notice, though Mrs Williams obviously had.

"Pitni, is how long it gwine tek yu fi drink one mugga tee? Mek haste and finish, yaa."

With two slurps, she downed the then cold tea and automatically slid into her drill, but for the fact that she stood, for a half a minute, at a loss in front of the washing-up bowl, with nothing left to do.

For the first time in her life, Tété was accompanied to school by her mother. The child felt an unusual combination of pride, confusion, fear and embarrassment. She knew by now that her mother had stayed off work because of Teacher Johnston. What was she going to do? Sally meant business, no doubt about that. She strode at a stately, but no messin' pace to the schoolhouse, Tété holding up the rear.

Schoolmistress stood in the doorway, scouring the district for the latecomer. She would really get it this time! She tapped her foot, tap, tap, tap on the wooden floor of the schoolhouse. More sturdy in its construction than the cabins, there was still something of the makeshift about the building, as though it had been decided that these people were not to be taken seriously in their interest in education. Two tiny figures appeared on the horizon. Schoolmistress shaded her eyes with her left hand, the better to see them. After a while, she was able to make out one figure. But it was an adult. Impatiently (foot deh tap tap pon di floor), she waited until the figures drew nearer. Then she had it. It was Tété. Tété and her mother! An involuntary gasp fled down her throat to seek allies with the bread and tea in her stomach. Sally, for her part, and having caught sight of Teacher Johnston, now assumed combat posture, namely she hoisted all her long skirts almost up to the knees and accelerated in the direction of the schoolhouse doorway. Schoolmistress had so far successfully avoided any contact with Sally, whom she considered too low, and who, she felt, was not above embarrassing her in public, completely disregarding her seniority. Simply to be seen with the woman was an embarrassment. Yesterday she had punished this woman's daughter and lo', here she was strutting to school looking like a chicken scratching around in a back yard whereas any other parent would have welcomed, indeed encouraged, such discipline. Really, it was too much.

"My goodness. Is so late already?" She thought it fit to return to the class, which she did, closing the main door after her. How long had Maas Bill been standing there? Anyhow, there he was, leaning against his broom, his grey eyes half closed, singing sweetly to himself like a man who has had too much of something good. He dug out his key for the main door and opened it, leaving it slightly ajar. Then he remembered a crack under the window which he had been meaning to fill. The window looking into Teacher Johnston's classroom. Yes, he would sit there and fill it, likkle bit...

The children, who had all flocked to the window as schoolmistress stood on the doorstep, now rushed back to their seats and were studiously unexcited as she swanned into the classroom.

"Good morning, boys and girls."

A few of the said tried to look at each other through the corner of the eye whilst hoping to deceive Teacher Johnston into thinking that she had their undivided attention. Others could not stop themselves from staring at the classroom door, willing it to fly open and for the fun to begin. Those near the window were hard pushed not to giggle as the grey woolly head of Maas Bill bobbed up and down to get a peep into the classroom, his right forefinger shoved to his lips, his whole expression conveying the never-ending lashing they would be in for if they ever brought to schoolmistress' attention the fact that he was on the other side of the window. It goes without saying that his tool-bag was nowhere in sight.

"Good - mar - ning - tee - cha - Jahn - stan!"

Sally stood with her daughter on the other side of the classroom door, both having, silently, crept into the building, Sally's skirts still hoisted dangerously high and on her feet her Sunday shoes.

Her only shoes. She had also removed her everlasting headscarf, revealing a head of fine, neat hair. Tété's heart thumped so much she feared she would not outlive the morning. What was her mother waiting for? Had she changed her mind?

"Now, let's see who's here, shall we?" Schoolmistress took the register with an over-generous friendliness in her countenance.

"Brown!"

"Here, Tee - cha - Jahn – stan!"

"Simit!"

"Here, Tee - cha - Jahn – stan!"

"Mary-Jane!"

"Here, Tee - cha -Jahn – stan!"

"Louise!"

"Here, Tee - cha - Jahn – stan!"

Schoolmistress hesitated.

"Inès?" her voice failed to maintain that carefree sing-along tone. The tightrope too high, her foot too big.

"Here! Miss – triss – tee – cha – Jahn - stan!" Sally marched into the classroom, dragging her daughter after her.

Maas Bill began his I'm-so-happy dance (batty deh jillap to the left to the right) beneath the window. He was mindful, however, not to take his eyes away from the classroom.

"*Mrs* Morley, what can I do for you?"

"Wat yu kyan do for me is tell me why yu beat me darta an stop her fram eatin lunch!" Sally's face almost touching Teacher Johnston's in a bitter kiss.

"Your daughter was -"

"*Don't* tell no lie pon Tété! She wasn't eatin no coc'nat!"

"I was -"

"Big grey-back big-man-foot woman like a yu deh listen to lie fram dat deh likkle doondoos[31] pitni! Yu tink yu is a s'mady? Yu tink bicars yu is schoolmistriss yu is better dan me? Yu is black, yu hear me, *black like me!* Yu tink yu is di only s'mady know someting? Well, *me* know someting yu don't know," and with that, Sally grabbed schoolmistress between the

---

[31] *doondoos* = albino, i.e. light-skinned. Sally is speaking about Mary-Jane

legs and held on with all her might, hand and crotch now vacuum-sealed. "If piss way easy fi piss, fowl wudda piss[32]!!" and with such words of indisputable wisdom, Sally ripped Teacher Johnston's crotch out, her hand swinging down fiercely to tro weh the piece of rotten meat. "An let me tell yu someting. If yu ever so much as lay one likkle finga pon my Inès Morley, me gwine lay *ten* pon yu!!"

Tété stood in the corner, horrified. What could she do with her eyes; what could she look at which would not look back, laughing in her face? Her eyes fixed themselves on her dusty toes. How would she ever live through this day at school? How could she ever feel right in this class, ever, ever again? Her mother had barged into the classroom with her skirts lifted and had grabbed the teacher's - down there. She had envisaged a match where each would throw fine phrases at the other. She would be proud of her mother for speaking such fine English and for beating Teacher Johnston at her own game. She did not expect her mother to make a grab at teacher's poonani she sincerely hoped the good Lord in heaven did have mercy she -

"Tété - sit down!"

The command came from Sally, who now lowered her skirts and smoothed them out. Her eyes challenged schoolmistress to a staring match but the latter had fainted into her chair. Sally marched out of the classroom, head held high. She hadn't premeditated an assault on teacher's poonani either she had only known that she would rely on instinct. The minute she heard that voice, that supercilious "*Mrs* Morley"... Still, Sally had no grounds to be displeased with herself; she had used no foul language and she had maintained the upper hand throughout. A daughter should be proud of such a mother.

"Hm–mmm, Sally, man! Dat was sweet, sweet, sweet!" The hole beneath the window could wait for another day, after all. Maas Bill no tarry deh, him make haste go round front to congratulate the winner.

---

[32] if it were easy for chickens to pee, then they would. This is a reference to teacher Johnston's childlessness

"Wuuuiii, wuuuii. Sweet as a shame! Walk about fi notting better than si' down fi so-so![33]"

"Gu weh. Yu too nosey. She likkle bit too important. Me his di only one in dis world wid di right to beat Tété."

"Is so yu tink?" The gentle question stroked Sally's face, eventually to rest on her breast.

"Is me di only one raise her, innit?"

"Fi who decision dat?"

"Me kyan't stannup ya deh labrish[34] di whole day. Me haffi go work, yaa." She departed, feeling those grey eyes, like so many fingers, touching, looking for a way in.

Spanish girl do the splits
Spanish girl show your knick -

Nack paddywhack
Give a dog a bone
This ol man came roll -

---

[33] going out without any expectations is better than sitting around half-heartedly because you could well get a pleasant surprise
[34] chatting

20

    Quizzical though it might at first appear to an outsider, all the tenants in Beswick Road were wont to stop -
for a fraction of a second -
whatever it was they had been doing each and every time the doorbell rang. This time round, that soft, apologetic press of a forefinger against the white, hard nipple of plastic gave unequivocal indication of the fact that that someone was not sure that he (or she) had the right to be putting his (or her) finger on that bell.
    Ding donnng... Ding... Dong???
One or two children, wrenched away from their momentary play place in the vicinity of the curtains by an imperative parental grab, unaccompanied by words, were pushed impatiently to some other corner of the room. The ring of the bell was not such that any of the tenants of this handsome terraced redbrick house in Beswick Road could say without doubt that they recognised it as belonging to any of the people they knew. (Uncertainty, like sister, Certainty, of similar intensity though of a differing hue, thus ear, eye, heart, experienced, never shall confound the gait of the two...) It might be door-to-door, some conjectured. Or election campaigners, others speculated. Worse still, it might be Immigrations. Or even the Police...? Not a soul, not even the cat- moved -
for a fraction -
of a second.
Miss Brown had quite categorically stated that if anyone ever, *hever* gave the Police occasion to come knocking at her door, that person could pack them bag and she and them would have to part company. So one or two wives shot their husbands a vicious look. And one or two wives were shot back an equally vicious shut-yu-mouth-woman. The doorbell rang again. Truculently, this time.

On this particular, somewhat agreeably sunny London two fifteen, when all the tenants of Beswick Road, and Miss Brown's cat, desisted from action for that fraction of a second, Rose happened to be down at Miss Brown's as she had got into the habit of doing on a Saturday afternoon. She had, by now, made the acquaintance of most of the other tenants, either on their way to the kitchen with a basin laden with soul food ingredients, or else on their way out again with a steaming delicious-smelling pot, but since no one had ever entertained the idea of inviting her to their room, Rose was not about to, either. Notwithstanding Miss Brown's inclination to chat-too-much, Rose welcomed the time spent in her company as a real taste from home. The two women cast reciprocal 'is-who-dat?' looks from beneath arched brows as the bell was molested for the third time.

"Carmen!"

Carmen emerged from behind the plastic stripey hang-up between the kitchen and the living-room door.

"If is door-to-door, me have it arlreddy. Look like him no mean fi go weh fore him run up me lectricity bill, yaa. Mek haste and get rid a im."

As Carmen went over to the window, Rose and Miss Brown followed with their eyes. Miss Brown tiptoed in the direction of the tv set to turn the volume down.

"Mum, it's someone black."

"Black?"

"Yeah. Black."

"Is who it is?" Miss Brown, now two-thirds away from the sofa and one-third from the television set, had evident difficulty in making up her mind to go over to the window. "Is who it is?" she insisted.

"How'm I supposed to know!"

"Move *weh* fram di curtain no mek him see yu!" Miss Brown's whisper thundered over to her daughter and cuffed her as if she had just done something without permission.

Carmen rolled her eyes to heaven as she moved away. "He looks like you, if you ask me," but she had done her bit, so she now walked back to the kitchen, unwilling to perform any more favours, muttering something it was just as well Miss Brown was too preoccupied to pay attention to.

Miss Brown stared at Rose, then beyond her, then back at her once more. Her eyes grew wide with horrified recognition. "Roy!" She gasped.

Rose's eyebrows said, Who?

"Carmen!" Miss Brown whispered as loud as she dared.

Carmen re-appeared in the doorway with her most fed up expression on.

"You did see if him have a bag wid im, like im gwine stay long?"

Carmen shrugged her shoulders.

"Go an let im in."

"Why me?" Carmen protested. "I don't even know who he is!"

"Child...!"

She got the message.

He rapped tap taptap tap tap on the living-room door as he wiped his shoes off on the doormat. Roy had not seen his sister in years. Only once or twice since they had arrived in *Hinglan*, first him, then her, him following his wife's family to settle in Birmingham, her, Miss Brown, deciding in favour of London. Miss Brown, not at all partial to her sister-in-law, refused to spend her hard-earn money on a visit. And now he was here, in London. After all those years. It has to be said that Miss Brown's brother did feel a little awkward, after all those years, so he decided the best thing to do would be to behave as though they had just seen each other the other day.

"Miss B?" he greeted her with a chuckle, as with an over eager display of his immaculate teeth that had won him innumerable lady friends on both sides of the Atlantic.

"Uncle Roy," Miss Brown stated a fact, not a welcome. She stood in the middle of the room. "Di door open."

A stout, cheerful-looking man going on for fifty stepped like a dandy into the room. He was better looking than his sister and had helped himself to a taste of almost all of her girlfriends back home, which fact had invariably led to a mash-up of friendships, for which Miss Brown had never truly been able to forgive him. When Uncle Roy followed his wife to England, Miss Brown had hoped that the cold would put him out of action likkle bit. He only ever remembered he had a sister when his wife kicked him out and he needed somewhere to put his head. Here he was now; fatter than she recollected, a few grey hairs beginning to make an appearance, and the paunch of good living pressing itself tightly against the waist of his trousers. But where was his bag?

"Come in an sit down," Miss Brown said indifferently. But she could not help herself, she had to ask, "Is where yu bag deh?"

Uncle Roy made himself comfortable on the sofa. "Marnin," he said to Rose.

"Marnin," Rose replied.

"Yu see dis madda a yours, her bradda kyan't even sit down five minute rest him leg before she want to chase him out," he stretched one hand along the length of the sofa, eyes on Rose.

"Is not me daughter dat, but is a member a di family, yu hear wat me saying to you?"

"Is what yu name, lovely?" He sat back and opened his legs likkle bit.

"Emily," Rose said as she got politely to her feet. "Miss Brown -"

"Emily. You warng know someting, Emily? These Jamaicans don't have no manners, you know. Nat like *we* British. These Jamaicans rough and dirty-up like a old stone in a back yard. But *we* British, we nice and mannersable. Our manners nice and pallish like a precious stone in a ring. Now tek me. When I hear seh someone deh knock pon me door, me don't lek im stannup outside till im catch cold, me open up and invite im in. And me don't ask him is when him going fore him even sit down, me ask him is what im would like to drink. Dat's di diffrence between *we* British and dem Jamaican dem." Uncle Roy brushed something off his trouser leg and waited.

"Miss Brown," Rose tried again. "I best be going."

"Alright, Rose," she spoke in Rose's direction, with her eyes fixed on her brother. "Yu gwine come down later fi a likkle a me stew peas?"

If there was one thing Rose could not say no to, then it was the way Miss Brown cooked her stew peas. The delicious reddened oxtail to suck the fat off. The plateful of rice soaking up the sauce and slipping down your throat in a manner too good for chewing. Carmen was in the kitchen right now keeping an eye on the peas.
"If you sure is not too much trouble..." Rose avoided looking at Uncle Roy.

"Trouble? Is no trouble whatso*h*ever," Miss Brown assured her.

"Well," Rose turned to the brother on the sofa. "I best be going. Nice to see you."

"The pleasure was all mine," Uncle Roy replied gallantly.

Miss Brown standing in the middle of the room and Carmen in the kitchen both rolled their eyes up to heaven.

"All mine," he assured the slender young woman. Nice young gyal.

As Rose started up the stairs, she just caught Miss Brown ordering Carmen to look in the fridge see if Daddy still got a few can a beer, and by the time Rose reached the top of the landing, Miss Brown and Uncle Roy were tearing up some raucous laughter about something. Or someone.

"So anyhow, is what you tink a Hinglan?" Uncle Roy made himself comfortable behind the generous plateful of food Carmen had grudgingly placed in front of him. He picked up his knife and fork.

"Wait till we say grace!" reproached Miss Brown. She clasped her hands together.

All bowed their heads, reverently.

"For wat we are about to receive may the Lord mek us truly tankful amen," and before anyone else dared open their eyes, Miss Brown's cutlery could be heard to clink the plate.

"Hinglan nice as a shame, ee?"

The shy smile from that 'nice young gyal' was to be interpreted as a rejoinder in the affirmative. Rose fussed some stewed kidney beans and oxtail onto her fork.

"Wen me come a Hinglan, me was one a di first blacks here, yu know. Nineteen hundrid and fifty. Me rememba how me did go a Kingstan an find out all me options. Me go to Elders & Fyffes Ltd. Dem have a 7000 ton passenger steamship tween Jamaica an Avonmouth. And me go to United Fruit Company, 40 Harbour St, Kingstan Jamaica, but me turn dem down," he swallowed a forkful of steaming rice. "Pass me di pepper sauce." Carmen complied.

"Tank yu."

"*De rien.*"

"I beg yu pardon?"

Carmen sighed, "It's French."

Uncle Roy raised and eyebrow, di child bright or just plain facety?

"You tink a Britishman was gwine sail inna any boat name ba-na-na pro-dyu-sa? Me is a ba-na-na?" He chuckled.

Rose and Carmen smiled at one another.

Miss Brown had heard it all before.

"Yu an yu styupidness 'bout yu British. British me back foot!" She mixed up the peas with the rice.

"Is how often me haffi tell yu? Nineteen hundrid and fifty me fly over wid me British passport. Nineteen hundrid and fifty his excellancy di gobnar Sir John Higgins was Captain-genrall an gobnar-hin-chief of Jamaica an its dependencies. A Hinglishman. Me nevver own a Jamaican passport in me whole life. So is wha dat mek me? British, or Jamaican?"

"Yu passport don't say notting bout who yu really is. Is just a piece a paper mek yu kyan move from place to place more easily, yaa. When di Japanese did win di war an tek over the British colony give you a Japanese passport, dat mek yu Japanese?"

"Cho man, yu too stubborn." If there was one thing Uncle Roy deplored, it was ignorant people carrying on as if they were intelligent. "Me find out all about British Overseas Airways twice a week from Landan to Lima. Yu even know where Lima is?" he challenged.

"Is wha me want to know where Lima is for? Me ever gwine want go a Lima?"

Uncle Roy snorted. "Santiago-de-Chilli, New Yark, Bermuda, Narsa, Kingstan, Panama, Lima. And British West Indian

Airways Ltd base 751/2 Harbour St, Kingstan. Pan Am deh fly daily via New Yark an Miami an cost £152. Four hundrid an twenty-seven Jamaica dalla. £235 return. Six hundrid an fifty-height Jamaica dalla. Me is a carpenta. A good job, dat. You want know wat a good job as a carpenta pay you 1950?" He looked at Rose and Carmen. "Two poun' a week. Two *poun'* a week! An four hundrid an twenty seven Jamaica dalla fi a one-way ticket. You work it out." He leant back.

Carmen and Rose did some mental arithmetic. Miss Brown no bother.

"KLM dat time deh fly daily via New Yark or Havanna, but dem Dutch not getting my hard earn money. Is dem and di Spanish start up dem colony business spoil up di chance fi we black people till di British come an put a stop to it. Look at how dem mess up South Africa."

"Eat up yu food fore it get cold," Miss Brown muttered, meaning im chat-too-much. As always.

"Me never beg fi come a Hinglan like yu see di Pakistani dem deh do. Di British government *h*invite me an give me a job when me come over even. Dat is wat I call service. Me is not one a dem people jump pon no bandwaggon. Me is a pioneer! Yessah!" He poured himself a glass of carrot juice. "Anyone else?"

Miss Brown held out her glass, deliberately forgetting her table manners afterwards as she was sure that his last comment about jumping on the bandwaggon was aimed at her. She had first gone to England after waiting to see how others were faring.

"An when tings start fi get tough di end a di fifties, dem mek new legislation. Commonwealth Immigrants Act, July 1962. Dem tighten up. Only if you intelligent and qualify, or if yu underage an yu parents legally in Britian, den yu cudda still mek it over. Hinglan look diffrent den, yu see! Wen me come over, dem did have one smog after four o'clock yu see! If yu nay know yu way home by heart yu never find it. Di number a times me walk round Birmingham an kyan't find me own front door! An dem still did have trolley bus dat time an no white line dem an di roads like dem have it now. An di pavement did high, yu see! You brok yu foot if yu no careful. But all dem tings nay bother me. Me deh look after misself since me was twelve, an di first pair a shoes me ever have pon me foot was when I go into di army at sixteen, so me more or less kyan cope wid anyting. Dat time dem still don't have no sirens yet. Di palliceman dem did hang out di window an ring a bell. Ting a ling ting ting! Man, Hinglan change up!"

Miss Brown caught Carmen stealing a look at her watch for the third time. "Child, is wha mek yu inna such a hurry?"

"Who? Me?" Carmen looked at her mother as if she hadn't a clue what her mother was on about. "I'm meeting a couple a mates later down at the youth club, that's all, and I don't wanna be late. S'it alright if I leave the washing-up for later? I'll do it when I get in."

"Youth club, or bwoyfren?" Uncle Roy interpolated, a twinkle in his eye. He sucked the skin of a kidney bean from between a slit in his teeth.

"Boyfriend?" laughed Carmen, nervously. "You gotta be joking!"

"You gots to be joking indeed!" Miss Brown retorted.

Rose stay nice and quiet. Even the cough in her throat have to wait likkle bit. At sixteen, Rose had already had her two children, so she knew Carmen was no child anymore.

"I wudda *buss* her head fi her if she ever so ungrateful not fi tek di chance I come all di way to Hinglan fi give her."

Carmen's head hung low, like her shoulders, drooped in a show of surrender. Inwardly, she fumed at Uncle Roy. Just as she was beginning to like him, he had gone and started to stir up trouble. Hopefully he would be gone by the time she got back.

"Keep your hair on, mum," she soothed. Other people thought Miss Brown hard, but Carmen had her ways and means. "If I say I'm off down to the youth club, then I'm off down to the youth club, okay?" She stood up. "See you when I get back, then."

"Come in an show yu face fore yu go let me see wat yu put on."

"If you say so," Carmen sighed an exasperated sigh, and tried to slouch from the room as though she really would rather not go.

Once she had gone, Uncle Roy sucked his lips thoughtfully, then asked innocently, "Is how old your Carmen is?"

"Sixteen," replied Miss Brown, glad that she had had Carmen, seeing that her other children were now too old to be allowed over. For Carmen things would be different. Were different. She had a wardrobe full of clothes, shoes on her feet and others lined up under her bed just waiting to be worn. Carmen did not know the meaning of the word hungry. If she was sick, her mother could take her to the doctor without paying a penny. Carmen would have chances. She would have a future. The colour of her skin would not matter; her shade of black or the nature of her hair. If she learnt well. She would get somewhere. That was Britain. Not Jamaica.

Sixteen, Uncle Roy thought, but decided that now was not the time for talking. He ate up his stew peas before, as Miss B said, them get cold.

21

"Jack!" Monica prodded him, "C'mon, you'll be late for work. Jack... you playing wiv yourself?"

"Wot time is it?"

"Time you stopped wanking and brought some money in!"

"Know wot? You're as common as muck."

She leant over, squashing her breasts against his arm, said, "Give 'ere, let me do that for ya..."

But he yanked the sheets back and marched his cheated hard-on out the bedroom.

They hadn't done it for ages. There he was, wanking off next to her and there she was, only too willing. Monica fell back onto her pillow, wondered what she might be doing wrong, but then thought *fuck* it, she snatched her cigarettes from the bedside table.

"Hello again," said Jack as he reached the bus-stop, wearing a grin so wide almost all his teeth were on show. "You and I must stop meeting like this or tongues will wag, you know!"

"I don't know what yu mean!"

"Don't you, now. We've met here at least a dozen times… wot'm I saying," he interrupted himself, "*dozens!* And I get a glimpse of you almost every day, or every other day. You never have a friendly word to say to me though I know you don't dislike it."

"Is what yu tink I can possibly have to say to someone like you?"

"Well, you could smile once in a while and say, "Hello, Jack, fancy meeting you here," or "Hello, Jack, nice to see you again," you know, something like that. Nice n friendly, like."

"Nice an frenly me back foot!"

"Wot have you got to be so defensive about, eh? I don't hiss or whistle as you go past like your lot do. Well, do I? No, I most certainly do not! I'm just nice n friendly, as I said. So wot's a young girl like you got to be so uptight about, anyway, eh?"

"If is woman yu deh look go look inna yu own kind an inna yu own age, yaah."

"I beg your pardon?!" It was far too loud to be a real whisper. One or two heads turned. Jack put his back between them and Rose, "How old d'you fink I am, then?" Did he look a mess? He knew Monica could look a damn sight better but he thought he wasn't doing too badly.

"Yu old enough to be me farda, yaah." Rose turn her face the other way look down the road.

"*Wot?* Don't make me laugh!"
But he did. "If I started having kids at fifteen like your lot seem to then I could be your father, grant you that." She had a nerve! Old enough to be her father indeed! "I'm only -"

"How old you is don't interest me."

"Wot does interest you, eh?"

"Wat me do is none a fi yu business." Is wat mek im no go weh an leff me alone, im is a blasted nuisance, she thought. An where di blasted bus deh?
No blasted bus, near or far, but Lou, as luck would have it, a little up from the bus-stop, Lou stepping out of the newsagent's and heading their way, hunched over her cigarette. From the minute she recognised that hunched up petite frame, Rose started to fumble at her bag till it opened, the better to stick her head in its jaws, rummaging around for she knew not what, the main thing being that her eyes were off the street. And the minute Lou caught sight of Rose, her eyebrows let go of one another, "Oh ello, Emily! On your way home, are you?"

"Yes, see you." She managed a meaningless exchange for a second or two, but glanced up only briefly at the voice that had so stabbed into her privacy and sliced her open.

"Wot you looking for, then? In a bag that small can't be too hard to find anyfing, can it? I mean there's not a lot you put in your bag when you're going to work not like when you're going out somewhere special I'm off somewhere nice tonight. Fink I might pop out again this aftanoon n see if I find somefing to doll me up a little bit noffing I hate more'n a woman who lets herself go, can't be surprised if her old man's eyes start doing the walkies, know wot I mean? Course, me n my old man we're just like we were from the beginning, wouldn't change im for the world n he wouldn't want no other woman, either, I see he's alright. No-one goes running after a bit a scraggy chop when he's got steak at home, know wot a mean? Anyhow I must be off, listen, you fancy coming out for a round of bingo sometime? All girls togevva, we don't half 'ave a good laugh I got noffing against you lot. My Michelle had a golly when she was little got it from her auntie Diane. Loved that little golly, she did. Really, must go, got a fousand n one fings to do before the day's done. Cheerio, Emily. See you tomorrow!"

You know them people who talk non-stop? No business if you show no sign of interest, just talk talk talk without them even stop to draw breath? This is a kind of person Rose could never stand, like a whistling woman and a crowing hen; they were an abomination. For one long, long, moment, Rose stood with her eyes closed and her head tilted back, as if knocking back some nasty cough syrup. Swallowed she did, too, then set her lips sternly before opening her eyes once more to find Jack turned to face her, not smiling, or self-satisfied, rather thoughtful, even sad. She would not look at him. Said,

"Here yu bus."

He continued to look at her.

"Look, yu gwine miss yu bus!"

"I'm not taking this one. Not today. I'm catching the same one as you are," then he ducked away from the vexed look she shot him. "No need to get your knickers in a twist, I'm not gonna follow you home or anyfing like that... where you getting off?"

Silence.

He sighed, "Look, you can't stop me from getting on the same bus as you. There ain't a law against it, far's I know. If you tell me where you're getting off I'll get off a stop earlier, how's that?" he tried to be cheery.

Silence.

"Am I talking to a brick wall or somefing?"

After a long, long while, "Me deh get off by Pallard's."

Jack nodded, as if contemplating a second option, decided upon:

"Pollard's, is it? A deal's a deal," but his cheerfulness made no impact on her. He exhaled with a slight whistle, his eyes on his shoes.

"Emily -"

Rose jump. He had said her name so sadly, so painfully, but never the pain which she had felt.

"...that first time I spoke to you and made you laugh, your face lit up so much it was an absolute beauty to see... you oughta laugh more often... really, Emily..."

Their bus ground to a halt at their feet.

"Ladies first." His arm outstretched gallantly to pave the way, Jack let Rose board the bus, then sat down next to her.

For her part, Rose hugged her handbag close to her chest and looked obstinately out of the window, much in the way certain Londoners had the nasty habit of doing whenever a dark-skinned passenger politely asked (and polite they always were) if the seat, that very same empty seat they were standing right next to, were free.

The West Indian conductor stopped in the aisle.

"Two please, mate."

Rose had no time to protest.

For his part, the conductor, whose one hand was holding the base of the ticket machine like the bottom of a babe in arms nestling on his chest, used the other to swing the arm of his ticket machine round till it ching chinged,

Ching ching!

He handed Jack the two tickets.

"Taa, mate."

Rose stared out of the window. If the truth be said, to look at Life from the window of a bus constituted a pleasurable, daily activity for Rose, the first taste of which was had in the taxi ride to Beswick Road on the very day of her arrival. The streets of London, though not paved with gold, nonetheless provided a plethora of noteworthy occasions for the eye and many a titbit to write back to Jamaica about. Not to mention that agreeable chug-

chug-broom-broom under your seat as the double decker steered through the streets like an oversized perambulator. Quite, quite nice. But not this time. Nor did she need to turn her head to know that every time he walked past their seat, the conductor let his eyes stray upon the two of them. Jack Dunbar and Emily Thompson sat upright. Not a word passed between the two a dem. Once, they brushed shoulders as the driver took a corner too sharply. Neither apologized to the other.

"Pollard's is the next but one, so I'll get off here, okay?"

She nodded.

He reached for the cord overhead, suspended from the back through to the front of the bus like a washing line. Pulled it.

Ting ting!

"Some money drop fram yu pocket."

Jack glanced down to see a coin lying on his seat. "Can't be mine. I keep my money in my wallet, here," he touched his breast pocket.

"Well, it's nat mine neither."

"You have it."

"Me say it's not mine!" she insisted, irascibly.

He picked it up as the bus lurched forward past the traffic lights. "I'll use it to pay your fare the next time... there will be a next time, won't there, Emily?"

She sat alongside the conveyor belt in her white overall and white cap. The meat pies soldiered by in rows of six, inspected by a battery of women, some more emancipated than others, all in need of money. Looking down the line, Rose never failed to be amazed at how many different colours a woman's hair could be. Those in possession of plenty bundled it under their caps, which were actually meant to enhance the idea of hygiene, but did nothing of the sort. Some of the women had delivered rather vocal opposition to having to remove their freshly applied nail varnish on their first day on the job; said what a waste of time and money it led to. Management even had the cheek to ask them to cut their nails, others had grumbled in their first tea-break, their gratefulness at having found employment not extending beyond the first hour.

"And have you heard? Their wanting to introduce rubber gloves? You won't catch me in a pair a rubber gloves! Whenever I see a hand in a rubber glove, I always fink someone wants to stick 'is hand up my -"

"You'd be lucky!"

And thus, the first friendships were sealed. Every now and then, Rose took a faulty meat pie off the belt to pack alongside others in a box at her feet. Some ended up on the worker's tables at supper time. Miss Brown's freezer was full of them. As long as her freezer didn't say no, she wouldn't, either, she said, and would finish with her standard joke, "Me get use to no sunshine in no time, but you tink me cudda live without dis here freezer? No sah! Lek dem back home keep dem sunshine, yaa. Me satisfy wid me freezer." The women chatted as they worked, filling each other in on whatever had been heard in the meantime. Allegiances were clear. Rose spoke when she was spoken to and belonged to no camp.

The few men on the shop-floor sat quietly, outnumbered, locking themselves away behind their eyes. Not much fun, working with all these women. Something demoralising about it, even if they did come off with a pound or two more on a Thursday night. Still, someone had to bring the money in and that was the man's role, so they sat there and got on with it, their thoughts elsewhere; on a new car, on the races, on the money, on a woman they fancied, and these thoughts pushed them forward, another minute, another hour, another day... Only the foremen strutted around, amusing themselves, but it could be a dangerous game, didn't they know it, for skill was needed to identify the venomous, or the unwilling, unless you wanted the next pay-day to be the last. Like Cheeky Charlie. A real goer, he was. Everyone liked him. Apart from the feminists. That was a new trend coming in and it cost Cheeky Charlie his job. On account of Mary. A tight-lipped woman who looked as though she'd never had it – that's what Charlie said later - so he had snuck up behind her and whispered to her earlobe:

>Mary, Mary,
>quite contrary,

let's 'ave a feel of ya
hairy fairy…

but she slapped his face and had him dismissed for sexual harrassment. Management had tried to hang on to him as he was such a good worker and that, but Mary was having none of it. Started talking to the unions, so Management had to let him go. She had to go herself not much after that when all the women ganged up against her. But fun was had by all, as a rule, and it helped make the time go by. Cheeky Charlie's replacement was a man called Derek. A nice, quiet kind of bloke, who looked as though he was daunted by so many meat-pie-inspecting women. They soon put him to the test.

"Derek darling, I fink you betta come n'ave a look at ma meat pie..."

"Oooh, Derek! I went to pick this pie up, an ma finga got stuck in by accident. Come n'ave a look at the hole I made..."

"Derek, petal," she stood up to let him get the full benefit of her 42D-cup, then began to stroke his shoulder, "how about you tasting my pastry, Derek?"
The young man pulled away, alarmed. One might have thought his very life depended on it, the way he was carrying on. His eyes frisked the shop-floor for an exit, but could only blunder from the one laughing face to the other.

"You *are* saucy!" someone shouted over, enjoying the performance.

"These are modern times, my dear. These *are* modern times!" 42D replied. "But I reckon I shot wide o' the mark. Seems like our Derek ain't into pastry, are you, darling?" and she went to stroke his brow, and would have done, had he not stumbled back at the last moment. "Nope. I reckon he's more in favour o' *bangers*!"

"Ooh! Ha-ha!" This was better than telly, and many were those who had to turn their head aside so as not to cry on them meat pies.

"You into bangers, are you, Derek?" they teased. "Go on, show us ya rubber gloves!"

A siren went off. The blue bulb on the wall near the exit started flashing. Derek fled through the swing doors, leaving the merriment to persist behind him. Those to whom the siren applied wiped away their last hiccup of tears and left their places for their ten-minute tea-break. Unwillingly, for a change.

In the yellow-washed tea room the flirtations persisted, even blossoming into a real, though short-lived affair from time to time. Workers, foremen, queued up for snacks and cracked jokes with the tea-lady. Rose sat at a table of women, smiling in on their vacuous exchanges. Privately she was chasing her own evil thoughts out of her mind. Bad thoughts, they were. Wicked thoughts. Forbidden thoughts.

22

"Jack, Jack, you'll be late for work... Jack... you playing wiv yourself?"
"Wot time is it?"
"Time you stopped wanking and brought some money in!"
"You know wot? You're as common as muck."
"Give here..."

He jumped from the bus. Dodging the traffic that buzzed around him like a swarm of bilious bees, he managed to cross the street and catch a bus going the other way. He wondered if she really did live around here, somewhere; wondered if he might perhaps bump into her if he were to idle through these streets on a Sunday, say. She lived behind one of these windows here; he might even be walking past right now without realising it. She might see him one day, from her window up there. Perhaps she would wave. Invite him up... South-West London was not really his neck of the woods. He bet she didn't live on a council estate. Nope, she had to live somewhere nice; with a front door with steps leading up to it and with one of them brass knockers hanging out of the lion's mouth. One of them posh houses, with a front garden and a back garden, with flowers and shrubs and that. Like the Jewish people in Golder's Green. In a street with terraced houses. And no dogshit on the pavement. He pictured her; her laugh, her bright eyes, her beautiful, dark skin. Darkies. That's what they were called. Tosh, and what not. Lots of them were already there. If you went to Brixton, you would think you were in Kingston, right there in the middle of London. He had never heard of Kingston till they had come along... We're only jealous, thought Jack. We're only jealous cos they come over n work harder n we do and make a little something out of themselves. And we don't like it cos they're always laughing.

Cos we reckon we ain't got nothing to laugh about, then we think they're laughing at us, but really, when it comes down to it, we're only jealous. Wot's-his-name's bought himself a nice Cortina. Good on him! Little bastard works all the hours God sends and his wife's holding down two jobs in one go and what do we do? We say he must a stolen it or he's got a couple of girls working the streets for him. We put him down, and that. Wonder how long it'll be before one of his tyres gets slashed... They're a good lot, really. Just a big bunch a boys, Jack sat back in his seat, warming at the thought of his relationship with his black colleagues; the jokes, the lingo, their immediate acceptance of his person. He thought about Emily; hoped she was warming up to him, that she would let him be nice to her. But then there was Monica, who tore up the picture like a jealous lover; shouting, scoffing, demanding, more and more and more and *more*. More money. More attention. More recognition of her so-called sacrifices, he could kill the stupid bitch, sometimes. And then there was Emily...

What could he say, he asked himself as he hurried through the gates. Alarm-clock hadn't gone off? Had to take one of the kids to the doctor? No, he couldn't say that; brings bad luck. What could he say, then? Waterpipe had burst and he had to wait for the plumber? Someone had been broken into and the police had come round doing door-to-door? Jack was already in the building and still hadn't made up his mind.

"Ello, Jack, how's ya back? You're alright, mate," Pete nosed in confidentially, "I already clocked you in."

"Ah, cheers, mate! I owe you one." He disappeared down the stairs to the locker room.

Lunchtime meant pub time. Many of them there were too, offering their dark, potent bosoms to oversized offspring, who, replenished, would reluctantly get to their feet once again, shrugging on their jackets to resume the duties of men. When the first blacks turned up around a decade ago, pushing their heads round the stained-glassed doors like a pack of foolish sheep, some of the inn-keepers told them straight that they weren't welcome. They moved on without putting up a fight. But they did put the word about. Reggie at the Horse and Crown said he didn't give a monkey, even when it turned out that the other keepers were doing good business with the blacks. He had only wanted not to offend his regulars, but they, too, began to wander off to the other pubs that the blacks frequented, towing their sunshine behind. There was a bit more life in the place with them around, the regulars said. There was something about blacks, I dunno, born entertainers, they said, remorse in their voice as they came less and less to the Horse and Crown and then stopped coming altogether. Reggie put some tables and chairs outside to attract Management, but the most frequent punters were the right-wing, who had started to fester in the darker corners around the dartboard and the pool table. And the barmaids didn't seem to want to work for Reggie anymore, even when he put their wages up, grumbling that those bloody niggers were costing him money. But a better wage was not enough. The barmaids had heard all the dirty jokes. Knew all the British beer tricks. They wanted to be chatted up by those dark-eyed Samsons who had a way of cocking their legs to suggest more than was good for a lass.

Jack sat cosily in the lap of one of the many noisy, smoke-filled pubs fringing the docklands, whose murky lights made a pretty enough necklace at night. He had seen the insides of most of them by now and had pilgrimaged from the Horse and Crown to the Dirty Duck to the Queen's Head to the Black Swan, which was his regular. For the time being. It was useful to have a regular, for everyone to know exactly where you meant when you said, "See you later down the pub, mate," and for the barmaid to know exactly what you wanted: "Ello, Jack. Usual, is it?" Jack was in a good mood, today. His friends were, too, one having been added to their number. The group propped up the bar and didn't much notice the barmaid wiping down the counter, swinging her udders.

"Lift them up so I can get under," she said with a wink as she removed their beermats.

"Jack, man, me muss tank you fi help me fren out. You is a real pal, bredda." Linford gave Jack's arm a grateful squeeze.

"Know your problem, mate? You talk too much." Jack removed the arm and gave it back. "And I ain't queer either, so keep your bleedin fingers to yourself."

Every one a dem laugh.
Jack, at home. The father of sons.

"What yu tell me work like a magic, yu see! I an I really grateful." Richard raised his glass.

"You n who?" Jack's beer glass, suspended in mid air.

"I an I!" reiterated the newcomer.

"Bwoy, no talk no rubbish inna me ears, yaah!" Linford styooped.

"Okay, boys," Jack assumed authority. "You wanna say you n you, Rich, it's alright wi' me. Just let me know which one o' you I'm talking to, alright?"

"Come, Jyack. One more drink before we go back, nuh?" Linford's hand was already jingling up some more change in his trouser pocket.

"Don't mind if I do," replied Jack, draining his beer glass.

"Wait man! Wait man wait man!" Richard interrupted. "Me bring a likkle someting fram J.A. fi special occasion…" and he produced a bottle of rum together with a small glass from the cloth bag at his feet.

The barmaid should've said it weren't allowed, bringing your own, but if she drew attention to them, they'd get into trouble, which meant that *she'd* get into trouble, and she really did kind of like this new one and didn't want to spoil her chances, so she just tutted in a soft reproachful way and squeezed her udders past the keeper to distract him for a minute or two.

"True Jamaican fire water!" Richard stealthily poured a glass, handed it to Linford, who downed it in one with a smack of his lips. Richard poured another glass, handed it to Jack this time, who did the same. The overproof rum took his breath away and caused his eyes to run water. He got a slap on the back to decongest him.

"Me bring a likkle someting fi yu, Jyack, let yu know me appreciate yu help." Richard pulled from his cloth bag a purple tie with green-yellow patterns on it. Very dashing. He almost didn't get the job because he looked too much like a lady's man in that tie, but the gaffer thought, give a bloke a chance, so he took him on.

"I ain't hanging that round me neck, I'll look like a bleedin pimp," but Jack was all smiles. "I'm only pulling your leg, Rich. Taa, now I'll have to find myself somewhere special to go with a fancy tie like this one. And a special woman to go with it!" He rolled it up carefully then slipped it in his trouser pocket, his mind on someone. "C'mon," he glanced at his watch. "Time we got back."

None of them noticed a white docker in a corner nudge his neighbour so the latter could witness Jack's drinking from the same glass as those two black men. None of them saw the darts of disapproval shot their way. Jack first felt the eyes of the group on him as he walked by, the way you just do if you are being stared at for too long. He proffered a friendly, lightly inebriated "Ello, mates!"

No reply.

"Suit yourselves." Jack ran to catch up with the others outside. So he missed:

"The only bloody lion I know of who'd rather be a friggin' ape, that one."

And he missed the Neanderthal, pre-verbal grunts that accompanied the exchange of bitter, pregnant glances.

"Is wa unnu[35] say?" Linford broke the silence. "Come round to my place fi dinner sometime." The three walked along, past the articulated lorries, past the cranes overhead. "Serve unnu up some real soul food, get Lucy fi cook mek yu mouth water," he grinned, revealing his gold strips. "None a dis bangers an mash dog food! Jack, is wa yu say?"

"Lucy?" Richard tottered, his head pleasantly warmed by the alcohol.

"Lucy is me woman. She name *juicy* Lucy…"

"Bamba!! An tell me, is what so juicy about dis Lucy?"

"Dat is fi *my* business!"

---

[35] *unnu* = you (pl)

"Bamba!"

"First of all," Jack found his way back into the conversation, "just to put a picture straight; it's no bleedin bangers n mash where I live, mate. Steak, every night o' the week!"

The two snorted their disbelief. They were pals. What the hell, it was only a joke, anyway.

"Count me in," Jack confirmed.

"Cho man, yu know yu no haffi harsk me. Where there's food, there's Rich!"

In a confident, cocky gait, the three headed for the docks, revitalized.

"Yu know so'um Jyack, yu is a real good white man. Me like yu fi true." Linford moved a little closer.

"Well, that's nice to hear, but you could do me a favour and drop the white-man-black-man bit, gets on your nerves after a while, know wot I mean?"

They did.

"Anyway, I know more about your way o' doing things than you do about mine."

"Don't talk no foolishniss, what any white man can know 'bout any black man?"

"Your language, for one. I understand every word you say so don't fink you can say somefing under your breath and I won't understand it, cos I do. So there!"

"Like what, den?"

"Well," Jack thought, "like all your sayings n that. I know wot they mean, you know."

"What den?"

"Well, all that about small-islands, Jamaicans and Africans not liking each other. I know all about that. And I know sayings like John Small and im got money."

"What? Yu know 'bout Jahn Small an him got money?" Linford teased. "Is how much money im got?"

"And I've heard that one about 'greedy choke puppy'. I know that one as well."

"T'raatid! Me ears deh play joke pon me! Jyack know about greedy choke puppy!"

"Greedy no choke no puppy, yaa," corrected Richard. "Better belly bust than good food spoil."

"That as well." Jack, pleased with himself. "And 'want want no getti. Getti getti no wanti'. Know that one as well," Jack said in quite passable Jamaican. "Anyway, I know more about you than you do about me. Bet you don't know wot a cup of rosy-lee is, do ya?"

"Rosy-lee? Cuppa Rosy-lee muss a someting fi drink."

"Somefing ta drink, he says! Somefing ta drink!"

"Well?"

"Somefing ta drink! Can't you get any closer'n that? Wot about: give us a tune on the old Joanna. Wot about that one, then? Haven't got a bloody clue, have you?" He slapped them both, harmlessly. "All you know about is juicy Lucy and wot have you. I tell you lads, I'm one up on you. I'm one up on all a you."

Richard gave Jack a playful shove. Took a faked swipe at Jack's face and ducked as Jack lashed out, his fists raised, ready for a round. The two sparred for a moment or two, scuttling like ants beneath the lofty necks of the cranes swinging with heavy containers from countries too far away to be real for the dockers purely intent upon clocking-out time.

"Get away wiv ya! Leave a man in peace so he can enjoy his lunch. See you later," and Jack pushed them on ahead of him.

Pools of men lounged or squatted by the quayside, their sleeves rolled up, their buttons undone, sunning themselves in their lunch break. The sky, a few clouds caught up in its net of blue, swam above them, pulling the birds along. Jack idled on, returning the greetings thrown his way. A beautiful day, it was. He looked up. Knuckly cranes fingered into the sky; combed the water's edge. He could hear the blue-brown mass, smell it even as it lapped up to him, inquisitively. Boats from here went all over the world. All over the blimmin world, Jack thought as he leant against a post and unwrapped his sandwiches. And people, they came from all over the world just to be here, too. He had never been anywhere. Been to the airport often enough as a London taxi-driver, but had never seen a plane from the inside. Seen more ships than he'd care to count, but had himself never disembarked in some far-away land, eager to mingle with unknown faces and hear the music of unknown tongues. Such things were not for the likes of him. His thoughts drifted to someone. Imagine that, a young girl like that coming all this way to make a new start. Takes a hell of a lot of courage, that does. They're prouder than we are, that lot. Braver n we are. He bit into his sandwich, but then imagined Monica cleaning her fingernails with a knife or the end of a spoon. Her n her disgusting habits. They don't bring sandwiches to work, they don't. Their wives send them to work with a chunk of meat. He wondered if she had a boyfriend. She don't mind showing she's not interested in the likes a me, he thought, downcast. I can be a real charmer, given half the chance. A real charmer... The sky swam on by, heavy and sultry. The water lapped in and out, in… out; a tongue in the head of the beast called London.

"I can be a real charmer..." He finished his sandwich, brushed his fingers clean on the leg of his trousers, and idled back.

The facts:

In 1950, 1,700 people emigrated from Jamaica to the United Kingdom of Great Britain and Northern Ireland. Twenty years later, in 1970, the number of emigrants had reached an alarming 23,000. The total number of immigrants in the UK in the year 1970 constituted, nonetheless, less than 5%.

Enoch Powell, a conservative politician, gave a controversial speech in Birmingham in 1968 on the topic of immigration, after which he fell into disfavour and was dismissed from the shadow cabinet.

The fiction:

23
London, September --, 19--

Dear Junie,

Greetings from an Englishwoman. (Smile). I know the children waiting for this letter because they know a little extra something in it for each of them. Give Marlene a big kiss from mummy for her birthday and give Leroy a kiss just as big. Tell them I love them so much and can't wait to see them and be with them once again. I'm working so hard I don't have time yet to go to the immigrations people and find out what the rules and regulations is to get the children over, but I see plenty people doing it so I don't see any trouble, only the trouble of getting the money together. I don't want to send for them one one because the one who left behind going to think I love him less so I want to save till I can send for them both in one go. Sometimes in the morning I just don't want to go to work. Just don't want to get out of bed. I think - when I could stay in bed this morning and do nothing, or do my hair. Then I feel so bad when I think my babies out there missing their mummy.
In England them got real seasons. When I got here last April it was cold and windy. Sometimes I just chill right through to the bone and wake up find the kettle water frozen. But then the trees start to blossom up make the whole place look pretty. Now the summer start to finish and we coming into autumn. Autumn is nice, too, over here. The leaves turn brown-orange and fall off. Everywhere you go, this warm brown colour and still enough green. Old and young at the same time, like a woman in her early forties. Don't laugh. It's true. When you come to England you start to think different. Feel different. A bit more sensitive some how. You think anybody in Jamaica ever sit down and think

about a tree? If them ever hear they would say I'm not in my right mind!

My landlady Miss Brown is alright. Her husband is alright too but him don't show him face much. Miss Brown is a nurse and she own the house I'm living in, so you see you really can make something out of yourself if you set your mind to it. Them got a daughter name Carmen. She's sixteen but if you ask me she behave like a ten year old. The people them over here generally young and inexperienced. Them don't know nothing about hardship. Miss Brown got one brother called Roy live somewhere in England called Birmingham. Him always want to come and stay and Miss Brown have to find excuse because she say him too worthless.

Junie, me shock to hear say One-foot gone! Is what make him get up and go so sudden? Did him have another woman the whole time you never know about? Or him fed up with the children? You say you better off without him but I know how much you did like him. I really sorry to hear it. Sorry for true. You must write and tell me as soon as it is too much for you to look after the children. I don't want them to be a burden to you.

Almost every second of my time occupy. Only Sundays I enjoy as a day of rest as God commanded. I'm learning to type now. When I can type I can get a better job. Where I work I sometimes write down a message or two when the telephone rings and nobody not there. One day the manager ask is who always writing the messages. At first I didn't want to own up because I thought he might think I using the phone for private calls. But when he look at me and ask me, I got to own up. Well, him say - Emily, when you got such nice handwriting you should be working in the office. Some of the secretaries here write like spiders I need a whole half hour just to work out what it is them trying to tell me. The secretary give me one look you see! Me don't business! It's him make me think about typing and when that coming along, I think I might even try a little shorthand. This factory work hard for a lazy Jamaican like me you see! But some of the English woman them liven up the place with them cheekiness. My whole life I never see so many people working in one place like that, but them tell me it's a small factory even. I glad for the job, of course, but when I see Miss Brown and what she manage to mount to, I don't want to spend my whole life in no factory. A woman must have a little ambition, don't you think? But the girls them over here jealous when them think you going to mount to anything is a shame. You can't tell them too much what you doing or them try to spoil up you plan. Black as well as white. One woman at work always talking about how nice her husband is. How him can do this and how him can do that. How him never lift a finger to hit her and how him treat her like a queen. One other black woman make sure she get in nice and friendly with her. Always round her house, always together till people did start say them is lover. Next thing you know, the friend run off with the husband and the woman so shame she leave her job and go look another one. Even the church sisters talk about how that one have on what she did have on last week and how that one don't iron her skirt good. Is what make people so wicked so?

Anyhow I so glad to hear say you like the wig I send you! I know you would like it. I always keep an eye open for something nice for you and for the children. Don't write me no rubbish about me rich. Me not rich at all at all at all. But me work hard. I work hard for the things that are worth working hard for, I know where my duties are, I know who I have to thank and who I mustn't forget. I pray to the Lord and He answer my prayers and keep me strong for another day. All round me people are complaining. Even the black people complain, so quick them forget how hard it was back home. Them want more of this, them want more of that. And everywhere you turn is advertisement tempting you to buy all kind of rubbish. You hard earn money can't even stay in you pocket a little while. Over here when you go to the supermarket there's so much to buy it turn your head. You can't just buy a little milk. You buy silvertop or redtop or goldtop. You buy it in a bottle, half pint or a pint, you buy it in a tin, or you buy it in a box. You can buy powder or condense or you can buy sweetmilk. And everything is like that. There is never only one of anything. When I think I did go hungry back home and how it break my heart to see my children almost skin and bone looking up at me with them hungry eyes. That look alone crush my pride and I did sit down and write to Richard relatives. I don't say they don't take advantage here - them sure get their money's worth out of us, that's for sure - but we don't lose in the long run. I would work 24 hours a day, walk a long long time on water if it mean my children can come over and get a good start in life. And the good Lord make sure everything work according to His plan, not according to ours.

Is so much me write? Me better stop before you fall asleep. (Smile). When the postman see this full up envelope from England, him going to think is riches me sending over and not pages full of foolishness. If him break it open him gwine disappointed, you see! Once again, give my love to the children. Marlene can wear the ribbons on her birthday, but after that only let her wear them on Sunday.

God bless you all three. To you Junie, always a friend. To Marlene and Leroy, always a loving mother. Rose

Row row row your boat
Gently down the stream

Merrily merrily merrily merrily

Couldn't've been

24

Then who?

Face-to-face, 1970

Hello. I'm Mandy. Mandy Green. I'm... four? Four. I got a mum n a dad. My brother's name is Derek and my sister's names're Cynthia and Wendy. I'm the baby of the family. We live in a house and we got a garden. And a car. That's why we're a happy family.

What you know, 1970 (Several months later)

I close my eyes when mummy washes my hair because it burns. Because if you don't, the soapy suds run in and then it's too late. If you close your eyes then, then you keep the suds in but really you want to keep them out. I don't like it and I don't like it after. It always hurts and Wendy is always first. I sit in front of mummy and put this hand on this knee and that hand on that. When she does the front I have to turn around. This time I didn't like it... there was a smell up there... sort of deep... I didn't like it but I didn't say anything. I just knew I shouldn't.

I know how to keep Wendy off my sweets. Nobody told me. I just knew. There - in my knickers! In my knick-knocks! They always have wrappers, never have sweets with no wrappers. Then my sweets are safe. I know one other way. Spit on them and let her see. Then she leaves me and my sweets alone. But sometimes I still put them away there. I know she won't want them now.

Free please, 1971

When I was free... no I wasn't, I was four. I remember now I was four, mummy said Wendy and Derek should take me with them to the Saturday morning picture show. I was really excited cos they always came back and talked about the super films. Some were cartoon and some were real. I was really excited! The cinema was on the main street and we were allowed to go, just the three of us. I couldn't wait! Mummy told them to be extra careful crossing the road because of me, to hold my hand and not let me rush out from the kerb. Anyhow the cinema was on our side of the road so we only had to cross the small road and not the big one. There were enormous pictures in the windows of the cinema and lots of boys and girls waiting to go inside. Ooh, I couldn't wait! Sometimes they tried to push in and we said, "Hey! We were here first, you're not pushing in!" When they tried to get in early with friends who were already there and that. If we let them push in, maybe we wouldn't get in. Sometimes we said, "Hey! The queue's that way, you know!" So many boys and girls!

Then it was our turn. The counter was really high up and I couldn't see inside, but Derek is really tall for his age, much bigger than the other boys, and he could see in and he had the money. I think Wendy could see in as well but I couldn't see in.

"Free for the Saturday morning picture show, please," my brother said.

The man asked something and my brother turned round and pointed down at me.

"How old is she?" the ticket-man asked.

I couldn't wait to get in cos I knew it was really huge and black inside with loads and loads of seats.

"She's six."

But I wasn't. I was four. I knew that.

"No I'm not, I'm four!"

Then the man said something and Wendy pushed me really hard. "She's really six. Really!"

And he said something else and they said, "Please, oh please, just this once, please, please..."
They dragged me away from the counter and started shouting and screaming at me, "You stupid fool! Now we can't get to see the Saturday morning picture show, all because of you!"

"Why?" I asked, "Why weren't we going to see the Saturday morning picture show?" But they just told me to shut up and dragged me all the way home. I cried because we didn't get in and they pulled me all the way home and made me trip up on the kerb.

Mummy shouted at us when we got back cos now we were in the way and everybody was horrible to me but no-one told me I should've been six...

I don't remember when we went again. I don't remember them going without me after that but I'm sure they did. I remember later going to the Saturday morning picture show, but the very first one, sitting in the big seat in the dark with all those boys and girls - I don't really remember.

Ding-A-Ling! 1971

I go to school. We learn a lot a things at school but some of them I know already. My teacher's an Indian lady and I don't like her that much. There's a teacher in our school called Miss Mummy and she's really nice. Everyone wants to be in her class. I do too! I have my own coat peg and mummy made me a plimsole bag. She's got a sewing machine. My plimsoles haven't got any laces. Wendy took me to school the first day cos mummy had to work. She's in the juniors. There are lots of boys and girls to play with. At home there's only Wendy and she doesn't always want to play with me.

> This old man, he played one
> He played knick-knack on my thumb
> With a knick-knack paddy-whack
> Give a dog a bone
> This old man came rolling home.

>   This old man, he played two
>   La-la-la-la la-la-la...

Do you know how to play hopscotch?

In the family, 1971

My teacher's name is Miss Ragoo. She's got rotten black teeth and rings under her eyes like uncle Fester. I hope she won't be my teacher next year. I hope I'll have Miss Mummy. Normally we don't get homework, but yesterday she asked us to get the names, birthdays and marriages of our families so we could draw our family tree and put them on the wall. I think it's a good idea. Then all the family trees go together to make one big tree.

But in our family, it's not so easy. Mr Harry is not mummy's dad. He married mama, my grandma, when she came to England but she'd already had five children by someone who ran away and left her to marry an older woman. They weren't married and some of the children have his name and some have hers. Mummy's got hers and my aunties have his. Then my mum had Cynthia and Derek in Jamaica before she got married and Cynthia has a different name. And there are uncles in Jamaica I know nothing about and one of my aunties has four girls and she's not married and the youngest has a different name to the others because she was born in England and her father's a tramp. He wasn't then but he is now. And my dad's got twelve brothers and sisters and his mum can't read.

Mummy doesn't like people to know all this. I don't think she knows I know all that much. I think she wouldn't like it, but when they're talking, they think cos we're playing we're not listening or we don't understand. Even if they whisper I can play and still understand some of it even if I look the other way. I asked her things but she got angry.

"Stop asking questions! Let her mind her own business, the nosey cow!" She got dead angry, my mummy did. So I stopped asking. I made it up a little. I gave everybody in the family the same name. I gave my aunt a husband. I told uncle

Fester I didn't know the birthdays cos my parents were too busy. She said alright and only gave me one tick when some others got two or three. I think she knew I was lying.

L-L-L-Lurgies! 1972

The doctor said that I've got scabies. Mummy said I can't possibly have. But I do. She sat on the seat behind me in the bus. That wasn't very nice. I can't help it. It's not my fault. They run away from me at home.

"Eeee! You've got the l-l-l-lurgies!" They make me cry. It's not my fault. Wendy's not allowed to sleep with me and Cynthia hates having her. I have a bed all to myself, at least. I'm not allowed to tell anyone at school, not even my teacher. They'll think we're dirty. But I don't know what to do when my friends want to hold my hand...

Joining in, 1972

Now that we're in the junior school, at assembly we all sing Christian songs. I don't know the words to all of them. I'm still learning. Boys and girls hold them up in assembly and stand on a chair so we all can see. It's not my turn yet. Some of them I know:

> One old lady, two coins small,
> Jesus was watching as she gave her all,
> And Jesus said as his heart was made glad,
> That she had given all that she had,
> All that I have,
> All that I have,
> I will give Jesus all that I have!

We don't sing the same one all the time otherwise I would know all the words by now. But the Asian kids in my class say it's not fair, they shouldn't have to join in.

Finding out, 1972

We've got a cat called Timmy. He's grey and white. He's a good cat. I think so. When he wants to go to the loo, he goes to the back door and meows. Meeaooww! Meeaooww! Just like that, he does. Then we got a cat called Sindy. She's black and white. We never buy cat food. They eat our leftovers. I'm sure they'd prefer the catfood on the telly, like I prefer the food on the telly to the food we get. But they must take what they get. Just like we do. One day there was this noise behind the sofa. Miiiaow! Miiiaow! Really high and squeaky. I pulled the sofa away and Sindy was there with lots and lots of kittens! They were dead small and couldn't really move but kept trying to crawl all over each other. They were nice and furry and could fit in my hand. Everyday I had a look, they were so nice. Miiiaow! Just like that, they went.

Then one died. I went one morning to have a look - and it had died. I got a funny feeling, knowing it was dead because it was alive the last time, see? Course I kill flies all the time and Timmy sometimes brings in a dead mouse and that, but that's different. Anyway I took it to the garden and buried it under our pear tree. Did I tell you we got a pear tree? Well, we have. So I buried it under the pear tree, but I couldn't forget that kitten, I couldn't. And a couple days later I went out... I went out... and dug it up. I was really excited! Then I buried it again after. But I still couldn't forget it... so I went out another time with my spoon: I got my own spoon...

Urgh!

It was horrible horrible horrible! It was all kind of... eaten away... there were loads a loads a white worms wriggling everywhere and over each other as if they were fighting to get at something there was only one of. Know what I mean? I screamed and ran away. It felt like someone had poured ice-cold water down my pully. I felt sick as well and my knees went all wobbly. I didn't want to bury it cos I didn't want them greedy white worms crawling all over me. But I did bury it and I never, never dug it up again.

Playing out, 1972

We have a big garden but we like to play out front with the others. There's Colleen and her sister, Denise, another Denise, her mother's divorced, a ginger head boy, Bradley and sometimes his sister, Vanessa, they live on our side of the street, and there's Jill, she lives opposite us. Sometimes we call for each other and go out and play. Wendy and I have to stay on our side of the street and are not allowed to go too far from our house, not around the block or anything. They can. They're all white but they haven't got the half of what we've got. Maybe Bradley.

I'm not allowed to talk to Jill anymore. Mummy says we mustn't cos she said her mum said we're black cos we don't wash. But her mum said it, not her, and she likes us really otherwise she wouldn't knock and ask us if we want to play. Mummy says she's got a face like a spoon but I don't like it when she says horrible things about my friends because I haven't got any more. Once I asked Bradley to be my boyfriend. Even though he's ginger.

"Bradley, will you be my boyfriend?"
"You wot?"
"You heard. Will you be my boyfriend?"
"Haaa! Colleen! Coll -"
"Ssh! Don't tell no-one!"
"Colleen! Guess wot she just asked?"
"It was only a joke, anyway! Shut your face! It was only a dare! I didn't mean it!"

But I did, really. I asked him again another time, later, and he said his mum wouldn't like it because I'm black, so I said, "Oh, alright."

Them n Us, 1973

Everything belongs to a group. You can group things according to size or shape, colour, feel, smell, age, anything. We group a lot in maths, but you can group anywhere. You can even be in more than one group at the same time; ten and twenty, for example, belong both in the group multiples of two and in the group multiples of five. Everything, absolutely everything belongs to at least one group, and that's good cos it must be a terrible thing to be all alone. If you listened to my parents, then my most important group was the black group. I never think about it much, but they're on about it all the time. They make it sound like war to me. Them and us.

Whites are different. Special. But they don't deserve it. Pakistanis don't count. They're too choosy, my mum says. They only choose themselves. Their kids aren't allowed to do anything, they're not allowed to play out or anything, and their parents speak rotten English. It always comes out sounding funny whatever they say. They live all crammed into one house and they have kids like nobody's business, that's what my mum says. We saw nine of them pile out of a mini once, me and Wendy. The fullest cars are always the ones with them in. That's a fact. Says my mum. Pick their noses and dig their bums in public, they do. Says my mum. And they spit on the street. Hawk it up and glob it out and they don't even feel embarrassed about it, that's what she says. And they're not allowed to cut their hair. And the boys wear it in a bun on the top of their head under a hanky. My parents can't stand them. I'm not sure if they actually know any. Personally, like. I do. The ones I know are nice enough. Most of them are well off. You know, they have sweet shops, newsagents, butchers, sari houses, that kind of thing. Always a bit of money in their pockets for sweets and they never live in council houses. We don't, either. The ones I know are nice, but maybe they'll change when they get older and become more like their parents - black teeth, bandy legs and smelly. My mum says. But the ones I know are really alright. So far. Apart from Miss Ragoo. She's got black teeth, too.

One of my friend's father is a doctor and he's sending her to private school at the end of the summer so that she'll finally start learning something, he says. She's not stuck up. She's not cleverer than me, anyhow. Pretty. Her name, I mean. Her name's Pretty. She knocked for me once. My mum says only Pakistanis and Africans can be relied upon to give their children such ridiculous names and she warned me before we skipped off not to take anything from her cos they never bought toilet paper and washed their bums with their hands. So when Pretty offered me a strawberry bonbon, at first I didn't know what to do. But I worked it out. I took one from the bag instead of the one she had in her hand for me, just to be on the safe side, although her hands looked clean enough to me. No brown stains or anything. I could never say no to a strawberry bonbon.

Once I asked Pretty what her parents thought about black people. She said they didn't. That can't be right cos my mum's always telling us how they think they're better than us. I tried asking her which ones she was talking about (at my school they're some from India, Bangladesh, Pakistan, Uganda, Kenya and other places), but it didn't matter. All of them, my mum said. Not only that, they throw their dead bodies in the river, or else they burn them and bash their skulls in. A family where we live got taken away by the police for burning their granny in the back yard. That's the gospel truth. One of these Halal butchers was on telly cos he murdered his wife and put her through the mincer and that's no word of a lie.

"My parents don't think about Pak- about you lot, either."

I really like Pretty. Lovely long black hair. Nice small feet and she could speak another language, isn't that super? I think, deep down, I would like to be her. Anyhow ten is a multiple of two as well as a multiple of five, even though two and five don't seem to have a great deal to do with each other. Other than that they're both numbers, maybe.

Who's that? 1973

One day mummy came home with a baby. Why did she go out and get another baby? She was always telling us we were a pain in the neck, and shouting for every little thing. And telling on us so our dad would lash us good and proper. What I would have been able to do if I hadn't had you lot, she was always saying. Always on about the stone she had to bear. Then she came home with another one. Well, it wasn't really another one cos it was the only one, but it was another one cos she had some already. I couldn't understand it. Grown-ups are so difficult. I prefer doing adding up and taking away. It's better when you simply do what you're told with grown-ups. The funny thing is, I don't remember mummy getting fat or going away. But then I didn't see Sindy getting fat and she had loads. I simply came home one day and she was upstairs with this funny pink baby. How comes she was pink and I was black? Something wasn't right. But she got blacker after a while, so everything was okay. Her name's Kim. Kimberly, really.

Chilly willy, 1973

Lots of people don't like the cold, but I don't mind. As long as it's not sloshy or slippery. We got sent home from school once cos the water in the heating froze. Lots of boys and girls were happy cos they don't like school. I do. I'd much rather go to school than stay at home.

I like waking up a morning when the bed's really warm because there's two of us in it and you can see outside that it's really cold. I don't wear socks in bed cos my mummy says if I do, it'll make my feet grow big and they're more than big enough already.

I like coming home at lunch-time and sitting near the window with my hot soup.

At the bus-stop, people always complain. Especially the old ones. This time I didn't want to walk to the academy cos it was so cold so mummy gave me my bus fare. I was standing there with my violin and this old white lady asks,

"You play the violin?"

"Yes," I says.

"Can you play it well?"

"Okay."

Then she starts having a moan about the weather. I knew she would. Then she says it must be doubly hard for me.

"We're used to it, I suppose, but where you come from, it's baking hot all the time, isn't it? That must be lovely!"

But I was born in London.

On my honour, 1974

> I promise that I will do my best
> to do my duty to God,
> to serve the Queen
> and help other people
> and keep the Brownie Guide law.

I'm a Brownie. Me and Wendy. We go to the hall on a Monday evening. Mummy bought us each a Brownie uniform. Some girls have lots of badges, but I've only got one. The housekeeping one. Now I want to do the cooking one. Sometimes we go to church to clean the brass and silver there and after that we can make rubbings. You put your paper over something nice and scribble over it with a crayon, then you get a print.

On a Brownie trip to the River Thames, I fell in cos I wanted to feed a swan that wouldn't come close enough. I couldn't swim and I could feel the tin cans in the water. Brown Owl's husband jumped in and saved my life. I had to take my clothes off because they were all wet. And my knickers. Mummy was really nice to me when I got home with Brown Owl and her husband. And Wendy, she was dead jealous.

Food glorious food, 1974

We go home for lunch, me and Wendy and Derek. And then Derek stopped coming home for lunch cos it was too far. Cynthia never comes home for lunch. After lunch we have to get on our hands and knees and pick up all the bits off the floor before we can go back to school. But we don't have to do the washing up. We come home and whoever comes first has to go to the chippy on the corner and buy a portion of chips to take home. Then we have it with sausages and baked beans. Or spam. Sometimes a beefburger or a fried egg. We always have to share a portion. We always have to share everything. I always only ever get half an apple and I always have to share with Wendy. Mum and Cynthia never cut it fairly and we fight about who gets the bigger half. "Cor, that's not fair, she's got more than her fair share!" Always fighting over the fair share and sometimes I'd refuse to eat my smaller half until mummy came after me with her hand in the air and I'd grab my smaller half and run.

Those who went to school dinners always had a sweet. At home we never did. They got really interesting things at school and I really, really, really wanted to eat at school, but I knew better than to ask. She'd only start shouting. Anyhow one night Wendy and me made up our minds to go together and say we wanted school dinners. We knew she'd start shouting and we were both afraid. Nobody wanted to say it.

"You say it."
"No, you!"
"It was your idea."
"You're older, you tell her."
"I'm not saying if you don't."
"Let's say together, then."
"Mum..."

She knew straight away something was coming and she was ready to shout.

"We... we want to have school dinners!"

After she'd finished, we kept saying to each other, "Told you so!" But we did get to have school dinners in the end.

Your class lines up behind the yellow line in the playground and you are brought into the dining room. There are about twenty long rows of tables. The dinner ladies are really nice and if they like you, you get a bit extra. Everyday there's something different and we have lots a pies and gravy and things we never eat at home. But the sweets are best. Always with custard. Mmmmmm!! Apple crumble, gooseberry crumble, cherry pie, spotty dick, sponge cake, treacle pudding, chocolate pudding, always with custard. *And* there is ice-cream and jelly, wobbly blancmange and sometimes fruit cocktail, where I always save the cherry for last.

Only at the weekend did we get a sweet at home but it was never a cake. Always fruit cocktail with ice-cream and jelly. I like to watch mummy making jelly and sometimes we get a brick raw to eat. It tastes delicious! Much stronger than when you put boiling water on it. Once Wendy and me asked if we could have sponge and custard. We got it! Sponge in a tin and you have to put the tin in a pot of boiling water and open it afterwards. And custard powder cos it's cheaper than ready-made and you have to be careful in case it goes lumpy. And then we discovered something scrumdiddlyumptious: pineapple and custard. A pineapple ring with a little juice topped up with custard, mmmmm!! I scrape the bowl out with my fingers afterwards.

Weekends we normally have something special. But it's always the same. Sunday breakfast is baked beans, bacon and eggs, sometimes fried plantain, or fried bread. We got a whole orange each on a Sunday. I try to get a big one but sometimes the skin is really thick and the orange inside small. Then they say it serves me right for being greedy, but they all do it, too. We have to drink coffee, even though I hate it. Then someone told mummy that grapefruit juice is good and now we have to drink a small glass of grapefruit juice, too. We all hate it but we can't get up until we've drunk it. Everytime we complain, we get the same story about the starving millions. I'm the only one who hates coffee but we all hate grapefruit juice. Sunday dinner is always rice and peas and chicken. Not green peas, but kidney beans cooked in the rice with coconut cream so the rice goes dark red. Or sometimes black eye peas. Gungu peas, we call them. We haven't got our own language, but we sort of half have. When my parents speak Jamaican, white people can't understand them and when Mr Harry speaks, I don't always know what he's on about. It's more or less English, but it's often wrong, like when my dad says "it eat good" or "it drink good" when he really means it tastes nice, things like that. Our Sunday dinner always tastes nice, bit it's always the same. Then we have a fizzy drink on a Sunday which we're not allowed to touch until we've eaten everything. There's no point asking. I always save the meat for last. I don't like the Jamaican bits we have to eat sometimes; yam, cassava, breadfruit. They eat it every day but we don't have to. Thank goodness.

Sometimes we have a glass of hot milk and sugar before we go to bed at eight thirty and I always try to finish it before the skin starts settling. Mum works until night and when she's gone, Cynthia sometimes fries chips for us. She's much older and she doesn't like us too much, but she's nice when she goes to the cellar and gets some potatoes and makes chips for us.

When my mum worked in a factory called Telfer's, she'd bring really nice pies and pasties home for us and we could have one each because she hadn't bought them. The sort of pies you see in the chippy but we're never allowed to buy. When she started bringing them home it didn't matter about the chippy. Only that they had saveloys and gherkins which we never had, but the lady in the chippy likes us and often gives us a good helping of crackling. When my dad's in a good mood, he buys fish and chips from the chippy but we were never allowed to eat from the paper, always on a plate. There are lots of things we're not allowed to do and we're never told why. Just so. We're not allowed to open the chips until we get them home. I wanted to enjoy my chips on the street like other people. Well, anyhow one time I went to the chippy to get them for lunch and I opened the packet, just for once, so I could have a chip. But I couldn't wrap it together again the way they did. I tried my best, but I just couldn't. So I shoved them all in the best I could and took it home. My mum saw straight away what I'd done and really beat me for it. I mean really. Not just a slap on the leg like the white kids got, but really smacks in the face and punches even. Really rough with us although it's usually ma dad that dishes it out. Still sometimes they're really nice to us and we can have one of the cheaper ice lollies when the ice-cream van comes.

But the best thing is, our neighbour, Mrs Longdon, she works for Trebor's and she's always bringing things home for us. She's got five kids and we've got five kids. At school we show off sometimes cos we've got sweets from the sweetie factory. Mrs Longdon is black, so we're allowed to take things from her. Sometimes they're still hot and you can stretch them for ages before they break. Then I'm glad to be black cos if I weren't, she wouldn't have offered me, or else I wouldn't have been allowed to take it. But I am and she is. And I don't have any fillings.

Sunday school, 1974

We're baptised but it doesn't really mean anything. We kind of mutter a prayer on a Sunday before we eat dinner. That's it. And we're supposed to say prayers before we go to bed, but no-one ever checks and I've forgotten the words at the end.

> Gentle Jesus meek and mild
> Look upon this little child...

Then I la-de-da the lines I can't remember and then it ends something like;

> If I should die before I wake
> I pray the Lord my soul to take.

Something like that. But he never gives me any of the things I ask for. You know what grown-ups are like.

On a Sunday we have to go to Sunday school. They never go to church, but they insist on sending us to Sunday school. Cos Wendy and I are Brownies, we have to go as Brownies. It's really boring but we can't say we don't want to go. One particular time we really didn't want to go. But of course we had to. Each of us gets two pence for the collection. As we got nearer, we absolutely didn't want to go, so you know what we did? We walked around the church block all the time until the service had finished and the people started coming out, then we went to the sweet shop and spent our money on sweets. They never found out. They've never once asked us what they talked about at church, so we know they're not really interested.

Do I believe in God? Yes, of course I do! Well, I think I do.

Cross your heart? 1974

My biggest secret? No. I ain't telling. If I tell, it's not a secret anymore. No. No, I can't. Stop asking or else I'm going to go. My second biggest? You promise you won't tell? Promise? Cross your heart and hope to die? Well, you know mummy's got a baby? She used to breastfeed her. Wendy and me were allowed to watch but Derek wasn't. I think he wanted to but he was never allowed to. Daddy watched sometimes, but Derek never. He always had to leave the room He's a boy. It looked funny. Not last night but the night before when daddy started night shift... she's glad to see the back of him cos he keeps getting on her nerves and they don't talk to each other half the time... she had Kim and then she put her down and called Wendy and me. You promise you won't tell? She told us... she told us to suck it but we didn't want to... she pulled us and made us, but before, Derek had to go out of the room. It was a horrible feeling. Like a dried raisin. It must be horrible being a baby. Then she told us never, never to tell anyone and when I went to bed with Wendy, we were afraid to talk... and I felt really lonely.

Our house, 1975

Our house has got three bedrooms. Downstairs is a double-sitting room which is always locked and it's got the best things in it, a dining room, a kitchen and a bathroom. We've got a big garden with a flower bed and a pear tree. We've got an apple tree as well, but it doesn't bear anything worth eating.

We have lots of nice things, most of which we're not allowed to touch. We have lots of nice glass glasses that we drink out of when we have visitors, but we don't have very many. Ordinarily we don't drink out of glass. Cynthia does. We have plastic cups, everyone their own. Mine's orange, Wendy's yellow and Derek's blue. Nobody's allowed to drink out of your cup and if you find it in the sink, then you know that someone's used it and you have the right to be angry. My cup's a bit bashed up, but it's mine and I don't have to share it with anyone.

Not like my bedroom. Wendy and I in the same bed, even. She always quarrels about the cover and starts shouting if I cross the line onto her side. That's only important when we're not talking to each other, though. We even had to share a potty. A big pink plastic one. It wasn't a baby's potty. We're not babies. Even mummy and daddy have one. A white metal one with a blue rim, and they're definitely not babies. Even my granny has one. It wouldn't surprise me if Colleen has one. I'm pretty sure Mrs Longdon has one. Even Pretty, perhaps. It's so practical. It was always on my side under the bed. Of course we had a toilet, but it was downstairs next to the bathroom and no-one wants to get out of a nice, warm bed in the dark and cold to go to the toilet. I know I don't. We were only allowed to do numbers 1s in the potty. If you needed to do number 2s, you had to go downstairs. We had to empty it every day but it always seemed to be my turn so we fought a lot about it. Sometimes when I was sure it wasn't my turn to empty it, I'd refuse to take it down. Wendy refused as well so it stayed there. The next day would have been my turn but cos Wendy hadn't emptied it the day before, it was still her turn, wasn't it? But she wouldn't bring it down, so it stayed another day. Then it'd get really full and you could even smell it. The more full it got, the more neither of us wanted to take it downstairs cos it'd be so heavy, we might spill it. We weren't allowed to, but sometimes we still did number 2s in it. When you'd eaten too much, it'd drop, *g-tonk,* into the water, well, wee, really, and splash your bottom. A horrible feeling, that was, especially when you knew it wasn't all yours, but still better than getting up and going downstairs. Sometimes it'd get so full, it'd be really too heavy for us to carry, so we'd put a piece of cardboard over it so they couldn't see how much was in it. Sometimes they got a whiff of it anyway and shouted at us and threatened to beat us. My mum's got an enormous nose and it's always shiny, like a conker. She always said never mind that it was big, it worked. And it did - nothing ever got past it.

Even though we had a potty, we still used to wet the bed. Only now and again, but we didn't do it on purpose... we don't anymore. Very rarely. Wendy always says she never does it, but I know it's me sometimes and Derek sleeps alone so he can't blame it on anyone. Then we really get it. I remember one time the bed was wet. Do you know, it makes these yellowy, greeny, bluey stains on the mattress and on the sheets, like the tie-dyes we made once in our painting class. Wendy said that I did it and they beat me for it. (Why do they always tell you not to cry when they hit you so hard? Cos they don't want the neighbours to know what's going on, that's why...) But the bed was wet in the middle and not on my side, so maybe she had done it, after all, but because I do it, did it more than her, they believed her and I got in trouble. Mum took us to the doctor and he said maybe it was emotional but mum said everything was perfectly normal at home. A few weeks ago the potty got a split in it and they threw it away and won't buy us a new one cos they say we're too nasty with it, so now we'll have to go downstairs to the bathroom.

Their house, 1975

I've been inside a white person's house before cos my friend Fiona always invites me to her birthday parties and I get to go to her house. Her parents are really nice. They hold hands and kiss each other. I think that's nice. I've never seen my parents holding hands or kissing each other. Maybe they do it when we're not there, but they did it in front of all of us and I think that's nice.

I'd like to have a birthday party. Wendy wants one. I bet she'll get one before I do.

Fiona's house is like ours. It's really nice and they have pebble dashing on the front, like we have.

You should see Colleen's house! I was in theirs once. You should see their living room! They use it like any other room, it's nothing special. They haven't got any nice furniture or anything, and guess what? Colleen and Denise have got their whole clothes for the week ironed and hanging up on nails on the living room wall. The living room! Where visitors sit! When I told my mum, she couldn't believe it. I wish they were allowed to look at my living room. That'd make them jealous. At least they don't have to get up each morning and wonder what they're going to put on. But not in the living room...

Pretty's got a nice house, but I don't see her anymore. It always smells different to our house because they have special things which they burn. I think it's religious. They have interesting pictures of their gods. Some of them have got six arms, or an elephant trunk - half man, half beast, but she doesn't know enough about it to be able to explain it to me. They've got lots of these pictures hanging up and when I go there, we're allowed to play in the living room. When I went there I should say, because I don't see her anymore. Her mum's really nice to me.

My grandma's living room is small and crowded and the telly's always on. Almost always. She sometimes gets visitors. Then they sit in the living room, watch telly and talk about old times. She uses her living room like an ordinary room cos she hasn't got a dining room like we have. All her visitors are black. They don't have any white friends. All her friends are Jamaicans. My gran can't stand Africans. Mr Harry's the same. The only white people who come in are the workmen. Then they have to be white cos Mr Harry says they're the ones who do the job well whereas black workmen are too lazy and always try to cheat you. Black people are their own worse enemies, he always says, but he speaks so fast, he speaks so much Jamaican, I don't always know what he's on about.

We don't have that many visitors, either. At Christmas the family comes round, but we always end up arguing. I wish we had more. You see people coming and going in all the other houses but not ours. When my dad's friends come, they play dominoes really loud and they get so worked up, mum always ends up shouting because they scratch her table. They slap them down really hard. Or they come round and drink beer and watch the cricket on the telly when the West Indies are playing.

My friends are not allowed in. Only in the passage. I'd like to play with my friends in my bedroom, just once. But I can't and that's why I like going to school, too.

Growing up, 1975

See that? I'm getting boobs. Well, I've got them already but they're only starting. I'm the first one in my class. We do P.E. in our vests and knickers so I know that I'm the only one. I didn't like it at first cos the others pointed at me and laughed at me but I don't care anymore cos I think they're only jealous. I'm an early starter, my mum says. It's true. I could read and write before I started school and I got a gold star from Mrs Hill when I was in the infants for my joined-up handwriting. She's the Headmistress. Joining up is dead easy, I think, but the others, they couldn't do it.

I grew up this morning before dinner-time but I didn't really know about it. I knew I wasn't wetting myself cos it was too slow and it didn't last that long. Miss Ryan wouldn't let me go to the toilet because we're supposed to go at playtime. When she came over in the end, I told her I was bleeding. Then she let me go. They were all whispering that I'd cut myself. I thought so too, but I wasn't sure because it didn't hurt like it should when you really cut yourself, like when you fall down skipping or you're trying to catch someone when you're 'it'.

Mrs Watts, our nurse, she's really nice. She gave me something for it and a pair of... fresh knickers. She keeps a spare set of clothes for things like that, she said. I had to wash mine out. I didn't want to touch it. Urgh! She hung them up and I had to come back for them after school. Then we had a little talk.

When Mandy went back at lunchtime, Mrs Watts also had a letter in a sealed envelope for Mrs Green. Mrs Green read it, put it back in the envelope, tucked the flap in. Placed it on the telly, thought twice about it, picked it up and slipped it into her trouser pocket. Wendy was also home for lunch.

"You know what it is, don't you?"

Mandy had told Wendy and Wendy had told their mum before Mandy summoned up the courage to give her the letter and the plastic bag which wasn't see-through because her mum had a thing about see-through bags.

"You're going to get in trouble!" was the first thing Wendy had said when she saw Mandy at the door in a skirt not her own.

"No I'm not. My skirt's dirty."
"You wet yourself at school!"
"No I didn't! I got my period. So there!"
Wendy fell silent.
"You've got to tell mummy."
"You tell her, go on."

"You know what it is, don't you?" her mother asked as she placed a plate of spam, baked beans and chips in front of her. Mandy nodded, her eyes on the spam. It looked like white people.
"Good." She went to fetch the squash.

Mum's going to buy me some pads and a training suit so I don't have to do P.E. in my knickers anymore. I'm going to get permission from Miss Ryan. I feel a bit like a baby but I'm not. I'm grown up. Starting to.

The motor, 1975

One good thing about our family's that we've got a car. My dad works at Ford's in Dagenham and we've always had a car. Some of my Indian friends have got a car, but Colleen up the road, Denise across the road, they're white and they haven't got a car. Colleen's dad works in the docks and he can only afford to ride a bike. He's always hobbling around cos he's forever getting knocked off it. Jill doesn't have a car either. She's the one whose mum said that thing about me.

Mostly we don't use the car, only my father, but in the summer holidays he sometimes takes us to the seaside. I remember he had a grey Ford Cortina, but that wasn't the first one. I know every numberplate he's had and the sound of his car so we know when he's coming home. Mum would cook, load the boot and we'd set off for the seaside. I liked to show off when the other white kids could only play on the street.

"We're off to the seaside. It's a pity you don't have a car. See you!"

If they didn't stick their tongues out and say something about blackies, then they'd ignore us, or else say, "Show off! Show off! Pick ya nose and blow off!"

I'm the map-reader, telling my dad which turning to take. We'd stop on the motorway and have a picnic and my dad'd always wee in the bush. We had to do it hidden behind one of the car doors, squatting down, but for us it was trickier and you sometimes got your leg wet. Mum always waited. When we got there, we'd walk up and down the promenade and go to the funfair and each get a toffee apple or a stick of rock. Once we saw this white girl. She was really young, about fourteen, I think, and she had an enormous pregnant belly. Everyone was looking at her and she kept looking away. You could tell she was ashamed. But she was so young, it must've been an accident. Then my mum went on and on about what she'd do to us if we ended up like that.

Those days were really great. Sometimes a friend from my dad's workplace would come along with his family and they'd have a race on the motorway. He'd go up to 100 miles per hour and my mum would always shout, but we in the back loved it and he is a good driver. We've never once had an accident. And there's a dog sitting in the back with his head nodding all the time like he's enjoying it as much as we are. Not a real dog. A fake dog that's a bit furry but shiny underneath if you've touched it too much and rubbed the fur off. When we got home, they'd still be playing out and I'd think, Huh! My parents are better'n yours!

Cynthia, 1975

Cynthia tries to be an adult, but she's not really. Not quite. She has to help out a lot in the home, doing mum's work when mum's gone to work. The three of us always have to go to the launderette. I hate it because it's so boring, waiting for the wash and Colleen and that lot always laugh at us when we're coming home from the launderette cos we have to work. I don't know what they're laughing about. We're not the ones who live in a council house and don't have a car... Cynthia hates doing the housework and she sometimes takes it out on us, but I don't tell on her. She can be really nice, like when she makes chips for us, or when she takes us to the park, but even then she leaves us in the playground so she can meet her boyfriend and makes us promise not to say anything.

Sometimes we're allowed to stay up and watch the Dracula films. She laughs when I hide under the table when the spooky music comes on. She's very good at basketball. She plays for her school and she goes to the girls' grammar school. Last week was very sad. They had some important game. Really important. County championships. She'd asked ages ago if she could play that evening and my mum'd said yes. She never asked him cos she didn't need to. But then, on the evening before the game, mum changed her mind and said she couldn't go because she needed her at home. Even though she'd promised, even though Cynthia was picked and everything, mum said she couldn't go. I felt dead sorry for her and she was really upset but she didn't want to show it, so she locked herself in the bathroom and cried. She tried to swallow it but I could hear her anyway. That's the first time I've heard her cry. You shouldn't do things like that. I never really felt close to Cynthia because she was practically a grown-up, but last week I did because she's my sister and she got hurt.

Finding out more, 1976

I don't tell Wendy anything. You can't trust her. She always ends up threatening to tell on you. Unless she's in it. Cynthia doesn't tell. I don't tell on her cos she doesn't tell on me. She caught Wendy and me kissing once. Under the sheets. It was just a game. Boyfriend and girlfriend. When I'm the boyfriend, I have to kiss and touch her, then it's her turn. My boobs are just as big as hers. Cynthia was ironing. We thought she didn't notice, until she said, "If you think I don't know what you're doing under there, I do!" But she didn't tell, and anyway, it was only a game.

The heavy hand, 1976

Why do I always say my mum and never my dad? Well, he's not really a part of the family. He's only there for beating us and helping out with the money. He doesn't play with us or talk to us or anything like that. We're all afraid of him. When mum says, "You wait till your father gets home!" then we know we're in big trouble. I don't think he likes me very much.

He can be so horrible to us. Terribly horrible. To his own children, just imagine. And for the stupidest of things. They'd throw a loopy if they found out I was saying all of this, but I don't care because it's the truth. We have a French woman living next door. Frenchie, we call her. As a matter of fact she's from Tunisia but she speaks French. Frenchie's got a really nice garden, much nicer than ours, with lovely flowers and stuff and a garden shed at the bottom. Well, anyhow, one day whilst Wendy and I were playing in the garden, we decided to pick some of her flowers. Just for a laugh, like. Children do things like that. Anyhow she saw us, didn't she, and came over to complain. Boy, did we get it! When he beats us, he sets his face really hard, he really wants to hurt us and he never stops even when mum says it's enough. He hits us with anything, whatever's handy; a stick, a piece of wire, his bare hand, but often with his belt, and with the buckle side, even. I hate him, I think. I used to dream about killing him. I remember dreaming about sticking a knife in his neck whilst he's sleeping, or telling my teacher how horrible he is and asking them to take me away, but if I ever told anyone...

There're lots of secrets and forbidden things which, if we break, we'll get in trouble for. Nobody's allowed to know what's going on at home, about personal things. Nobody's allowed to know our business. Skeletons in the cupboard. Loads of them. When we were younger, Wendy and I always used to wear the same clothes and because we were around the same size, people were always asking if we were twins. We had to say yes, because it was nobody's business that we weren't. Things like that. Skeletons and stupid rules. My school's on the same block as our house on the parallel street almost directly behind our house, but I was only allowed to walk the long way round, coming out of my house and turning left, not the short way round, which went past the chippy. Don't ask me why. I had a friend I wanted to walk home once. Last year before I started having school dinners. She lives on the short way round. What difference could it make? If anything I'd be home quicker. So I walked her home, but when I reached the corner to where I lived, I got scared. What if someone saw me? I thought about going back and going the long way round, but then I'd be home late and get into trouble for that. So I went the short way. Just as I was almost safe, my mum comes out and looks over the garden gate. The look in her eye! I knew she wouldn't hit me on the street, but she did once we got indoors. Just a few punches in my back but enough to make me cry. Then the magic words, "You wait till your father gets home!"

He's really rotten to Derek. Really rotten. He tied him up and locked him in the cellar because of something he'd done. He's always criticising. He hates it if we have bogey in our nose and shouts at us, but once when he was in a stinking mood, he grabbed Derek by the neck and cleaned his nose out with a corkscrew. Derek's face was covered in blood afterwards but nobody said anything and I thought, you animal, one day I'm going to kill you. I hate my mum as well, sometimes, because although she generally doesn't beat us the way he does, she never interferes when it's going on. If you hate children so much, why do you have any? I can't remember him hitting our mum, though. I think he's scared of her. She's always laughing at him behind his back because he can't do anything. Any little thing that needs doing around the house, he has to call someone in because he can't do anything. He put a new plug on the hoover once and we all ran for cover because we thought he'd blow the house up. Mum included. But it worked and you could tell he was annoyed that we all thought we were going to die. I'm sure he only got it right by mistake, anyway. He's really ignorant. I can read and write better than he can because he never went to school. He's never hit mum, but one day they had a fight, a swearing fight, and he threw a bottle of coffee at her head and only just missed. He really went for her and she had to run. Wendy and I were under the dining room table, dead scared. We were crying. She was crying as well. He doesn't like Cynthia but he never hits her. She's bigger than us and I just found out he isn't even her dad. I wish he wasn't mine, either. If he likes any of us, then he likes Wendy. She can get away with blue murder, but not us.

I'm sure other kids get hit at home and I suppose it must be right otherwise they wouldn't do it, but I think you can go too far. He goes too far. A smack on the leg would be enough. Hitting's never the same as explaining. They never explain, they just bash. Sometimes I think anyone who can bash their kids like that can't really love them even if they say they do. Have they ever said it? Well, they've never kissed me or held my hand or any of that stuff. That's not their way. But the dinner ladies let you hold their hand. Well... no, they've never said it in so many words, but I suppose they love me. They have to, don't they?

On the line, 1976

I play the recorder and the violin. I'm quite good at it actually and I've passed a few exams. The music academy is about half an hour from my house. I normally walk up there so I can have some time alone. I like to be alone. Wendy has her own friends and she thinks she's better than me because she's at secondary school, but she knows I'm cleverer. Whenever mum tells her to let me help her with her homework, she flies off the handle, but really she doesn't want to admit that I'm better than her. Being loud, all the time. As my mum says, empty bottles make the most noise. We give a lot of concerts at the music school but it really annoys me that my parents never come. They're always too busy or too tired, but all the others, their parents work as well. Sometimes it's embarrassing when the others are waving at their mums and dads in the audience and I just pretend to rearrange my music. I have six music certificates on the living room wall and people are always impressed which makes Wendy even jealouser so she starts doing acrobats because she's better than me and she's double jointed. Then my parents show me off, but when it comes to buying a ticket...

I wanted to do a weekend intensive course with the music school. It cost money and I needed a signature. If you got the signature, you could pay later but only the first ten handed-in signatures could go. The problem was, my mum was at work. I had to ask *him* for it. They never gave me money for other things, but generally I got the money if it had something to do with the music school. So it was only a question of the signature. I didn't like talking to him but there was no way to get around it. So I explained and asked for his signature. He held the pen in a really funny way, as if he didn't quite know what to do with it and it took him such a long time to write his signature, I felt sorry for him. Then I suddenly realised my mum signed everything that needed to be signed, and organized the bills, ordered from the catalogue. Everything. Then I didn't feel sorry for him anymore. I felt ashamed. Mum was right. He was hopeless. A stone we had to bear.

They were always never talking to each other. Tell your mum this, tell your dad this. Mum said this, dad said that. I hated it. When they weren't talking to each other, I'd be the one who had to write letters to his mother. He'd tell me what to say and I'd put it into good English. I hated these letters, he always spoke a load of rubbish and his stupid old mother, she can't read anyway, someone else has to read it to her. My mum always made fun of that. And then I'd have to finish; "Always your loving son." Don't make me laugh.

One last word, 1976

Am I like them? I have some things in common with my mother, yes, that's true. I got my brains from her, she says. She could have done great things if she hadn't started having kids and got lumbered. I've got her big feet. I hate my feet. But other than that, I don't think we're similar. I hope not. I wouldn't shout so much and I'd give the children a chance, but I'm not going to have so many cos that's like putting a rope round your neck. I'd listen to them and play with them the way some other parents do. If I get married. If I find someone good enough and not throw myself away on someone who doesn't appreciate me. I'm very mature. She says I've got an old head on a young body but when I know about things she doesn't want me to, then she calls me forced ripe. I don't think it's nice to take the mickey out of children. Certainly not your own. They always take the mickey because I've got big lips, calling me liver lips, saying "tulips from Amsterdam" and "look at those l-i-p-s!" They know I don't like it but they do it anyway, her and Wendy. Wendy gets to do things I can't, that's not fair. If I call her a dunce, I get told to leave her alone. She didn't get in trouble when she stuck bubble gum in my hair on purpose at night because my hair was longer than hers and mum had to cut it out. I would have done. Mum says go away from me with those big lips, I don't know where you got those big lips from. Once I asked her if I didn't get them from her and I didn't get them from him, then where did I get them from and she just flew off the handle for no reason. Maybe she has the right to get angry because she works her fingers to the bone and gets no word of thanks for it. That's what she says, anyway.

I wouldn't say I was really happy but then again, I wouldn't say I was really sad. I don't think about it like that. It's just a normal childhood like anyone else's. We've got our own house and we've got a car... I've got some nice clothes. Maybe... don't tell anyone I said this, but... maybe if I had a nicer family... nicer parents, like... But anyway, it's not over yet, not quite, and maybe it'll get better. Yes, I hope it'll get better when I start secondary school at the end of the summer. I'll have lots of work to do. Yes, it'll probably get better then... the angels will roll the stone away like they do in the Easter Song... and if not, well, when I'm grown up, it'll be my turn.

> The angels rolled the stone away,
> The angels rolled the stone away.
> It was early Easter Sunday morning,
> The angels rolled the stone away...

Jesus had a sad life as well, didn't he? I mean, they killed him in the end, didn't they?

One two buckle my shoe
Three four knock at the door...

And eyes and ears and mouth and nose
Head shoulders -

Stop it! Leave him alone, go on, skat!! I'll tell your mums!

25

A benign, a bright Saturday morning; so bright that even Rose's cupboard of a room push up under the roof like a sparrow's nest managed to steal a ray or two for itself. The flower-pots she had placed on the windowsill had gone a long way towards making the room a place to which one might want to come home; a place worthy a verse to grace a tea-towel on the kitchen wall, although she both left her dwellings before she could make the most of the cheering sunlight and returned when the best of it had already gone.

Not on Saturdays, however, when, true, she did have to get up at seven o'clock in the morning, yet throwing back the covers and stretching a lithe leg down to the fake tigerskin rug, Rose was conscious of having enjoyed two glorious hours more than the days before in her bed, whose lumps and bumps she had learned to live with. Tuck, pull, tuck; pull over, pull under the mattress, Rose made up the bed, fingers g-l-i-d-e--- over yellow-blue roses, cavorting on the sumptuous candlewick bedspread first spotted in a shop on her way home from her early-morning cleaning job. For four whole weeks she had followed the price, first standing in front of the shopwindow, then popping inside to check how many they had in stock, convinced it was the perfect thing for her bed, and already thinking hard to see what she could possibly do without in order to scrape the money together. For four long weeks she would stop off to see if 'her' spread was still there. But after these four long weeks of speculation, culminating in her conviction that the price would not be coming down, Rose had gone in with the request to place a deposit. Not the sort of person to buy what she could not afford, and, admittedly, somewhat afraid of being laughed at, such was Rose's desire to own that candlewick bedspread that she had gone in and, in her best English, had gone ahead and asked anyway, ready to walk out with her head held high if ever she should have the misfortune to be served by one of them skin unnu teeth[36] show-off think you is s'maddy dunce dunce white gyal deh work inna shop bicars she doesn't have di *brain* fi office work. The English girl, no older than herself, who was idling behind the counter, parted her cherry red lips:

"Yes, of course you can, ma'am. If you would like to select one, I will put it aside for you."

As natural as can be. *Ma'am*. Kuya! So Rose fastidiously picked out the crispest packet for that nice young shop assistant to put aside. Every week, with her pay packet from the cleaning job, she had gone straight to the shop to pay installment after installment till the day that bedspread ride home in the bus with her. There would be no more treating herself to anything for a long while after that, apart from intermittent pangs of guilt, for the money she had spent on that spread could have gone towards bringing Marlene and Leroy back to her sooner.

The bedspread had been her pride and joy for just over a week now. Rose stood back to get a better view; g-l-i-d-e--- her finger. *Nice...* Later, much, much later, she would treat herself to two new Woolworth's sponge-filled pillows, which she would puff up each morning to make them sit up on the bed. Miss Brown had given her whole books full of greenshield stamps which she had started saving but couldn't be bothered with anymore. Rose had taken herself down to the Co-op and traded in the appropriate number of stamps for a transistor radio. The three remaining books of stamps were wrapped in a plastic bag pushed to the back corner of her wardrobe. The radio sat on the bedside table next to the picture of Leroy and Marlene. Next to her Bible. Rose stood in front of the mirror, combing her hair, singing along to a song on Radio One. Half past eight; the news would be on any moment now. A child gurgled, happy on the floor, out of sight, but apparently ready for a new round of attention.

---

31 *skin unnu teeth* = grinning

"Hello, Laetitia. Hello baby." Rose got down to take the tiny hands in hers and swung them from side to side, much to the infant's delight. "What a way dis baby so soft and trusting..." What a way this baby, born a Hinglan, lucky. What a way... Miss Brown had heard of a woman seeking a childminder for Saturdays; a black childminder, a young black childminder who had children of her own, for the woman Miss Brown did hear of had no intention of entrusting her one and only child to some unknown white woman and most certainly not to some barren black woman whom jealousy might tempt to do harm. Rose picked up the child to bounce her up, bounce her down in the crook of her arm in time, round and round, to the music. Rose was looking good, had lost some weight; her bottom ripe in her bell-bottomed trousers, her waistline neat in her new denim jacket with its long, pointed lapels and circus-red buttons down the front. She carried the child downstairs to the pram taking up all the space by the front door.

"Me not here, Miss Brown."

"Alright, Rose – oh, Rose?"

"Hm?"

"Is market yu deh go? Yu can bring me back a few finger a green banana and a nice piece a yam from dat coolyman pon di corner?"

"Sure!"

"Tank yu, darling. How's Laetitia?"

"She fine."

"Sweet pitni dat!" Miss Brown came into the hallway. "Guess who phone me dis marning want to come 'visit' me?"

"Who?" Rose felt a flurry of fear.

"Roy! Look like him wife boot him out again an im deh look somweh put him useless head."

Sigh of relief. "So is when im coming?"

"Me tell him me no have no space fi him, so wid any luck im will stay where im deh. Me too old fi another pitni, yaa. Time fi him stan up pon him own two feet. Big old crusty man must can look after himself. Me only hope im no come come bother me. Him and hard work no fren, you know. All him can do is talk politics. Anyway me can see yu have tings to do. Me won't keep you," and Miss Brown retired, leaving Rose to tuck the baby in and steer the pram down the front garden into the happy London morning.

He could not believe his eyes when he saw her leaving Woolworth's, pushing that enormous pram; felt as though someone had punched him in the stomach, knocking the wind out of him. That could not possibly be her pram! Could it? Not knowing what he was doing or what he would do, he followed her.

The stuffiness of a launderette was a thing Rose felt she would never, ever, get used to. The women sat there, backed up against the hot, vibrating machines, nattering, whilst Rose sought out an empty bench, trying to pay them no mind; trying to empty *her* mind.
"Is fi yu pitni dat?" He stood over her, testing his best smile.
At first, the voice had not registered; sounded only vaguely familiar to her, a voice from her childhood. From home. Pleasant, seductive, but for that something querulous that made her look up…

And see Richard.

26

    Just back in from work that very moment, Jack was standing in the hallway, and although he hadn't been round the flat yet, hadn't even taken his jacket off, although the flat was making all the noises it usually made - telly buzzing, fridge wheezing, waterpipes, the lot, he sensed in an instant -
    "Nina? Ben, where's ya mum?"
    "Dunno. Said that she was going out n that you're not the only one who's got cronies."
With a sigh, expelled from the caverns of his fed up lungs, Jack:
    hung his jacket up next to her empty peg,
    pushed his working boots into place along the skirting board next to where her outdoor shoes were missing,
    threw himself into a chair in the kitchen.
Them in the flat upstairs, trampling around again. Why couldn't their kids just
    s-i-t
    d-o-w-n
and behave themselves, sit down and watch telly quietly like his kids did.
    "Oy! You up there!" one hand cupped over his mouth. An angry voice carries far. Propels saliva. Turns the veins that scale the temple hard, blue.
    Giggling.
Pack of anti-social bleeders! What he wouldn't give to get off that council estate, but it was hopeless; with only two kids? They would need another *three* before getting on the list for somewhere bigger. He felt sorry enough as it was that his two had to stay cooped up in the house all evening, all day when they were on school holidays, but he would not have them mixing with the kids round there. Not that he had anything against his two inviting a friend home so they could watch telly or play upstairs, but they

would not be going out. A few months back it must have been by now, when Ben had run in crying because some of the boys on the estate had thrown stones at him. His father had simply tutted with even greater disdain for his son than he had shown for the gratuitous violence impregnating the headlines of his local newspaper, had just said, "Stop crying, you sissy. They're just jealous. Riff-raff like that don't know the meaning of the word family. Next time they chuck stones at you, you pick up a couple yourself and pelt them back good and proper." The following evening, Jack had braved the cold, had gone down with Ben to practise pelting stones at a wooden wall, some of them council kids watching at a distance.

"Look at em," Jack head-butted their way, "gawping like they've never seen a son having fun with his dad before."

Ben pelted, harder, like a cricketer, imagining them council kids yelping every time he slung a stone, every time he got them right where he wanted to, egged on by his dad, teaching him the right angle, guiding his pitch. Inside, behind the ostentatious ruffling of hair or vocabular praise, it pained Jack Dunbar to have to teach his son how to pelt other boys, poor little bleeders they were, with all the cards stacked against them no wonder they turned rough. They pelted for ages, till their shoulders ached and them council kids had wandered off, one by one, driven home by hunger and the cold. The next time Ben asked if he could play out, his father still said,

"No."

Them in the flat upstairs didn't stay quiet for long. Jack's ceiling shuddered as they chased each other up and down, knocking over furniture. What could a man do but sigh? A slip of paper at the other end of the table caught his eye. Swallowing down that something inside him which recoiled from the idea of getting up to have a look, he pulled himself to his feet after a minute. *I'm fed up with this mess*, it said. *Need a change. A good one. A bloody long one*. Near the bottom: *Monica*. And below that: *dinner is in the oven*.

"*Bitch!*" He flung the note at the window. How long would she be gone this time? Maybe she was just trying to shock him. Maybe she'd creep in tonight at four o'clock in the morning. By God he'd let her have it this time, whenever she came back!

"Ben, what time did your mother leave, then?" he shouted from the kitchen to the living room where the television blared.

"Ben!"

"I don't know."

"What d'you mean you don't know? What time did your bloody mother leave?"

"I don't know!"

"Come 'ere when I'm talking to you!"

Ben dragged his feet from the sofa, over the carpet, across the lino, then stood blinking up at his father.

"Sorry, son," Jack pulled up a trouser leg, bent down to Ben's level and tried again, "it's not your fault... now, try again. Try to think," he put his arms around his son, rubbing him gently. "Were you watching telly when your mother left?"

Ben nodded.

"Thanks, son. You're magic!" He smacked Ben on the bum as the boy turned round to leave.

It was then that he first noticed the pile of dirty dishes in and around the sink. Dinner in the oven was still warm; fish fingers, potatoes and green peas. From a can. A skin had formed on the gravy.

"You two already eaten?" he shouted through to the living room.

"Yes!"

"When did she go, then?"

"Oh, she left just before I got home from work yesterday. I don't know what the hell she's playing at."

"Wot is it with you young people, James?" She had given him such a nice name; James Dunbar, she couldn't bear the way he let everyone call him Jack, as though he were a commoner. "I ask myself why you young people can't get your act together, eh? I'm sure I don't know."

"Mum, are you gonna stay wivva kids this evening till I get home from work, or ain't ya?"

"Someone around here has to have a sense a duty..."

"See you this evening then. Oh, and mum," quick peck on the cheek, "Taa."

Nana Irene lived a few streets away in the upper half of a maisonette, although she had submitted numerous applications to the council's housing agency to get them to move her down. On account of her legs, but that stupid young thing at the desk seemed more interested in her nails than in Irene Dunbar and tried to give her the impression she was being ungrateful. "I ain't looking for charity!" Irene had tapped on the counter, indignantly. "My husband's fought in two world wars and I've brought up four respectable kids, so I'll not 'ave you reduce me to begging, you silly little tart, wot I want is my fair due!" But Irene had given in now. The only way she would be coming out of that maisonette was feet first. That's how grateful society is. Do your duty, then they treat you like a sponger. The only ones to ever show any appreciation were the grand-children, Irene smiled as Nina and Ben pressed themselves lovingly against her, delighted by her surprise visit.

"You doing well at school, Ben?"

"Course I am!"

"And you, Nina, d'you like going a school now n having lots of boys and girls to play wiv?"

"Yeah!" Nina liked to wear her hair in pigtails when she went to school.

"That's good to hear! Now, go and put your clothes on and then you can come and watch telly with Nana, okay?"

The pair pounded up the stairs to their bedroom, where there was a wardrobe for the two of them, a bunk bed squeezed in behind the door, and the table Monica had put by the window. For homework. Monica had likewise submitted several applications to the council's housing agency, but the council said; two kids in a two-bedroomed flat? And both parents earning? Count yourself lucky.

The phone booths were always pissy round here, and the doors too heavy to be kept ajar with your heel. Monica had to leave her overnight bag:

a pair of slippers

    a hairbrush
    two pairs of nylon tights
    a bundle of underwear (her best ones)
    a dress (she was wearing one already)
    a skirt
    two tops
    a photo of the children in their school uniform
    another one of the two, taken by the door-to-door photographer in August

outside on the pavement. She dialled the number; had wanted to laugh, to sound carefree, yet no sooner had the receiver been picked up at the other end, then shame, rage, helplessness and all sorts of other vehemently felt inarticulations raced in a salty flow from her eyes and nose, so that all she could splutter was thanks, she knew she could count on her. What? Oh, just a couple of days, she said.

27

She looked away, annoyed that he should have seen her looking up and down the street. Looking for someone. His grin got wider with every step he took, teased by every novelty he was able to detect about her, even from that distance – new hairdo, make-up, nails, new clothes (nice little figure), my God – so that by the time he had reached the bus-stop, James Dunbar was brandishing the irrepressible smile of an admirer.

"Good marning." She could hardly keep her smile back, either.

After swallowing, "... who's the lucky man, then?"

"Is wa yu mean?"

"You off to get married, or somefing?"

"Me? Married? Yu too styupid! Yu tink if me going to get married me would stan up here at di bus-stop?"

"That's right. A Rolls for you... anyhow I'm glad to hear you're not getting married." He couldn't tear his eyes off her.

"So am I."

"Emily... you... you look absolutely stunning. Took my breff away when I saw you just then."

She chose to say nothing.

"I think about you quite a lot, you know, Emily. I know I don't stand a chance, but I like to think about you."

She remained silent.

Jack: We've been meeting all these months, an I really look forward ta seeing you every time. Seeing you warms me up so much, it makes me start the day on a good note, know wot I mean? Anyone who had you for a girlfriend should think himself lucky...

He'd been practising for ages, all the things he might say, he could say to get her to go out with him. He had worked out how he would stand and what he would do with his legs, with his hands and that. And now that she was standing there before him like some beauty queen, he could feel himself bursting to say something, but dammit, he couldn't remember his lines.

Jack: There's a mixed couple round where I live they look so good together. They're the other way round, mind. She's white and he's -

He'd never actually said the word *black* to a black person before. He didn't know if she would like it.

Jack: Well, they're the other way round. Not like -

and that word *us* got stuck in his throat.

Jack: Always holding hands, they are. Real in love, like. (*sigh*) Lovely, innit?

Then, wetting his lips,

Jack: Emily...

Jack's inner voice: Go on, Jack! Get it out. Now or never!

Jack: It'd be so nice if I could just take you out one afternoon. You know, we could go for a walk somewhere nice and have a nice meal somewhere... the summer's over, we won't have that many sunny days left n it's already getting darker quicker in the evenings...

Jack's inner voice: There! You see! Weren't that hard, was it? Give yourself a pat on the back, mate (*laughing proudly*). A whacking great pat on the back!

Jack: Emily, what do you say?

Emily (in a no hurry): I'm a very busy person. Me don't have no time for tings like dat.

Jack (panting): Whenever you're free, I'm free. What about weekends?

Emily: You tink me gwine go out wid some white man me know notting 'bout part from him name Jack?

Jack: What about a Sunday afternoon?

Jack's inner voice: She hadn't said no outright, had she? She hadn't said no…

Emily: Must tink me nay have someting better to do wid me time…

Jack (persisting): Nobody works on a Sunday afternoon…

Emily: ... tink we let go and loose like fi unnu woman dem.

Jack: Emily?

Their bus chugged its way up to them he ignored it they could catch the next one -
Jack: Emily?
Emily (irritated): Cho man, me ears deh eat grass! (*shrugs her shoulders at some botheration*)
Jack: Beg you pardon?
Emily: Say me fed up a hear about it!
Ding ding! The conductor rang the bell twice. The bus, obedient, tame, pulled away. Jack hopped round to the other side of her.
Jack: Wot is it you're afraid of, tell me. You afraid you might actually like it, perhaps?
Emily: Me nat afraid a anyting you can do me. Me got me Protector.
Jack: Then why don't you come! (*imploring*) Emily!
Couldn't she see what she was doing to him, couldn't she feel that he would walk the earth for her - could she really not?
Jack: It would do us both the world of good...
He could think of nothing more to say as he stood beside her, staring ahead sullenly, irked by the mindless chatter of the people around him *why the hell didn't they just shut their traps!*
Battle break out on Emily Thompson face but she keep her mouth tight shut, yaa. The next bus just turn the corner and she can't afford to miss it -
Emily: When?
Jack: Shall we meet at one?
Emily: One is too early, man!
Jack: What about at two?
Emily (brief pause): Where?
Jack: Wot's wrong wiv 'ere, at the bus-stop?
Emily: Good.

    Ding ding!
    "Two please, mate." He held his hand out for the tickets, "Taa, mate."
Both stared straight ahead, their bodies erect, not saying a word to each other, like a couple after a quarrel trying to play it down in public.

"Pollard's is the next but one," he said, still smiling. "Shall I get off here?" his head inclined a trace in her direction. Red fingernails, she had. Just like a lady.

"Not if yu don't want to."

"Oh, right," he whispered.

Rose tug on the cord and it go *Ting-ting!*

Jack scurried to his feet, holding his unbuttoned jacket against his chest, out of her way before he took his seat again, his eyes on her the whole time.

Rose looked down at him, wanted to say -
then made her way to the back of the bus.

"Hello lovely! Y'arlright? Wat a way yu look pretty dis marning!"

"Marnin," said Rose, brightly, surprised to see Uncle Roy in the front yard, obviously waiting for someone to let him in. Miss Brown had put him up for a few days the last time before passing him on to a friend of hers. Miss Brown was a nurse and a businessman, she said to Rose afterwards. She couldn't be wasting no space on tenants who had no intention of paying. Acting on Miss Brown's advice, her friend Renee had only given Roy a key after he had given her the rent in advance. Renee called her friend regularly to find out how best to handle him. Both secretly hoped his wife would be taking him back soon. Which she did. But here he was again.

"Is how long yu deh wait?"

"Too lang. Yu tink seh anybaddy wudda open di door an let me in? Bwoy, ignorance is a ting me not too partial to, yu hear what me saying?"

"Miss Brown not there?"

"Me no tink so. She normally back by now, and me just feel like come round fi a chat..."
No bag in sight, but maybe he had just left it at the station like he had done the last time, to make a false impression.

"She bound fi come back any second now. Yu can wait in di entrance if yu like, or in di kitchen upstairs. Me gwine change me clothes an do a likkle someting."

Rose opened the door and stepped into the dark hallway. Uncle Roy following.

Visibly annoyed to see her brother cluttering up her entrance, Miss Brown, when she got in around half an hour later:

"Uncle Roy," she kind of grumbled.

"Miss B.? Lek me help you wid yu shopping." He hurried to relieve her of a few of her plastic bags. Uncle Roy put on a calypso cassette to make the unpacking of shopping more jovial.

"Miss Brown?" Rose knocked, tap tap, before she put her head round the door.

"Come in! Di door open!" Miss Brown called above the music.

"Me can't stop," she took a step inside the room. She had changed her clothes, but something lively still clung to her face. "No. Me really can't stop, me haffi go a work. Just to say a quick howdi."

"Mm-hm. Arlright," as she packed away a few remaining bags of rice then stacked two tins of ackee and two tins of callaloo on top of one another. "Some other time." She herself was on night shift. Now that Uncle Roy was there, she gave herself up to the fact that she would be getting nothing done that morning. The ironing would have to wait, and she would have to hoover some other time. The only thing she would manage to get done was the dinner, which she would have a plateful of before going to work and leave the rest for Carmen and Daddy.

Uncle Roy came over to stand in the doorway and watch her peel a big yam. " Mercy! Is wat a big yam dat!" he exclaimed.

His sister need not answer straight away…

"Yu gwine stay fi a likkle dinner?" she did as she had to.

"Well," Uncle Roy tried to sound surprised. "Dat wasn't my intention, but if it's inviting me yu inviting me..."

"Me not inviting you," Miss Brown said as she dropped the thick peel in some old newspaper. "Me *arsking* you."

Back in that handsome redbrick house in Beswick Road later in the evening, Rose could hear the calypso, still on, and be witness, yet again, to Carmen's skilful soaping up of her mother in order to procure the permission to go out. With alacrity, Rose had accepted the invitation to an hour or two in front of Miss Brown's telly in the hope that it would provide the necessary distraction from the thoughts racing round in her head.

"Wat a way you did pretty up pretty up dis marnin!" Uncle Roy commented from the sofa as soon as Rose had come down later. "Anyone in particular?"

"Me did have a job interview," Rose lied.

Miss Brown turned the music down and the telly on.

"How much yu want to bet yu get di job? I tell yu, Hinglan is di right place to be. Yu got di white dem who prejudice, but nobaddy don't prejudice like a black man. A black man is him own worse enemy. Im never mount to notting bicars a him greed an prejudice. Look how long dem is in Hinglan, an dem still deh do di dutty work an factory work. Tek di Pakistani dem. Di Pakistani dem not here half as long, and yet on every corner dem got a shop open all di hours God send, and dem go to work inna suit an briefcase when dem work fi di white man an not inna no overall. Even Pakistani doctor me deh see inna di hospital dem. Yu ever see a black doctor in a hospital? Miss B, you ever see a black doctor in a hospital in Hinglan yet? Dis nigga nottingness, you see..."

"Uncle Roy, if yu tink we gwine si' down here an listen to yu tripe dis whole hevening, tink again. Me work in a hospital. Me is as good as a nurse. Di house me deh live in belong to me, and no man can march me out on account of no laziness - or should I say no woman," she looked at her brother sternly, "and di only nigga nottingness I know 'bout is dat no-good nigga who always deh run himself down instead a pick himself up."

Roy laughed, victoriously. In a way, he loved these talks with his short-sighted sister, felt he always managed to run rings around her and prove just who it was who had the brains in the family. "Di only reason yu can sit there an proud a yu house is bicars yu get di money from a white bank. Di bank in J.A. no good. So soon yu put yu money in, so soon di managa siphon it off tek it go a Merica an declare himself bankrupt. Black people can't see further dan dem own greed."

"Is what yu know bout?" lashed back a rather irate Miss B. "Yu ever see di inside of a bank? Evry black person I know got dem own house, is di woman yu got fi thank fi it. Di men dem can't put one farding aside. Mi never see a woman kick out a her own house yet, but strange enough, di men dem always deh end up pon di street."

Uncle Roy chose to overlook the provocation. "Me know a woman got one son back home. She come a Hinglan an work hard save all she could send back to dis deh son fi build a house. Years later when di house finish, she send write him when an when she coming back fi him fi pick her up from di airport. Anyhow, when she arrive im neh di deh[37], but im send one fren fi pick her up. An dis fren drive one route dat not di normal route, an di madda ask him is where im deh tek her. An dis fren stop di car an turn round look at di woman. Missis, him say, me gwine give yu a piece a advice. Tek a plane go back a Hinglan. Yu son give me five hundrid dalla fi kill yu but me just can't go tru wid it. Lek me tek yu back to di airport. An di woman go back a Hinglan an turn mad deh walk round pon di street an talk to herself till lorry knock her down kill her." Uncle Roy looked at the two women. "Greed an prejudice, I tell unnu."

"Yu see anybody deh murda an kill wid no reason like di white man dem?" Miss Brown counter-argued. "If somebody kill somebaddy back home, at least dem got a reason fi it. Di white man dem just deh shoot any old anybody, an pitni an tings like dat. An dem don't shoot an finish, dem deh tarcha[38] an mess round wi di woman an chilren dem. You just look inna any newspaper. Me don't know *one* black person yet kill dem own child chop it up an put di pieces dem in a dusbin liner dash weh[39], but me read more dan one story like dat since me inna Hinglan, an dem always, *halways* white. Now, you tell me." Miss Brown crossed her arms; matter of fact.

Rose, flipping through a magazine, stopped at an article about a black American singer who had married her white stage manager. The two, cheek squashed against cheek, and she had a fat

---

[37] *neh di deh* = wasn't there
[38] *tarcha* = torture
[39] *dash weh* = throw away

diamond on her finger. "Yu see dis, Miss Brown?" she asked, spreading back the pages for Miss Brown to see.

"Hm-m, me read it already. Wid a ring like dat me cudda bring di whole family a Hinglan."

"Is who dat?" Uncle Roy asked, looking over. "Christel Jahnson? She marry dis ole white man?" he grunted. "Di woman gat no pride. Nice young gyal like a dat hook up wid one hole crusty white man, is what she tink she doing?" He got up and turned the cassette off as a good film was about to start on the telly. "I can't stand a black deh run after white meat. Any black who mount to anyting always go run marry into a white family instead a keep dem likkle wealth inna di black community. Dem seem fi have a real identity crisis. Dem need a cerfiticate remind dem who dem really is."

"Is wat yu say dem need?"

"A cerfiticate."

"Bwoy," Miss Brown laughed, "mind big word no brok yu jaw-bone, yaa. Yu ever see a white face in my house? All me tenants black, an di only white face dat show itself round here is fi your face. Anf now shut up yu mouth, Clint Eastwood gwine start."

28
London, September --, 19--

Dear Junie,

Greetings from your fellow islander. I got a little time on my hands, yet not the will do anything tiring, so me take a seat and pick up a pen.
How are you all? I hope this letter finds you in health and strength and that, like myself, you may report that you have fallen on better times.
Miss Brown and Uncle Roy, I wish you could meet them one day. When they tell me them old time story and their tales of England, time just fly past quicker than Lester Piggot (a famous jockey over here and him small like a squirrel). Not all that glitters is gold, as you know. Over here, this is as true of the pavement as of the people. Miss Brown tell me is black people move England forward. The English didn't want to buy houses because they said another war would come and bomb it. Is black people first come over and start to buy property then them follow suit. Even though Uncle Roy won't tolerate one bad word about the British, they still seem to have taken him (our whole race, I must say) for a jackass and try to teach him things like a baby when we learn from British books and British educated teachers. The number of time he tell me how much more he knows than them! When they show him how to measure one third, eighth, quarter, half and five-eighths of an inch, them can't believe a man can pick it up so quick, so him just let them know that in Jamaica there is a thing called school where you learn the foot rule and all the measurements up to thirty-six inch make one yard. Still, the character of the English is a thing Miss B and her brother will never be in unison about! Uncle Roy seems to be quite an

educated man and when him put him mind to talk fine, him talk fine as a shame! You ever hear anyone but a preacher or a judge can say something like 'if there is one thing I have established a personal distaste for then for persons light on knowledge, with but a deflationary understanding of the facts.' You ever hear a Jamaican talk like that without him bite off him tongue? And the ladies like it, you see!

Miss B, even though she come here and make the most of her chances, she not too keen on the locals, my dear. You remember how me did try to learn the national anthem in case somebody ask me? Well, if is come over you want to come over, don't bother wasting your time on foolishness like that because nobody cares a hoot. You don't have to know and you don't even have to like the Queen. Miss Brown let me know: Him Royal Highness no like we, you know. Him is one racist and a jackass at that. Him not even English! Change him name to Mountbatten so the German them don't come and hawl him backside off to a workcamp. If him did ever know seh Liz got one African man lover. So me hear. And Margaret? She di black sheep in di family; she like her drink and she like her drug too much. She gwine come to a sorry end, just you wait and see!

It is thanks to Miss B and her brother, and their eternal squabbling about politics but also their million stories that I feel so at home. I thought I would be sad on this far away, cold, lonely island but now I feel my life with both my hands and thank the Lord. I thank Him, I tell you! One day I hope He will allow you to come and see for yourself.

Life over here is so different in so many ways. The children are different. I am sure it is the same hard work, and not one school on God's earth that can prepare you for it. But the rules are different. When we were young, you mother and father tell you to do something and if you don't them box you down. Them just have to call your name – Tété! – and you stand there dutifully in front of them. Here you have to explain and you can't lift a hand to your children. Them turn out any better? I wonder if Marlene and Leroy will be the same when they come over here, or, like Miss Brown's Carmen, they will turn English? You should hear the way she talk! But I don't want to appear to be criticising, they are all nice people.

It's going to take much longer than I thought to save up the money bring them over. Maybe I will have to send for them one one after all. If I don't bend over backwards to bring them fare together, is two big s'maddy gwine stand up deh when me go a airport pick up me children. One big humman wid hip and breast, and one big young man, all dress up and solemn like a Sunday sermon and don't even reocognise him own madda (you like patois? Smile). All them childhood years will have passed, and no letter that can ever, ever give you them back.

Junie, as soon as I have the opportunity, I'm going to send you a picture of myself in England. I won't have the time to go to a photographer, but over here you have door-to-door photographer come by every now and then. If he come by on a Saturday afternoon I stand a good chance to catch him.

All my love to you. All my love to Marlene and Leroy. Let them know I write and that they occupy the most cherished place in my heart.

Your faithful,

Rose

The facts:

Edward Heath was elected Prime Minister in 1970. The 68th Prime Minister in the history of the British parliament, the conservative Edward Heath replaced Harold Wilson, the only labour Prime Minister in the last twenty years.

Enoch Powell, dismissed from the shadow cabinet two years previously, was most saddened by the fact that his participation in the party's victory could only take the form of his rather vocal support in front of the television set in the lounge of his comfortably furbished detached house.

Jackass.

What a naughty boy was that
To try to drown poor pussy cat
Who never did him any harm

And killed the mice

Ran
Down
Hickory tickory...

...Tock

The fiction:

29

    Gertrude hardly ever bought flowers and almost never received any. Her husband Winston was, alas, neither amorous nor romantic. He forgot their wedding anniversary with a tenacity it made her seethe. He forgot the children's birthdays. Her forgot hers. He never forgot his, and would brood and fuss the whole day if no-one called to send him their best wishes. If the children didn't send him a card. If Gertrude hadn't bought something special for him, cooked a nice meal for the occasion. He had been rolled home drunk by friends she vehemently disapproved of that night seventeen years ago as she had started having the contractions that would give them their first child. He had spewed all over the stairs, then had cried like a baby; just as well that he was too drunk to see the loathing rumbling in her eyes.

    Two days later he would poke his head sheepishly around the door to the ward where she lay with the other proud but sore mothers. The sight of him made her close her fatigued eyes. He had brought her a rose the Lord only knows where he'd dug it up from for it hadn't even been freshly cut. Its outer petals flopped about spinelessly. Gertrude's eyes switched from him to the rose. Spineless. And that swanky dip in his walk. She felt the grandiloquent bouquets of her fellow mothers smile upon her, condescendingly. How she hated him for turning up with his more-dead-than-alive piece of a flower, for giving it to her, the only black woman in the ward, in front of all the others, with his swank and his dip, feeling he had the right to be pleased with himself. He kissed her on the cheek with his hands pinioned to his side. Showed her the rose proudly, placed it in the vase where it bobbed around like a soggy crumb in a teacup.

    Was that the child?
Gertrude closed her eyes, sighed. It's a girl. Her name is Joy.

Joy, he repeated, Joy. A pretty name. When yu coming home?

She looked at him, her jackass of a husband, knew what he was getting at, closed her eyes and sighed.

Yu tired. Maybe me should leave. Me will come again in di marning.

He could visit this afternoon if he wanted to.

No, he'd better come in the morning, he said.

The woman in the bed next door hauled out a massive white breast and fed it into the newborn's face, awkwardly.

Winston looked away. Me will see you in di marning, if me kyan mek it. Look after yusself. And Joy. He smiled. Look after her, too. You tink she tek after me, he asked, cautiously.

Gertrude's eyelids batted a *I-hope-not* to the accompaniment of a faint snort as she rearranged her tight, heavy breasts.

She was tired. Any fool could see that she was tired, Winston smiled. Me not ere, and he went.

As he left, she followed him with her gaze. He hadn't even sat down.

She always resented it when she had to buy other people flowers, not that she would ever admit it. Never. She entered the florist and was assaulted by a prolific burst of colour and odour. She wouldn't buy anything showy. Something... discreet. Yes, discreet. She wandered around between the buckets.

What was madam looking for? Anything in particular?

Gertrude coughed her polite cough. Yes, she was looking for a small bouquet, not too showy, not too expensive, but, she smiled, a bit better than average.

Was it for a special occasion?

No... no. Just a small bouquet. A few of these, and a few of these. Made up nicely with a bit of green, if you don't mind.

Mind? Certainly not, madam!

Yes, of course, thank you.

She cradled the bouquet in her arm as she alighted from the bus. She would stay for half an hour, then leave. It was a steep uphill walk that registered itself in her calves as she click-clacked over the uneven paving stones in her fragile Italian shoes. As the shops receded behind her, the din of commercial activities faded into a warm soup at the bottom of the hill, leaving her defenceless against the thoughts which came crowding in. The truth was, she did not want to go. She would sit out her time, like a dutiful child, if ever there was such a thing.

    Imposing iron gates reared up ahead in the long brick wall which had been shat on and graffitied on as seemed to be the destiny of all clean surfaces. Typical, Gertrude thought. No respect, not one ounce. People were so destructive. Getrude blamed it on their upbringing as she walked through the gates into the hush. Three schoolboys on their way past the gates just then with their bags slung rebelliously behind them. One, two three, they whispered, stuck their heads through the railings and sang:

> Them bones, them bones them *dry* bones,
> Them bones them bones them *dry* bones,
> Them bones them bones them *dry* bones
> Now hear the word of the Lord.

Gertrude did not bother herself to turn around. "Upbringing," she said aloud, her grip tightening around the bouquet. Deeper and deeper she walked into the hush until there, ahead of her, was her goal; not too showy, not too expensive but yes, she liked to think, a bit better than average. She would give herself half an hour. What time was it now? She looked at her watch. Ten. Right, then. Half an hour.

30

Excitement possessed her like a demon, snaking its way through her body; injecting its hot juice. Every molecule in her stood to attention, spizzed, swayed, finally to lean intimately against one another, exuding a deep, secretive glow. It had happened. She had thought his interest in her malicious, convinced as she was of her unattractiveness. She was ugly, her mother told her, matter-of-factly. So ugly, they hadn't taken any baby pictures of her. What? Take pictures of her and waste good money? They would not. Hard-earn money yu no throw weh.

When the door-to-door photographer came, mother had smiled. Please, come in and take a picture of my children. If their white neighbours could afford it, they could afford it.

"Oh, yes," mother Englished, "do come in, do come in. I'll just call the children. Do take a seat in the lounge, they won't be long."

The lounge, the children heard her say. Did they have a lounge? Wow, they had a *lounge*...

"Robert! Amy! Come here and get your picture taken! Where's Joy? She might as well come along, too." Mother ran to get a comb. Pulled their hair till it was presentable. Ran to fetch two ribbons. "You come and put on some better things. Put on that dress I just made you. Go and wash your face and put some lotion on it." She popped her head around the door and smiled at the photographer. "Just one moment, please."

"Hm? Oh, yes! Yes of course!" He smiled back, his eyes dabbling in the room. The lounge. So, this was what a black house looked like from the inside. Mother glued her eyes on him. Just you keep looking. But don't you tell no lies on me. You tell the truth and tell it good. A nice house, she knew. Cared for it as for a child. She had unlocked the door to the living-room, the lounge, and shown him in. Just you keep looking, but don't you tell no lies on me, she thought. The children came to a halt in front of her in the hallway. Nervously. There was a white man sitting in their living-room and he was going to take a picture of them. Of me too, Joy thought. My first real picture. She had washed her face twice. Mother attached the bow with a hairpin. They didn't have good hair, her girls. Dry and roll up. Bitty bitty. Amy was pretty, though. Maybe her hair would pick up when she got older. And she wasn't as dark as Joy. And her feet were nice and small. Joy already had feet like a slow boat to China when she was as young as Amy, Gertrude opened the door to the living-room. The children hung back, bashfully. Get in! She ordered them with her eyes, but didn't dare shout, for there was a white man sitting in their living-room and the door was open. The children went in. He lined them up against the wall. Girl-boy-girl.

"Lovely little girls. Twins?"
Mother smiled a curious agreement.

"Well well. Fancy that! Right then, look this way. Fine! Say "Cheese!" Got ya! One more - lovely! They'll be lovely pictures, I can guarantee that, Mrs… ?"

"Simon, Gertrude Simon."

"Gertrude Simon? Sounds like a jazz singer. Are you a singer?"

Gertrude lowered her eyes and laughed a don't-be-so-silly softly. Who knows? Maybe she would have been, if Fate hadn't cornered her in some dirty side-alley with a jackass for a husband, who knows what she might have been. The flash went off, sending Joy staggering back with her arms splayed, her eyes darting around to see if anyone had noticed she had done something wrong. Mother was looking at her sharply.

"They'll be lovely pictures, Mrs Simon. Much nicer than your neighbours on the left. Your three are really photogenic." Soap up her pride, that's the way to do it. "Are you sure you don't want another one? One for each set of grandparents? That'd be lovely! Just look at them standing there! Aren't they pretty?" The siblings were eyeing their mother.

"Yes, maybe one more."

"Okay, you three. Look this way, say: *Cheese!*"

She paid for the pictures and they came back two weeks later. She showed them to Winston. Not bad, he thought. So-so, she thought. Hm, nothing special, that's for sure. Is how much yu pay fi dem? She told him. He made a note in his mind to deduct it from her next shopping money. Jackass. If you ever did know…

    Of course she had had her picture taken at school since then, but her mother never bought them. Didn't want pictures like that sitting on her mantlepiece. Too ugly. Almost as ugly as her sister's baby. Now, *that* was an ugly baby if ever a baby was ugly. Face all squashed up and hairy as a monkey.
    "You're not that ugly. But you're ugly enough. They take a nice picture of you and I'll buy it, but I'm not buying these."
Joy took them back.

    He didn't think she was ugly. He wanted her to be his girlfriend. He wasn't kidding around, either. He'd sent her a letter. Chucked the torn off piece of paper from the cover of his exercise book on her desk on his way out. Now it had happened. They'd met quickly after school and kissed. He had put his tongue in her mouth and she had put her tongue in his! She had wondered and wondered what it might be like. And now she knew. He had weighed her breast in the cup of his hand and had guided her hand to his hard penis. She wasn't even scared. Not so as he'd notice. It had happened! Her heartbeat hadn't knocked him out – he'd pressed himself against her and made her swell and grow hot. They'd heard footsteps. Broke it up quickly and disappeared in opposite directions. She pulled up her school socks and fingered the zip on her schoolbag. Headed for home. What did she care now that she hadn't been allowed to have her twelfth birthday party two months ago. It would have been good, this being her first year in secondary school, and that. Her birthday a month after starting, and that. Would have been a golden opportunity to catch herself a few friends; people would've been nice to her if they'd known she was going to have a birthday party. But now, she didn't care, not one bit. And what did she care what she might be getting for Christmas. She'd got something that day, and on the last day before the holidays as well, that made everything else childish and unimportant. She was special now. And secret. She hurried home to lock herself away and chew the whole experience over again and again. Oooh! What a feeling snaking its way through her body. Don't you ever stop!

31

Gertrude slid her hand inside her blouse to finger her breasts. They weren't ever going to be big. Not big enough to bounce when she walked, or big enough for the boys to want to whistle at her as she walked past, or make nasty suggestions. She was too dark for most tastes and her hair wasn't as nice as it could have been. Never mind, her girlfriends would say, and she never knew if they were serious or not; every hoe got him stick a bush. Other girls her age had real boobs; boobs to be whistled at, boobs jiggling on nasty suggestions as the girls sucked in their breath and swung their hips whenever anything older walked past. Gertrude had tried it, too, but she had too much bottom and not enough breast, so when she pulled her stomach in, it only made her look hungry and the men laughed, "Kuya! Big black batty an no boosam!"

They were growing, but not quickly enough. She sat on an upturned beer-crate under the mango tree's thick shade, her book open in her lap and a hand on her breast. Her toes played with the leaves underfoot. When would she get the chance to do it? Some of her friends had done it already and whispered about it excitedly. It was so big! So big, she couldn't get her hand round it. Eyes widened.

"Big as me wrist! Im did want put it inna me mouth, me tell him fi gu weh, him too nasty!"
They shrieked, wished, dreamed.
"Wen him do it, it nice, yu see! Nice as a shame…"
They lounged along the hot dusty road, the group of girls, all wanting to get home in a hurry to the chores awaiting them, to spare themselves the scolding they would be in for if they didn't get home on time, yet none of them so bold as to want to be the first to break it up. They lounged along, kept an ear open for

trucks that would mean men, thus the chance to pull in stomach and swing hip.

When would she get a go? She closed her eyes and fingered her breasts, out of view, under the conspiring shade of the mango tree. Her nipples grew hard. She rolled them around like peas between her thumb and first two fingers. It was kind of nice, but she knew it wasn't the same. When would she get a go?

Joy shoved the shoe-box with her secret diary and her writings in it back to its secret place when she heard footsteps on the stairs. Those were Amy's footsteps; so loud and arrogant, just listen to her, you can tell she was spoilt. Amy flung the door open and strode in.

"Wotchya."

Joy stared at the pages of her book.

"Wotchya, I said."

"Can't you see I'm reading?"

Amy stepped out of her school clothes, left them all over the bed, pulled on a pair of jeans. "Dinner's ready. Ya coming or ain't ya?"

"In my own time."

"Suit yasself." Tomp tomp tomp tomp, down the stairs again.

Joy retrieved her shoe-box and finished the day's entry, locked her diary and hid the key elsewhere. Good. She put the box away. Reluctantly, she went downstairs to join the 'family' for dinner.

32

Typical. Just typical. Fourteen years old she was but they treated her like a child. They were going up to Manchester for the weekend. To a funeral. A friend of the family's whom she had never seen but from whom they always received a tacky Christmas card with a dab of glitter. Amy and Robert were going.

Joy said she would not.

Gertrude said she reckoned Joy had no say in the matter, anyway.

Joy said, oh yeah? She reckoned she did.

There ensued a bitter quarrel. Quarrels. The beat, the rhythm of her days. Gertrude called for Winston, who instantly withdrew himself from the whole affair. Shadow of a man. Impotent. Joy watched him retreat up the stairs.

You a man or you a mouse? Gertrude shouted up the stairs after him. Heard the bedroom door, Bang! Spineless, she thought. Swung round to face her intractable daughter, Well, if she thought she was going to stay in the house on her own she had a next thing coming. Right then, Gertrude hissed, she would jolly well have to go to Stockwell to her grandmother's for the weekend. She spun and left the hallway. That child! Driving her to drink! Once so quiet and withdrawn. Intelligent children normally were. For she was intelligent. Gertrude was, too. My God, how her life would have been different if she had been born now! And here! The possibilities she would have had! That Joy had. And didn't deserve, ungrateful wretch that she was. Quiet as a mouse she was, then one morning she woke up and had turned into a real cow. Suddenly thought she was something special and carried herself so arrogantly that whenever Gertrude looked at her she just wanted to slap that smug little head right off her shoulders. Slap her down from her high horse. A bitterness had got hold of the relationship that had never been a loving one, if only Gertrude could, would, admit that to herself. No, she had never loved Joy. Didn't love any of them, not really.

I hate her, I *hate* her! Why should I like her only because she's my mother? I hate her and she hates me, and I'll have nothing to do with the whole hypocrisy! Joy stamped up the stairs and burst into her bedroom. And you sit there pretending you don't know a thing, she pushed Amy's legs, which hung over the bed and in her way, impatiently aside.

"Hey! Wotch it!"

"Just belt up and mind your own business!" she snapped. Amy got up muttering and went downstairs to her mother.

"You two are so bloody pally!"

They had been invited to a party, her grandparents had, and she would have to go along. There was no getting round it. She resolved to sit in a corner and think about all the nice things that had been happening to her. Things her mother kind of suspected and that's why she had turned so nasty. Joy knew girls, could talk to their mothers openly about periods, and boys, and dates and things. Girls whose mothers were really friends. They were the girls who didn't get into trouble. Joy wouldn't get into trouble, either, even though she never had a mother as a friend. But she had grandma.

Her grandfather was a terrible driver, always cutting in on people and risking red lights. Grandma would get worked up and push up her face. Then she'd start on about his drinking.

"Yu know yu not s'pose fi drink and drive, so yu just watch it dis time, yu hear me? Yu just watch it, or mek haste give me me taxi monni fi come home."

He ignored her. Knew it worked her up even more.

She started on again.

"Shut up yu mouth," he cut in. "Yu can drive? Mek haste learn fi drive, yaa, an drive yuself home. Yu not dead yet, or is a ghost me have inna me car deh nag me like dis? Cho man, all yu need now is di curlers, an den yu just as bad as Hilda Hogdan." He looked in the mirror. Saw Joy suppress a smile.

"Oh yes! Me is Hilda Hogdan?" He had her in a right little fizz.

"Shut up yu mouth fore me mek yu get out and walk." He winked at Joy.

"Oh yes? Fore me get out and walk, me wudda box you facety head right from yu shoulder. See wat yu tink 'bout dat!"
Grandpa accelerated through the amber and turned right without indicating. "Yu listen up and listen up good. Me is no Stan Hogdan. Yu hear me! Tink me gwine si' down and tek a beatin from me wife? Fore yu cudda knock off me head, me wudda brok yu two hand put yu out a action a likkle while."

"Is so yu tink?" Her voice, high and merry. "An when me two hand brok, no forget seh me got me good strong teeth. Good strong teeth, yu hear me?"
He sucked his teeth, "Ol woman, yu see! Look if me find meself one nice young gyal a dis party..."
Grandma bantered, "as if a nice young gyal gwine intress in a ol' horse like yu! Kuya! Did anybody ever see me trial!"
They all laughed, Joy in the back, too.

"Yu si' down deh deh laugh. Me gwine find a nice young gyal come rub me up pon me belly an treat me nice, yu see!"

Let them get on with it. Joy locked herself away in her mind to re-activate her latest experience. Closed her eyes and let the well-fed cat of a car purr through her. She had fondled the experience until it was now soft at the corners, yielding, dog-eared. Fondled it until the sweat of her excitement had lessened the colours, until the whole thing watered down, pastelled away into a cloudy dream.

Ian Lovelace. How could anyone have a name so pretty? He wasn't much to look at but who was she to complain. He had sought her out, had no need to fear that she might spurn him as he had been done by the prettier girls. He wanted to learn, too, and so did she, so they more or less drifted over to each other; silent, grateful. They met at lunchtime. A good idea; save yourself the trouble of lying when you come home late after school. Both his parents were at work. His sister, too. Her first job. Nothing special. Some secretary in some office. Somewhere. He didn't give a toss what the neighbours might say. Joy was helping him with his school-work, he would be ready to say. They weren't allowed in the building during the breaks, and in the playground it was too noisy to concentrate. Joy was clever. Look at her schoolbooks. Look at her marks. And he thought privately; she isn't even pretty. They won't think I'm carrying on with *her*.

They walked over to his place with a book open and Joy should act as if she was explaining something to him. He thought it a brilliant idea. They went in. Went to the kitchen at the back of the house. If anyone unexpectedly came home, they'd have enough time to get themselves together before the person reached the kitchen. Never, *never* go upstairs. He buttered two slices of bread. Put them on a side plate. He would say he was just about to offer her something to eat. The backyard wall was high. No-one could look into the kitchen. Anyhow, the neighbours on one side were a house full of Hindus and an old white couple on the other. They mind their own business. Only black neighbours would put their nose in and ask if his parents knew he was coming home at lunchtime. Well, they saw the books, didn't they? Could see that he was learning something, couldn't they? Got them where you want them if you say you're learning something. Go man go if you say you're learning.

Both had stood there not knowing how to make the first move.

D'you want somefing ta drink?
She said she didn't. You?
No, he didn't, either.

He swallowed hard. Decided to go for it. He kissed her, his fingers roaming over her plum breasts. She fell to tingling. Instantly. The feeling she loved. The feeling she couldn't get enough of. Joy balanced herself against the cupboard. As their tongues circled in each other's mouth, she thought; it's happening! You see, it's happening! To her, who had feared no-one would be interested enough in her. He was circling his tongue in her mouth and fingering her tits! Her mouth was quickly filling up with spit so she tried to swallow, but their teeth clashed noisily and she had to say; oh, sorry. Ian timidly unbuttoned her blouse. Left the top button done up. Touched her skin. Grubby, bitten down fingernails he had. He fiddled around at the back of her bra. Fiddled around. "At the front," Joy worked out around his tongue. He snapped it open to expose her tuppenny nipples. Dark and hard. He was looking at tits. Real tits! He kissed one. Turned its button around in his mouth, sucked on it hungrily. Joy closed her eyes and held firmly to the cupboard. Everytime he sucked - sometimes the sensation went in, like a screwdriver, sometimes out, like a string. Like someone was pulling a long string out of her. He came back to her mouth. She reached her hand down for him. He was hard. He pressed himself against her. Reached up under her skirt. Under her skirt! His fingers were in her hair and played with her. She heard herself slurping down there and it made her feel embarrassed, good thing her eyes were closed. She was so hot, her blouse felt tight and prickly at the collar. And there was a throbbing down there, as if it had a heart of its own. He watched her face, slipped a finger inside. Her eyes sprang open. He smiled. She smiled. After a while. So this is what it's like to be fingered! It didn't hurt. Not at all. He drove his finger in and out. Faster. So now he knew what it was like to finger someone! She was warm and moist. Ribbed part of the way. He brought his finger to her mouth. No! She drew her head back. He smiled. Undid his zip, smiling into her face. It didn't stand straight off from his body as she'd imagined it, but pointed slightly upwards, around eighty degrees, from his torso. She rubbed him up and down a few times then suddenly he was in her mouth. She must have fallen to her knees, but all Joy could remember was that he was in her mouth, and that it seemed the most natural thing in the world to do. Sucking on him, like he'd sucked on her. And it was nice. And he slurped too. If he did and she did, then it had to be natural, hadn't it? This made her feel much better. She stroked his thighs and played with his balls, with his buttocks, which were small and knotty. Ian couldn't believe his good luck. He was getting it all in one go. But he knew he didn't want to do *that* to her, suppose she... in his mouth? Urgh! Boy, it felt good! She was sucking his dick!! She was sucking it, and liking it! And he had secretly feared that no-one would ever want to do that to him. Look at her! She was loving it!

C'mon, get down on the floor. He eased her away. What for? She asked apprehensively. We're gonna do it. He watched for her reaction. No! She said, pushing him away. No! Her eyes were frightened and she stole a look out of the window, feeling self-conscious all of a sudden. Now what had he gone and spoiled? C'mon, he pleaded but he knew he was wasting his time. No! I said No! Joy did her bra up and buttoned her blouse. Damn it! He'd spoiled everything, he cursed himself. Damn it!

Wot time is it, she asked, looking around for her bag. She had to get out. She had to get out now. Quick!
He looked at his watch. Said it was quarter to.

Quarter to? She pulled her socks up. I'd better go.

Was she sure?

Yes, she was sure. I gotta go. You coming? She couldn't look at him. She had to get out!

Me? No, not yet. I got somefing to do. I'll see you back at school.

Okay.

Okay, then.

Right, see you.

See you, he said.

She got her bag.

Bye.

Bye, she said, making her way to the front of the house.

He waited for the door to slam. Sat on the chair. Did it to himself; he just had to.

They were waiting at the traffic lights and the couple in the other car looked them up and down. How did she do that without falling to her knees? She couldn't remember falling to her knees and she couldn't remember getting to her feet again. Strange, weren't it? Party was going to be a bore, of course, but she'd just sit it out in some corner with her thoughts for friends. Might sneak a few glasses and get a bit tiddly. Help to pass the time. They were alright, her grandparents.

As they entered the housing estate, they heard the steady pulse of a reggae rhythm further on. Groups of youths hung around on the landings, eyeing them as they went by. Standing at the front door, Joy could feel the music reverberating in her neck. It was insufferably loud. She realised this was her first party - her first real blues. They had to ring four times before they were heard and grandma had worked herself up again in the meantime. A stout man with greying hair and three gold teeth opened the door. Hot air, sweet and sticky, swam out in a thick gruel.

"Missa Simit!" He held out a broad hand weighed down by gold rings. "Glad yu cudda mek it. Me see yu bring yu missis an yu gyalfren!"

Grandma styooped. "Dis here is my grandarta Joy an she is only fourteen years old, yu hear what me saying?"

He stepped back gestfully. "Cool it, missis, cool it! Ol' humman, you see man! Missa Simit, a young gyal yu need, rub yu up pon yu belly mek yu feel good. "

All three waded their way through the air into the house. To Joy's relief, there was a regular sprinkling of the younger generation. Older than her, of course, but not all as old as them, grandma and grandpa.

"Go an enjoy yuself," said grandma. "Me gwine si' down here and talk me business."

Joy stood in the doorway to one of the rooms crammed with people and the Lord only knows what they had done with all the furniture for there wasn't a stick of it anywhere except where the older ladies, including grandma, had gathered to hold council, like hens. Even the carpet had been taken up. The music so loud, Joy could hardly breathe. Monster-ugly boxes blotted out the windows and boomed voraciously. And there were Rastas in the house. Loads of them. White Rastas, too. White Rasta women with their hair in dreadlocks, their emaciated hips under long skirts, from which peered, now and then, skinny, blood-drained ankles in Jesus creepers, swaying sophisticatedly to the beat. So this was a blues party.

33

    Gertrude hauled her purchases home along the long, familiar dirt road. She kept as close as she could to the edge, sometimes having to pick her way through the discarded rubbish strewn along the way; to step past the rusting Coca-cola cans or the squashed Red Stripe. Boxes, wrappers, bleached by the sun, skirted the road with their dry leaves or else formed a grey mash after the rains had fallen. Every now and then, a tree cast its shade thoughtfully over the villagers on foot with their heavy bags, their chickens hanging upside down, clucking away at a nervous premonition, or the children who grew tired along the way and tried to play up. The sun lashed down on Gertrude as she stopped, put her bags down for a fraction, changed them over and picked them up again. How she wished that for once, just for once, someone else would put this hour-and-a-quarter stretch behind them. Two strapping brothers, but it was always her. They'd lie around doing nothing, sit back with a beer in the hand or else be off gallivanting somewhere whilst she, she had to work like a horse for them. Buy and fetch and carry and cook. Wash and iron. Sweep and wipe. Polish and pluck and peel. And there was no use protesting. She was her mother's only girl. Their father had upped and left as they all did sooner or later, having been brought up with very little respect for their female counterpart, and immune to the notion of responsibility. And if, by some chance, you found yourself with one of the good ones, you'd have to beat the other women away with a stick and plague yourself daily with the thought that today someone else might have won him to her. So you question and you dig for secrets and sooner or later he can't stand it anymore so he ups and goes anyway. Menfolk. Sought and coveted and pampered and loved. Attacked, hated and forgiven. Soft as a raw egg? No woman will respect you. Hard as a stone; you'll find those who like it, but every woman – every head in a scarf, every heart in a chest, every bottom in a tight skirt – was on the lookout for a piece of toast; hot and rough but melting in your mouth... golden brown, coated with a spoonful of honey to run down the side and stick to your fingers... Laugh, flirt, drink beer. Spit. Strut. Slap. Sing. Fall into a chair and wait for dinner. Pull you close. Touch your breasts. Ride you. Love you. Leave you. Need you; Menfolk. What else was there to do but to resign to them, yield up one's flesh and string together those precious happy moments, like pearls, whilst you still could, then collect your due in the perfumed balm of sisterhood.

Her eldest brother, One-son, was impatient for her to come home. Where was she? Is where she deh? He passed the used dollar bills from hand to hand. Dirty, oily notes. They even smelled fishy. Like mackerel, he thought. Thick and penetrating. Then he saw her, shuffling down the road towards him. Quickly, he stuffed his dollars in a back pocket and reached for his beer.

"Is where yu been?"

Gertrude breezed past him in the direction of their modest home.

"Is you me talkin to, yu know." He had to behave as normally as possible. Not appear too excited or too interested in her.

"An when yu tink yu can do it quicker, what mek yu no go get di tings dem yuself?" She disappeared inside the house.

"When yu put down di bag dem yu haffi go a Maas Roach pick up some fish." He took a slurp of beer.

"Mammi nay tell me notting bout no fish."

"How she can tell you someting she herself know notting about? Me help Maas Roach fix something and im gwine send us some fish fi say thank yu."

Gertrude re-appeared in the doorway with a hand on her hip, wondering how her ten-thumb brother could be of use to anyone, even a fisherman, said instead, "Oh yes! Im gwine send us some fish fi say thank yu? Me wudda like to know since when fish can talk."

"Don't facety wid me. Just go and collect di fish. And quick, bicars him say him want go out."

"Wat mek yu never tek it di same time?" On her feet. On her feet. The whole day she had been on her feet and she had so been looking forward to a little rest.

"Child, you just do as me tell yu. Me wudda like to know what mammi gwine say when me tell her how Maas Roach generous enough fi give us some fish and yu say yu no want go pick it up. Go long, yaa, di man want fi go out."

A few minutes it took for Gertrude to pack the groceries away before she re-emerged into the sunlight. He watched her pass him without a word, watched the ponderous roll of her buttocks, watched her until she was quite far away, then raised himself just so much that he could retrieve his reward and begin, once again, to pass the used dollar bills from hand to hand; one dalla, two dalla, tree dalla...

Mister Roach's wife had left him. That happened too, from time to time; that a woman decided she'd had enough and just upped and went to another district. She couldn't stand his smell anymore, the fishy perfume constantly in the house. He couldn't help it, he said. A fisherman smelled of fish and that was that.

"Yu stink worse dan stale piss! Wa mek yu no do su'um fi get ridda di smell?"

He washed his hands, took a bath in the river once in a while, what more could he do?

"What den? Wat den? Yu tell me how a fishaman s'pose fi smell like rosewater, to raated!"

And then he would climb into her and she would smell for days, just like him. Fish. Mrs Roach decided she had had enough. A lady's not supposed to smell like fish. Monthly smells were bad enough, but them and fish? No. She left him. And this whole long time he had had to go without, had been so yearning for it that he saw pussies in everything; the fish's thick-lipped mouth... a wet and fleshy half-peeled mango... flowers, velvety and red, in everything he saw a pussy just waiting for him, tempting him until one day he said; no, this can't go on. A man is a man. Then he had that talk with One-son. Now here she was, coming up the road. He ran away from the window, dashed from one corner of the cabin to the next, touching everything in sight, as if pleading with it all to be on its best behaviour. In the bedroom, he sleeked a finger over the bedsheet.

"Maas Roach!" she shouted in through the opened door. "Maas Roach! Yu is home?"

He had a sudden erection. "Come in, chile! Come in!"

Suddenly Gertrude found herself picking up gifts for her brother once or twice a month. Picking up gifts, collecting things he had forgotten, taking things back. Never did she come away without… without being compromised. She said nothing to anyone, and then she thought, I've done it! I'm not a baby anymore. She repeated the hymn to herself to drive away a bitter disappointment:

I've done it...

Then she nursed the memories like a child, passing them on to no-one, stringing together her pearls for the necklace she would one day wear nostalgically as evidence of her allure. And Oneson cussed and quarrelled when their mother Ruby asked where he had got the money to buy that fancy shirt, and he stormed out of the house with a swank and a dip. Ruby watched him strut off down the road, thought; my son, just don't end up in jail and bring no shame on my family, that's all I ask. No. More. Shame. And she turned to Gertrude. And Gertrude looked the other way.

34

He said he would write. He said he would. She should have known better. She had her letter already written and learned by heart and was only waiting for him to do the decent thing and contact her first. What did they know about decent? Five agonizing days she had been on the lookout for the postman, who had come, but with nothing for her. She began to lose hope. He had used her. She was only a stupid little schoolgirl he'd met at a blues. A schoolgirl who lived on the other side of town. A schoolgirl he could dump easily. He was nineteen. A working man. A bricklayer. What did he want with a schoolgirl! She tortured herself, buckled over her diary, scribbling furiously. Her secret writings grew and grew as she wrote her sorrows off her heart, so engrossed in lashing the rowdy herd of her reflections in the right direction that she became sloppy about keeping watch. Amy had barged right into their bedroom.

"Wotchya."

Joy sprang like a jack-in-the-box. Too late. She found a new hiding-place for her writings. Checked them more frequently.

What was that? That noise? Could it have been... the flap of the letterbox? Joy sprang from the bed, dashed for the door then, checking herself, swanned, casually, down the stairs. Three letters on the doormat. One from abroad, another, most probably a bill, and the third, she couldn't tell. It lay face down, giving nothing away. She bent down to pick them up. Watched the trio tremolo in her hand. The one in the brown envelope was a gas bill. Long brown envelopes were always bills in this house. In fact almost everything which came was official; typewritten, postage paid or the company's name would be plastered all over the front. There was hardly ever any private mail apart from the obligatory Christmas cards, my God, didn't they have any friends? She turned the white envelope over... It had a window in it, too. Something in Joy turned its back on her and grew cold. He was not going to write. She had made a fool of herself. Had let him kiss her and touch her. Had let him put his tongue in her ear and rub his frighteningly stiff penis against her. Had let him whisper nastiness to her and grind her against the wall... but he was not going to write. Her fingers surrendered the envelopes to the floor. They crashed in mid-air, tutted at her, fell, well anyway you'll have to put us where we should be so come on, they glared back at her. Down she bent once more, skimming their details without seeing them for a long time, but... really... Really? *Really?* Yes. It was for her she snapped it up and was gone.

One-son had bought himself a new pair of shoes. New leather shoes. Mother was anxious. Knew she couldn't ask. Mother was anxious. Don't be, he said. Went to her. Put a hand on her shoulder. Don't be. Gertrude sat in her corner, trying not to listen. Don't be anxious. He wouldn't end up in jail. In the meantime, he had two girlfriends collecting for him so he didn't turn to Gertrude so much. It was hard for her. Of course it was hard. Bread - after cake - it was hard. A bitter blow for a girl of fourteen who could only lie in her bed and press herself against the lumps in her mattress. Until the day she asked her brother as he was manstepping past her room if he didn't have anything she could bring back for him?
He looked at her long, looked ather hard. Wanted to slap her.
No, he said. Wait a minute -
She lit up. Sat up. Swung her legs down to the floor -
She could bring him a beer.
The smile treacled from her face.
He thought; yu wortless piece a trash. Then his girls might be busy and he would send Gertrude, whose gratitude was overwhelming and as she practically raced off, he spat into the dirt; wortless piece a trash fi true. Woman dem! And he spat again.
Mother was anxious. Don't be. He gave her a dollar. She looked at it and was afraid of it. Don't be. Here's a dollar for Ricki when him come in. He smiled. Crossed the room to Gertrude. And here's a dollar for my baby sister. Gertrude stared

at it on the table in front of her, and fell to suspecting... He stood in the doorway. Mother looked at him; my son?

"Me is fine. Just fine. Just doing fine."
And he was gone.

The letters came. She read them over and over again. Over and over. Found a new hiding place just for them. She read them with her heart in her mouth, with her groin pressing into the bed. He wanted to do it to her; he wanted to lick her, kiss her, give it to her, make her scream. He wanted to fill her up. Pump her full. Ride her into paradise. She bucked about on her back, her thighs doing the tadpole, a finger whippng her startled, slippery clitoris to, through and beyond her first orgasm.

She had heard the gate squeak. Was at the door in a shot; caught the letters before they even had time to fall to the ground. There it was. Yet another airmail letter with the stripes crossed out and her name printed laboriously in the middle. She was used to it now although she still couldn't accept it, thus suffered every time a portion of that deep disappointment which had booted her the first time she had seen that airmail letter with the stripes crossed out and her name printed laboriously in the middle. Telling her everything she needed to know about him. Telling her - she had run and run and run, and nevertheless run straight into the arms of one of *them* how could that be? She decided to make the best of it. Only, when could they meet? Soon. Please, dear God, make it soon.

Her shoebox was gone. Panic throttled her so that her heart seemed to burst out through her ears. Her shoebox! Frantically, she turned the room over. Her things. Amy's things. The letters were still in their hiding place. She stuffed them in her jumper. Turned the room over, panting. Crying. Blind with anger. Her shoebox... Her shoebox... Amy had a drawer full of dirty knickers and socks. Joy rummaged wildly. Grabbed them all and threw them to the floor. Yellow-stained. Brown-stained. Caked on secretions. She threw them all out, tossed them to the floor. Socks, stained by leather, stiff with dirt, she threw them all out. Drawers with T-shirts and bras, she threw them all out. Lunged for the wardrobe, dived into the pockets. Their contents, she threw them all out. Under the bed. The chest of drawers. Behind the radiator. Behind the wardbrobe. Her shoebox... where was her shoebox! Joy thundered down the stairs, stampeding into the dining room where Robert and Amy were watching television. Mother was in the kitchen.

"Where's my sheobox?" she roared.

"Your wot?"

"You know damn well what I'm talking about!" Her voice so thick with tears she could hardly control herself.

Amy, slowly, got to her feet. "Wot shoebox? How'm I sposed ta know where your shoebox is?"

"Where's my shoebox!" Stiffened in her rage, she glowered at Amy, saw, from her fear, that she must be telling the truth. Amy didn't know where her shoebox was. Didn't even know she had one. Joy turned her eyes to the kitchen where the door was open but mother still hadn't come out to find out what was going on or to break it up. Joy stared into the kitchen and had to steady herself. Amy inched her way past Joy and went upstairs...

Gertrude was turning some meat. She held her face back from the heat of the oven as she flipped the pieces over with a fork.

"Where's my shoebox?"

Gertrude stirred the sauce.

"Where's my shoebox!"

"Is who yu tink yu talkin to!"

"Where's my shoebox!"

Gertrude closed the oven door and lifted the lid from a pot of potatoes on the stove.

"Where's my *shoebox*!" she was angry and ridiculous because she was powerless and her hatred wasn't enough to hurt. Always, always, she would be the weaker one. And her hatred grew. "Where's my shoebox!" And she took a big step into the kitchen.

Gertrude was alarmed for a fraction of a second, revealed her fear for a fraction of that second, before she pulled herself together.

"How dare you go through my things! How dare you!"

Gertrude smiled a victory smile, brushed past her daughter, went over to the sink.

"How dare you!"

She turned around and there was Joy, brittle with rage. And she had the carving knife in her hand.

"How dare you!"

"Wat yu tink yu doing wid dat knife!" But she couldn't hide it. She was afraid. "Put it down! Me say put it down!"

Joy did not budge. Her face jittered a warning for a second or two, just before her eyes glazed over.

Lord in heaven, Gertrude thought, the pitni turn mad.

Amy burst into the kitchen to complain. "Mummy!-"; fell silent.

"Put the knife down!"

"Where's my shoebox..."

Lord in heaven, Gertrude heard, with a chill, some strange voice coming out of the child's mouth. What's happened to her? Perhaps, this time, she had gone too far? She lunged at Joy, boxed the knife out of her daughter's hand; boxed her daughter back to this world. Joy came to herself. Still rooted to the spot, but her eyes regained their focus and Gertrude saw; she'd turned, she *had* turned... She grab up her daughter by the jumper and smack her viciously. "Yu tretten me wid a knife? Yu tretten me wid a knife?"

Joy raised her hands, tried to pull away.

She's here, she's here Gertrude could see now, and anger, shame and gratitude exploded into vicious blows. "Yu tretten me wid a knife!!"

Joy struck back. Lashed out at her mother. Boof, boof. And got her. She stumbled free. Out of the kitchen. Out of the house.

Gertrude inhaled, deeply, as if trying to snatch back every gram of air that had got away. Then she saw the carving knife on the floor. And Amy in the doorway, poised as if ready to run should she have to. Gertrude picked up the knife. Looked at it as at an unknown object.

"Mummy..." Amy tried again, taking a step back from the frame of the door.

No reply. Mother dropped the knife in the sink and staggered to the toilet.

35

Please please please, she begged over and over again as she pressed and pressed and nothing came. Gertrude looked into the cracked empty bowl. Nothing. She pressed again, harder. Nothing. She closed her eyes and sighed. Returned to the classroom with her head; down. Please *please* please... She would do anything. *Anything*... She woke up in the morning; today's the day. She went to bed, quietly. She woke up the following morning; today's the day. She went to bed, disturbed. She woke up the day after; please… She pressed and pressed and nothing came. She went to bed, frightened. Please please please, she begged. Over and over again. She would do anything. *Anything*... She woke up on the tenth day; today would not be the day. Nor tomorrow. Nor the day after. Nor would it be for a long, long time. She went to bed. And cried.

Nobody was allowed to speak to Joy. What did she care. Did she care that Amy didn't speak to her? Who was Amy, anyway? A spoiled little brat. Did she care that Robert didn't speak to her? Who was Robert, anyway? He was practically still a baby. Did she care that *they* didn't speak to her? Who did they think they were, anyway? They were doing her a favour, let the truth be said; she had nothing to say to them, anyway. Nobody was allowed to speak to Joy. What did she care? But she did. She suffocated in the silence and her wounded soul would not heal.

Gertrude's silence was attracting attention. She grew absent-minded in class; less eager. The teachers talked. She alone did not joke, did not laugh, whisper and shriek as the girls sauntered home, talking their girls' talk. She was too busy figuring. She thought about running away from home. Going to another district where she was unknown. But where would she live? What would she do? What about school? She could perhaps work as a maid in someone's house. A maid in someone else's house... being touched up by the man and suspected by the woman. Enslaved by the need for money to keep bodies clothed and bellies full. She, who had a good brain and had wanted to work in a bank or become a nurse. It was unfair. Unfair? Who says it's unfair? Did anybody tell her to drop her drawers and spread her legs so readily? What would her mother say when she ran away from home? Who would be there to help her? How could she run away like that and leave her mother to the gossip and the pointing of fingers? Pointing of fingers? They'll be pointing fingers where she is, too! Never mind her mother! Everybody must look out for number one. But her mother, she could help, and that way Gertrude might still make it to the bank or to the nursing school. If she ran away, she could kiss that goodbye and spend the rest of her life dreaming about what she might have been.

"Gertie, is what di matter wid yu?"
She shook herself back to reality to behold a pack of eyes studying her. "Is wha yu mean what di matter wid me? Notting di matter wid me... me was just thinking."

"Bout wat?"
She felt them watching her critically. "Notting in particula."

"Huh! Notting in particula me back foot! Is lie yu deh lie!"

"Cho man…"

"Is lie yu deh lie, yaa. Want to know wat me tink? Yu deh tink 'bout some seecrit or another."

"Cho man -" Gertrude started.

"Yu see! Yu see! Is true!"

"Shut up yu rubbish!" She protested as she tried to continue on her way.
They cornered her.

"Tell us yu seecrit, nuh?"

"Me no a no seecrit." She felt like one of the frogs the boys so gladly tortured. Pulling at their legs, letting them think they were free, catching them, trying to open their mouths. And then killing them when all the fun had been sucked out of the game so far, death alone opening a new chapter; dropping a rock on them, smashing their brains out. Taking a leg in each hand to tear the frog apart. Dropping them in a tin can with a stone on top and setting it on fire. They nudged in round her for the kill.

"Tell us yu seecrit, nuh? We talk our seecrit let yu hear and yu got yu seecrit don't even share it."

"Is how many time me haffi tell unnu? Me don't have no seecrit!"

"Yu too lie!"

"Me know wat it is!" interjected another from the group. "When is so she deh carry on, is pregnant she pregnant."

Gasps all around.

Gertrude shot her a look, then laughed. "Yu too styupid!"

"Gertie? Pregnant? Yu styupid fi true! No man don't even look at her. See how she eat up we conversation like seh a bread and honey. Is hungry di poor gyal hungry, yaa. Gertie need a man - dat's her problem." She laughed the melodious, condescending laugh of a ring-leader. She had done it first and she knew all about it. She felt sorry for her, in a way. Poor Gertie, black big-batty Gertie, who wasn't getting it and it was making her turn peculiar. Every one a them laugh. "Nevva mind, Gertie. Your time will come. Every hoe got him stick a bush." They laughed as they sauntered on, pulling in belly and swinging hip.

Winston was at his happiest when he could slide into the background like a shadow. Slip away like a silk scarf fallen from a polished wooden chair. He had brought trouble upon himself, he could tell as he folded the letter and returned it to its airmail envelope with the stripes crossed out, with his daughter's name written laboriously across the front. He would show it to Gertrude, maybe she'd speak to her. Yes, that was her duty. She was the mother. Mothers must talk about such things with daughters. Fathers were there to talk to their sons. Yes, he was sure she would. And yet... He was the one who had taken it. She might use it as an excuse to drag him out of his cosy corner into the piercing light of action. She just might. If only... He looked to see if he could reseal it convincingly, but no. If only... He placed it on Gertrude's pillow and went to work.

Ruby checked her from the corner of her eye. Checked her daughter bending over her book, but not seeing a goddamn thing that was marked on the page. Ruby could smell trouble from afar, it having acquainted itself with her so intimately for so long. She looked at her daughter. And knew. Watched her. And waited. She herself would do nothing. Was Gertrude waiting for her to charge in and accuse her? She would not. Gertrude would have to come to her. Her thoughts turned to her eldest son. My son, she thought, I did you wrong. I did you wrong...

A gospel broke from her lips, pushing its way up from the back of her throat. Curling and twirling like smoke around a spotlight. Gertrude turned an ear. And knew. The melody swirled over to her and told her what it knew. Told her of pain and shame. Of faith and broken pride. Told her of visions and promises. Of endurance. Ruby closed her eyes, bulbous tears flowing on the inside to the bitter-sweet tune outside. She hummed the melody which spoke to her daughter as a secret mother tongue. The last time she had sung like that was when her man had taken it into his head that life would be better without them. He went. Ruby had sung the whole evening. She never sang when there were men in the house. She sang now, and Gertrude drank her pain and shame. Stroked her faith. Her broken pride. Saw her visions. Heard the promises. Witnessed the endurance. And she felt dirty. Too dirty to be in the company of this woman with gospel curling from her mouth. Ruby closed her eyes and sang. And when she sang, the music unbuttoned her pain with its gentle fingers and stood aside to watch it chiffon to the floor. And when she stopped, the air was full of her presence, and she knew that she was now sitting there alone.

36

The first thing she saw as she came in was the opened letter on the shelf. She didn't touch it. No. Inching her way over to it, on her guard; yes, it was what she thought it was. But she still couldn't bring herself to touch it. It had been torn open by impatient brute fingers, and she knew at once *he* had taken it. She leaned over the date; must have arrived at least two days ago... Finally, she did pick it up, two-finger fashion, and withdrew with it to her bedroom.

Amy would not look at her, and in a shot she knew that she'd read it. They'd all read it, and her indifference sparked into a hatred that curdled to disgust.

"They wanta ave a word wiv you," said Amy, her eyes fixed elsewhere.

Joy chose to ignore her for a while. Dropped her schoolbag on her bed and kicked off her shoes.

"What about?"

"How should I know?"

How should I know, how should I know, Joy mimicked silently. How should I know to respect a person's privacy. How should I know not to abuse my authority. How should I know to love my children, to help them instead of hindering them, how the fuck should I know... she changed out of her school things. Took her books out of her bag.

"They're waiting for you."

"Well, let them."

She looked at the letter lying on the bed. She was the only one who hadn't read it. And now she didn't want to. She wanted to tear it up and dash the pieces at them, if they only knew how much she loathed them all! The minute she was in a position to leave, she would be off, and they would neither have sight nor sound of her again. But she wanted to come out with the truth, tell all about what went on behind closed doors; about the spite, the hatred they were fed on until it made them spew up, I've got to get out, her angel cried, get out or I'll go mad! But how? Where could a schoolgirl of fourteen go? But if she got pregnant... the thought came sneaking up to her on its belly and hissed at her ankles. That would slap her mother in the face; her and her fake respectability. Joy'd get state support that way, and a flat, and she'd be free. Free. If I have to stay here much longer, I'll end up... what if she told that she was being sexually abused? There was a lot of that going around lately. Yes! If I told, and stuck to my guns, who're they more likely to believe, me, or him? Her, of course, I mean why should she lie, whereas he would have a bloody good reason for lying, so they'd be on her side. Wouldn't they? I could say he forced me to, that's right, then they'd take me away and lock him up into the bargain. And mother darling, she would have to suffer the shame of it being plastered all over the front page of the local daily; the nudging and the whispering which she wouldn't quite hear but would know damn well what the sniggering was all about. The more she thought about it, the more Joy liked the idea. And if she said, I can't talk about it, and maybe if she cried a little, they would understand her trauma, course they would, they'd dole out sympathy and not push me too much, could well be, taking it as even stronger proof that what she said had really happened to her. And nobody could disprove it. So easy, lying. Well, don't they always go on about how I take after my mother? The visitors, in front of whom they had to monkey good behaviour so the guests would sit up and clap, Bravo, mum and dad; would toss a sweet or a penny in the children's direction, and smile as the pickaninnies picked it up shyly, saying three times thank you. Old boiled sweets. Cheap boiled sweets. So old, so cheap, they had stuck to the wrapper so you couldn't really enjoy them anymore with all that plastic on sticking to your gums.

"That's a very serious accusation you're making, young lady. Are you aware of that?" the Superintendant towered above her, speaking solemnly as befitted the occasion.
Joy gave a weak nod of the head.
"Yes. But it's true."

"Well," he said, unconvinced, "wait there. I have to fetch a female colleague before we can take this any further."

Suppose she asks me to go into details, what can I say? Will she be able to tell from my voice that I'm lying? No, course she won't be able to. I'm under stress, she'll see that. She'll be nice to me and take my side, won't she? What if she asks for details? Well, I know what one looks like, so that won't be a problem. But she'll want to know when we last did it, won't she? What shall I say? Yesterday? Last week? A couple of weeks ago? She might ask me why it's taken me so long to report it, I could say I was scared. Didn't want to hurt the family. I'll say yesterday. Yesterday. Wait a minute! Will they want to examine me? Stick something in me to test if I've really done it? Will they go scraping for sperm, or something? What'll I do?

What if *she* were the one who ended up in jail? In a borstal, with delinquents, the sort she moved out of the way of, or crossed the street to avoid if she saw them heading her way? And what if none of this happened, and she just had to go home in disgrace and continue to live in that house with them? What would they do to her? She knew what she would do to herself…

"I'd go down if I were you."

"Well you're not me, are you?"

"Thank goodness."

Right then, thought Joy. Let's see what they've got to say. Time to face the music.

Gertrude was putting on weight. At times she felt so sleepy she would curl up in a corner to doze like a puppy. She wouldn't swear on it, but she thought her skin was changing. The colour ripened, the texture, well, and her boobs, they seemed to sprout up overnight like mushrooms so that her two bras were suddenly too small for her and her flesh jostled querulously in the middle. Her breasts were sore at times, and she would have to thumb them quiet. The whispers grew louder.

She lifted the latch to the back door and stepped into the kitchen.

"Good aftanoon," she said to her mother.

Ruby looked up from her sewing, "Good aftanoon." Her foot-operated sewing machine stood in a corner, but whenever it came to stitching up hems or sewing on buttons, she would sit in the kitchen and listen to the garden noises. Taking the thread between her teeth, she would snap it in two, and think; thank God she learn a bit of sewing before him come along... She had no time for those women in the village who thought they should stay at home with the children and the man should bring in the money, is who dem tink dem is, white? A woman must have a trade and can earn her own money so when him bugger off she don't stand there stupid. And she would think what might have happened if she hadn't had hers. She heard Gertrude moving around the kitchen. What can she do, Ruby thought, what is she good for now? She got her brain but it no good for nothing if she no finish school. Ruby became impatient, angry. The one girl she got and she turn out worthless. She knew, alright, and she had been waiting over two months and Gertrude had not said a word. She watched her move around the kitchen and was furious.

  She had been planning it, planning it all the way home from school; what she would say to her mother. How. She knew she knew, and couldn't understand why her mother didn't come right out and accuse her. This made her afraid. Fear smothered her resolve. How would mother take it, the news? Would she beat her? Would she throw her out? At the back of her mind she hoped her mother wouldn't be hard on her because she herself had fallen into the same trap. Gertrude didn't know how to start. She came in and could only say, Good afternoon. She helped herself to a mango, bit off its beak, eyed her mother then,

  "Mummy - "

  "Wat yu want," her mother snapped back.

  "Me... me need some new bra."

Ruby knew the time had come. And she was angry.

  "New bra? Is how come yu need some new bra all of a sudden'?"

Gertrude looked at her mango. Just say it. Just say it!

  "Me is pregnant."

Ruby's hands fell still. She didn't want to shout, to slap, the way she had been. No. Just stay calm. Do the right thing. She put her sewing aside.

"Oh yes? Is how long yu know?"

Gertrude was silent.

"Well, me arsk yu a question!"

"Dis likkle while now."

"An?"

"An wat?"

" '*An wat?*' she arsk me, like seh she no know is wat me deh talk 'bout. An who di farda?"

"Dat's nat important," she said quietly.

Ruby's head jolted up. "Nat important? Nat important? How yu mean seh is nat important?"

"Is nat important," is all she could repeat, foolishly.

"Yu mean seh yu no know?"

"Me mean seh is nat important."

Gertrude waited. And waited.

"Tell me someting. Is where One-son deh get all dis monni?" She studied her daughter's face for changes. And found them.

"How me spose fi know weh him deh get him monni? Tink him tark to me 'bout wat him deh do? Me no know." She looked at her feet, and waited.

"Yu wortless piece a trash," her mother said quietly to herself as she resumed her sewing.

Gertrude didn't know what to do. She hadn't been slapped. She hadn't been thrown out. Not yet, in any case. She hadn't even been shouted at, yet she stood nailed to the spot as the tears gushed down her face.

Mother sewed.

Daughter cried.

Mother started to turn a tune around in the back of her throat, then broke it off, as if Gertrude wasn't worth it, muttering to herself, "Wortless. Wortless."

And when she heard the tune broken off, Gertrude felt her worthlessness fill the room and her tears would not stop.

You worthless piece of trash, her mother had called her. And for the rest of that day neither spoke another word.

37

As Joy returned to the bedroom, Amy tactfully made herself scarce. One slipped in and the other slipped out and neither said a word. Joy, strangely enough, was not angry. She was weary. Fed up. Why not: give in and be their goody two shoes? But even as she rolled the thought listlessly around in her mind, she knew it would come to nothing. She knew she would not give in, and certainly not to them, who were not worth her little finger. Look at how they had spoken to her! They were afraid of her. Of her growing up. And her mother, she had talked about Cut you down to size, Knock you off yu high horse, showing her Is only one woman in dis house, and all that rubbish a sensible woman would never let past her lips. Spoken with such venom... And then she had begun to say when she was young - then broke it off.

If she thought she was such a woman, then she'd better look after herself. Her mother refused to do anything more for her. Here were five pounds, her weekly allowance to do her own shopping. Mother would neither cook nor wash for her. If she thought she was a woman, she would have to look after herself. Father just sat there; a stupid donkey, his yellowy eyes on his fat, black carrot fingers. They were giving her five pounds a week? Joy had looked from one to the other, and smiled; she needed at least one pound a day, what were they trying to prove? She tossed the money on the bed and it landed near the letter. The letter; she still hadn't read it yet. It lay near the edge of the bed. But hadn't she left it in the middle? Ha! Amy had read it a second time. She laughed bitterly. So, she's started growing up too, ha! Then she tried to think how the whole hostility had all begun, from which point her mother had stopped liking her, had started hating her; tried to remember the incident which had sparked the whole thing off, and could not find it. There was this letter, of course, but before that there had been nothing concrete for her mother to throw back in her face and accuse her with. So where did it all begin? How was it she simply woke up one day to find herself in a raging war? This, she really could not answer, nor the thought hot at its heels; when, where, would it all end.

Five pounds a week. Independence at last! Only, the money wouldn't stretch for three meals a day. She decided in favour of lunch. In the meantime, Joy had become a stranger in her own house. When hungry, she would sneak down to the kitchen like a criminal, make something quick and drastic, wolf it down and slink off back to her room, her sole concern being that she bumped into no-one. Someone in the kitchen? Then she would wait. Listen. Smell. Hunt the opportunity. Slink in, gobble down, slink out. She wanted to see none of them, who were still under orders to have nothing to do with her, and would look the other way when she entered a room, or else get up and leave. She squatted in the den of her portion of the room. Went down as little as possible. If there must be silence, then let it be her own. A big lunch, she decided, would keep her through the evening and spare her the painful confrontations. But she could not afford a lunch as big as it would have needed to be. She trained herself stubbornly. Did without and called up her pride when hunger sank its teeth into her side. She would show them. She would not let them break her, give them the pleasure to see her crawl back and beg for forgiveness. She would not. Only, the weekends, they became the longest in her life... And there would come more, for the holidays were around the corner.

38

  Ruby studied the child but could find no resemblance to anyone she knew. Looked it over. Its feet. Its frail fists. Its scrunched up face. The lungs pumped and pumped, rocking the entire vulnerable frame. Ruby looked over at her daughter lying, exhausted, in a moist pool on the bed, almost asleep, the deep scent of her screaming perforating the thick air. It had lasted for hours, for hours Gertrude had screamed and screamed, her eyes exploding with fear and surprise. She hadn't given it much thought, what it would be like, having a baby. She knew about the pain, but no-one had told her about the *pain*; betrayed, her eyes sprang out of their sockets as she screamed, as her hands seemed to want to push her away from that bloated belly grinning up at her as she thrashed around on the hard bed. Ruby had tried to be of assistance to the midwife. It wasn't in her to hold her daughter's hand or mop her brow; she had never done it before and failed to see why she should be doing it now, so she said, "Come, now... come, now," and when Gertrude's screams ripped into the air, she shouted irritably, "Cho man, yu nat di only person ever give birth, calm yuself down!" and she thought; you want be a woman? Well, now yu know. Yu damn well learn to live wid pain if yu want be a woman, yu hear wat me saying to yu? She wrapped up the child and left the house.

  Gertrude saw her mother leave. Watched her through the corner of her eye. Started crying softly; my baby... my baby... The midwife looked over, said, "Hush now. Yu done good. Hush," as she sat in her chair near the window, looking out into the yard. She only wished the mother would do her business soon and get back home so that she could be on her way. She did not want to get involved. Listened and nodded as Ruby told her the story she was all too familiar with, as Ruby explained how she had had to beat her daughter into seeing reason, that the last thing

an intelligent young girl needed was a baby. A baby. No money. No man. Just the baby. Complained how the young people had no self-respect and that when she was young -
then she broke it off.

My baby... my baby... The midwife sat in her chair, looked out of the window and tried to close her ears to the girl's plea. This child was sensitive; it is not every mother you can take a child away from. Some of them turn, and this child, she could feel Gertrude in the room and her nose was full of the young girl's motherhood, she had them easy-hurting eyes. Gertrude's voice rose, expanded, taking on the features of a song. She toned it, nursed it, and at some point beyond naming, where pain takes on some amorous quality that breathes a mysterious beauty, Gertrude, for the first time in her life, found that she was singing. No words, not even really a song, but beyond her control; the secret language, and it wafted over to the midwife in dolorous clouds to smoke a dance before her eyes. It danced of pain. Of shame. Of broken pride. It circled the room in search of promises. Stroked the panes in need of visions. Rose from the girl on the bed who could not have her baby. The girl, taken over by a voice so new it was almost not her own. The midwife was lifted to her feet and carried over to the bed. She looked in Gertrude's eyes, and knew. Not from this one, oh Lord. Lowered her hand to Gertude's hot brow.

Hush now. Hush now.
And at her touch Gertrude fell asleep.

Ruby hugged the child to her chest and ran and ran. Ran into the bush. Clung to the child and weaved her way deeper into the bush, closing her eyes as the leaves slapped into her. Springing. Ducking. Darting. She stopped, panting wildly. Dashed her head to the left. To the right. Listened. She heard nothing but the birds and the music of the wind and trees. Rested likkle bit, her heartbeat stepping down the stairs, carefully, to the landing at the bottom we call normality, only then did Ruby seem to remember the baby. Gently, she peeled back the cloths and gave it light. It was asleep. She studied the child. Ran a finger across its brow.

My baby... She sank to the ground with the child in her arms. Her baby must have looked like this. She placed the child's head against her breast to soothe it with her heartbeat.

Her baby... Gertrude hadn't been beaten the way she had. Hadn't been knocked to the ground, been kicked in the back the way she had. A worthless piece of trash, her mother had called her and went to the chickens outside as her father rushed in, knocked his 12-year-old daughter to the floor and kicked her in the back till his Sunday shoes lost their shine. Kicked her, and with each new blow hoped to kick out the child he had no right to put in her. Where was her baby? Her very first baby, where had they taken it to? At fifteen Ruby fell pregnant again and ran away from home. Nobody, *no-bo-dy* was going to take another child away from her. But her very first child...What had they done with her baby? She hadn't even been allowed to take it in her arms. She looked down at the little bit of warm living, touched its soft arms, pink soles, peanut nose. Took out a breast and gave it. Leant against the tree and closed her eyes.

"My baby," she said as the child, after pulling two or three times on her nipple and realising that it had been deceived, threw its head back and wailed bitterly, its arms and legs stiffening. Ruby took a nipple between two fingers and guided the child's head to it.

"*My* baby."

39

She heard the flap of the letterbox and darted from the bed. Too late. Her mother had dashed from the kitchen and snatched up the two letters which had arrived. They were both for *him*. She placed them on the shelf, throwing a glance and a twisted smile at her daughter as she returned to the kitchen.

Thanks to the school holidays, she could catch the post every day. She had written to let him know. To let him know she needed him now more than ever. If she could come and live with him, if he could help her in any way. Anything! He had to let her know! Please, she prayed, please. The morning came. She hoped today would be the day. The letterbox flapped, but there was nothing. She left for the library, clothed in her indifference. The following day came. She hoped today would be the day. She took the stairs two at a time. Mother had been sitting in the living room on the lookout. Nothing. She slung her bag over her shoulder and strutted out the house. Then came the day after. The letterbox flapped. She was sitting on the bottom step waiting. Gertrude almost fell over her feet trying to get there first, then saw her daughter sitting on the step and knew she had made a fool of herself. Joy laughed out loud as she left the house, stepping past her mother who had had to get down before her daughter's derisive eyes and pick up the flimsy brown windowed envelope which she still held in her hand as the front door went, Bang. Alone in her room, Joy prayed. Please please please. Please *please* please. In a way she had hated them, but if only, if *only* she would receive one of those blue airmail envelopes with the stripes crossed out and her name written laboriously in the middle. Please please please, she prayed over and over again. Please please please. If only. If *only*... The fourteenth day came. He normally wrote within five. The letterbox flapped and she heard it from where she was. On her bed. Undressed. Why the hurry? Today would not be the day. Nor tomorrow. Nor the day after. Nor would it be again. Ever. She rolled over. Closed her eyes. Tried. It was no good. Even sleep had turned its back on her.

    Ruby could see her house from the dusty road and knew that something was wrong. She quickened her pace. Pushed the back door open, breathlessly, called, "Gertie?" to be greeted by an almost expected silence. She hurried to her daughter's room. The bed had been neatly made. The cupboard was bare. Ruby lowered herself carefully to the bed. Gertie was gone. She looked out of the window, seeing nothing. Where had she gone? In search of the child? The thing was now eight weeks old. She had thought it best to make a break right from the beginning. Less painful that way. Was she looking for the child? Ruby had got home that day, looked into her daughter's eyes, and knew she had done wrong. But what future would her daughter have? Tell me! Tell me! A young gyal wid a pitni and no man and no monni - is wa dat s'pose fi be? Is yu best interest me have at heart, yu hear wat me telling yu? Yu best interest! Finish up school and go look a job. Dem is di tings dat count, yu hear me? Wat a young gyal like yu want do wid a pitni spoil up yu life? But that look in Gertrude's eye; so far-away, wounded, impervious to reason... Eight weeks now since the child had been born and Gertrude hadn't spoken a word. One-son had wanted to beat her to her senses but his mother had snapped, "Don't you lay one finga pan her, yu hear me! Nat yu!" and she had daggered her forefinger through the air at him. What did she mean by her "Nat yu!"? Ruby had pulled her headscarf tight and turned her back on them both, leaving One-son looking at his sister. At a blank defencelessness where fear would normally be warbling at his threat. He had snorted at the two women. Yes, even he could see; his sister was a woman now. Even if a mad one. He had sucked his teeth. Strutted out for a beer. Ruby sat still on the neatly-made bed and all around her was out of focus. She thought and thought. Remembered. Asked. Thought some more. Until she grew angry, All di while me did tink di gyal have a brain an she styupid, to raated. Well, she on her own now. She is woman inuff? She on her own. Ruby went to the garden and murdered a chicken.

    Gertrude had thirty-five dollars left from the money she had stolen from One-son. He would be furious when he found out. Let him. She needed it more than he did. They all bumped along together in the bashed-up bus, calypso music blaring from the radio, the passenger them just deh chat. Gertude's first real bus ride. She sat up straight, taking in everything going on outside the windows. She had a hell of a lot of money in her bag and it made her feel uncomfortable. Strange, people think they know all about other people, and they don't know a thing. Who would guess that she had so much money in her bag? She lodged the bag under her breasts. Looked out the window. Little boys ran up to the bus offering their wares whenever the bus appeared to slow down, as it did every time it came to a cluttering of houses where somebody might like to get on. Sharp ears they had, those little boys, who heard the bus coming long before it came into view. They snatched their makeshift trays and sped for the main road, more often than not the only road, if one can call a hill-an-gully dirt track a road.
    "Cool jrink! Cool jrink! Cool jrink!"
One jumped up so the dirty bottles bobbed up and down in the window-frame, trying to pass themselves off as palatable.
    "Ice lally! Ice lally!"
    "Roas' chicken, home style! Roas' chicken home style!"
They stopped to tank. A swarm of boys fell upon the bus, bothering the passengers, some of whom got out to stretch their legs. See what was going on. Pee up a tree. Women let their children out to run around likkle bit, stay where me kyan see yu. Some littl'uns hung back by the entrance to the bus, unsure, eyed belligerently by the local kids intent upon stating their claim to the territory. A young man stepped from the bus, full of himself in his new clothes and his fake gold chain. Strode over to the café-shack and let himself be seen. For Gertrude it was enough to observe it all through the window. She sat near the back of the bus, fanning herself with a piece of broken-off cardboard.

An old stringy, dignified woman groaned up the stairs into the bus.

"Roas' carn... roas' carn home style... roas' carn..." she moved down the aisle, stepping over the boxes, over the bags that no-one seemed to want to leave in the boot and out of eyesight.

"Is how much yu want fi di carn?" a man in a window seat asked, sweat dripping from his brow, his shirt grimy and tight.

"Twenty-five cent. Roas' carn home style... roas' carn..." her eyes roamed, indifferently.

"Twenty-five cent! An di bwoy dem deh offer it fi fifteen?"

"Roas' carn... roas' carn home style... roas' carn..." the woman continued. Her eyes flitted about like befriended butterflies, finding nothing interesting enough to arrest them.

"Twenty-five cent too much, man."

He slapped at the little brown hands jumping up at his window trying to attract his attention.

"Roas' carn... roas' carn home style..." she persisted. "Tell me so'um, yu got a ol' granny a doors? Roas' carn..." and her look wafted through the bus in a never-ending tiredness.

"Gimme one a di carn," he muttered, ashamed. "Big one."

"Tirty-five cent. Roas' carn..." she continued almost asleep.

"Tirty-five cent! Ol' woman try fi cheat mi, yaa. Twenty-five cent!"

"Big one tirty-five cent... home style... roas' carn..."

"Tek it, me no want it!" He shoved the corn back at her.

"Yu tink anyone else want buy dis deh carn after yu feel it up feel it up? Look pan yu finger dem how dem dutty! Look like yu deh dig inna yu nosehole and deh scrape inna yu batti di whole time! Just give me me monni!"

He threw the money into her basket, cussing.

She stirred the coins like tea-leaves, deftly. "Me say *tirty-five* cent, nat twenty-five! Home style... Nice roas' carn home style?" she addressed a woman, who looked into her basket then turned back to the woman sitting in the seat next to her.

He chucked another ten cents.

"Mean likkle *bar*stad! Me know your granny gwine haffi *beg* fore she get a cent outta you!" She worked her way to the back of the bus. "Roas' carn... roas' carn home style... roas' carn…"

"Gimme one a di big carn an one a di likkle, please," Gertrude asked.

"Two carn, darta?" she wrapped them in paper and reached them over. Her thumbnails were long and filled with gunge. Her cardigan had long lost its buttons. A baby security pin with the colour worn off kept her breasts covered and her mouth was forever pushing itself up as if she were sucking on a sweet or something.

"One dalla."

"One dalla?"

"One dalla," replied the old woman, pushing her lips up resolutely.

"How much di small carn?" Gertrude interrogated.

"Twenty-five cent, darta."

"An di big carn?"

"Tirty-five cent."

"An yu mean seh twenty-five and tirty-five mek one dalla?"

"One dalla. Roas' carn... roas' carn home style..." her head drifted from side to side.

"Ol' witch!" said the man at the window seat, biting into his corn but not able to enjoy it anymore.

Gertrude gave her one dollar.

"Bless yu, child. Me can see yu is a good child. Child fi mek one proud. Bring up right and mannarsable. Child like a you look after her ol' madda in her old age, mek she grow ol' wid a likkle res*pect!*" and she pulled herself up to her full height and tugged at her cardigan.

Gertrude, choosing to ignore the cold spit which had caught her in the face, lowered her eyes.

The old lady turned, headed for the front of the bus once more. "Roas' carn... roas' carn home style... roas' carn..." and when she got to the man at the window, she clapped him on the head.

"Me is a witch?"

She showed him the hair she had got from him.

"Wat di *raated* - "

"Mek me tek dis deh dutty head, stink like I don' know wat and tek it bring one hobia man[40] me know."

"Wuuuiii! Wuii! Yes, man!" The people in the bus them liven up.

"Tek it give one hobia man me know *real* good..."

"Cho man!" he slung the corn out of the window and cussed a long round of "*bamba claats*" and "*t'raatids*" as the passengers turned in their seats to gobble up the free entertainment whilst the little boys outside fought over who would get the discarded corn.

The driver, returned to the bus, skillfully manoeuvred his stomach until it fitted snugly around the steering wheel. He honked twice. The children came back. The young man came back. Men who had done their business in the open wiped their hands on their trousers as they climed up the steps. The bus spluttered on, leaving the settlement to the things that settlements do when the hustle and bustle of the bus had hustled on.

Gertude got off the bus in the big city. It didn't take her long to find out where the well-off lived, and she headed immediately for that part of town. The big city. There were more shops here than she had ever seen in her lifetime. And people! Black people dressed like she never knew they could. And women in high heels and make-up. It made her feel unattractive and primitive. She'd never look like these women who swung their hips and pouted, touching their styled hair and talking back to the men who stopped to enjoy the sight of them and whistle nastiness. Look! There was a black lady with a little bitty dog on a lead. A dog. On a lead. She wore a long blonde wig, tottered along in her gold high-heel shoes and the men were just about going crazy over that blonde hair and them high heels. One stopped his car in the middle of the road, hung his head out the window, Hello lovely, wha mek yu no get in it, lek me give yu a ride. She said No, she didn't want a ride, she knew *he* did, she

---

[40] *hobia man* = witch doctor

chose to wiggle on her way, sweet-smiling to a chorus of tooting, of whistling and "pussy sweet!" Gertrude stood there in her country frock and chunky plaits. Me is a quashie; a real country bumpkin. Closed her eyes and sighed. Never. If she had finished school and got into nursing college... but she pushed the thought back to where it belonged, out of her mind.

Two parts of town Gertrude had to go to. The well-off black district and the well-off white district. She could have taken a bus but she had time. Besides, the one case she had wasn't even heavy. A bashed-up, scratched-up, thrown-out-by-some-indulgent-white-man-seemed-like-centuries-ago old brown suitcase that had been in Gertrude's family longer than she herself had. Some grandparent or great-grandparent had brushed it off and taken it home. A woman, no doubt; the men too proud to sully their fingers with a handout however badly they might need it, nevertheless making full use of it and only too quick with the word *my* when it went missing and they went crazy, threatening to bust up the cabin and bust in heads if it didn't turn up that minute. Ruby had taken it with her when she had left. Weren't nobody in that house going nowhere apart from her. Apart from downhill. She had given it to Gertrude when the latter had brought home the best grades in the whole school together with a letter of congratulation from the headmaster. One-son wouldn't be needing the case, the way things were going, Ruby figured. Ricky, neither, so she had given it to Gertrude, unceremoniously, telling her; wen is time fi yu go away an learn some more, yu gwine need a case put yu tings inna. One of the hinges was loose and the handle was fraying, so you couldn't load it too much. As Gertrude walked down the street, the suitcase tap tapped reassuringly against her leg with every other step.

First she enquired in the black district, but no-one was looking for a maid. Not at the moment, so she said thank you and continued on her way, past the white-washed houses of the black people well enough off to have someone wash their clothes and cook their food. Houses lived in by women who looked like they came from the movies and went to the hairdresser's every other day. If she had finished school and got into nursing college... She passed a freshly-painted white fence with a car in the drive and a big sign saying Dr C.G.R. Riley. A black man doctor! A real black man doctor with a car and a sign. And a black man wife... Brown, more than likely. High brown. At the very least. Unless she were the one with the money. And all the maids would be dark girls like her, Gertrude. The uglier, the better. She hurried on to the white district. It was all a little bit bigger and a little bit better, with some houses even having two cars in the drive. Walking along a meticulously tended road, Gertrude heard a child command impudently, "Sally, bring me a lemonade!" then a mellow voice answer, "Yes, Maas Arnol. Right away. You too, Miss Louise?" and the children played further, ignoring her.

The occasional black face passed her, looked into her eyes, saw she was from out of town, said, Marning.

"Marning," she replied, nodding a greeting.

"Yu deh look a job?" Stated more than asked. A thick-set black woman, hauling two bags of shopping to a house where there was certainly a car idling in the drive. She eyed Gertrude's frock. Fabric like dat don't sell in these parts.

Gertrude said she was looking a job. Fi true.

"Yu can sew?"

She couldn't.

"Yu can cook at least?"

Yes, she could do that, but nothing fancy.

"Well, yu can always wash. Anybaddy can wash. Fren a mine did leave by Judge Parker yestideh. Im did seem to think wat she got inna her drawers b'lang to him, yaa. Narsty ole man. Im live up deh, round di corner. Big white house look like a wedding cake. Ask if yu interest."

Gertrude thanked her.

As she arrived, a young black man was polishing the impressive car in the drive. He rubbed it with love, talking to himself.

"Marnin!" Gertrude intruded into his world.

He looked up from his work. He was dark and slim with little weasly eyes squatting atop a broad flat nose. When he stood up straight, Gertrude saw that he was not as tall as he should have been.

"Marning," he replied, resting his hand on the bonnet. "Come in, nuh?"
Gertrude opened the gate and walked across the drive. The garden was immense, well-kept, the flowers and trees as perfect as you could imagine them. The house didn't look like a wedding cake to her at all at all at all. It looked like a palace. Would she be allowed to work in this beautiful house? She stood in front of the car.
"Me looking a job."
"Oh yes? Me looking a wife. Yu interest?"
She didn't know what to say.
He laughed, "Is joke me deh joke. Don't tek it serious."
She smiled. "Yu know 'bout any job?"
"Yu want work fi me?" he grinned.
She didn't find it funny. He was cocky. And ugly. In a way he reminded her of One-son. She walked past him in the direction of the back entrance.

She was to be paid two dollars a week. She wondered how much her mother earned. How much Judge Parker earned to be able to pay all his hands two dollars a week. She resolved on the spot to save as much of it as possible. Maybe she could still make it to nursing school. The chief housemaid had brought her to the old Mrs Parker, who had only glanced at her out of the corner of her eye to satisfy herself she that was ugly enough.
"She'll do."
And the chief housemaid shooed her out of the great room as Mrs Parker made herself more comfortable in her chair, fanning herself through hours of stifling boredom. Gertrude was given a tour of the premises. Allocated duties. Introduced to the other workers. The chief housemaid seemed to think she was a black Mrs Parker, talking down to the others who called her Mrs Burke although she took the liberty of being on first name terms with all of them. They stood near the drive.
"Dis is Winstan. Winstan respansible fi heavy jabs an gardening."
Winston smiled, "So, yu get it?"
Gertrude nodded.

"Nice... nice," he said softly.

Mrs Burke looked from the one to the other. "Winstan, dis is Gertrude, but seem to me you two well enough acquainted arlreddy!" She pushed Gertrude on. "Don't tek up wid dat one, yu hear wat me telling yu?"

"Tek up wid him? Me no even know him."

"Two dollar a week is a lat a money fi a young gyal like a yu. How old yu is?"

"Fifteen."

"Got any chilren?"

Gertrude hesitated. Said, "No."

"Good. Me won't ask yu why it tek yu so long fi answer. Dat is none a my business, but yu listen to me, you mek sure yu don't get any, yu hear? Young gyal an two dalla a week? Yu can save it up an mek so'um out a yusself. Build yusself up to a nice nice s'mady. Me? Me too ol' now, an me got more dan dis one mouth fi feed, but you, yu watch yu step and no slip up. Use yu brain and mek someting out a yusself. Tek it as a piece a madda's advice. Me know wat me deh talk bout, yaa. Right," she pushed Gertrude in the direction of the kitchen. "Less a di labrish."

She had been saving her money and living on chips the whole week so that she would be able to have something nicer for the weekend. All things considered, Joy was pleased with herself. As pleased as a person half starving for two months could possibly be. Convinced as she was that she was managing, she failed to see how her flesh had fallen from her like a discarded garment or how her eyes had lost their shine.

Amy had charged into the room once, had caught Joy lying on her bed in her underwear. Had let out a shriek of horror at the skeleton that used to be her sister. Joy shot up, ready to shout, saw the look on Amy's face.

"Don't you know to knock before you barge into someone's room?" she got up. Got some clothes.

"It's my room as well," Amy countered instinctively, born as she was into an undefined confrontation with her sister. She stared with disbelief and growing queasiness. At the chopstick collar-bones jutting out. At the ribs. The bony hips. The fleshless arms. Witnessed the effort it took her sister to cross the room to the wardrobe. She still wasn't allowed to speak to Joy, wished she was, started to, then realised she didn't know what to say. So she went.

      Joy came in once to find a piece of paper on her bed. At first she thought it was a letter and pounced on it. Fool. She should have known better. That was the last letter she would receive from him, the one *he* had intercepted and opened. She didn't know what they'd done or said, she only knew they'd managed it. S*he*'d managed it, Joy knew from the self-satisfied smirks she let off, fat smug bitch; thought she had the upper hand? Thought she was winning? Well, just for her information, Joy hadn't cried once. Not one single time, so she could wipe that stupid smirk off her face. It wasn't a letter and she should have known better. It had an arrow on it. 'Under the bed'. That was Amy's writing. What did she think she was playing at? Was this some sort of stupid joke? She snatched the paper and scrunched it up. Chucked it out the window into the garden. Lay on her back on her bed. For a while. Thinking. Emptying. In the end, she couldn't stand it. Rolled over onto her stomach and worked her way over to the edge of the bed. Hesitated. Listened for the stairs. All was quiet. Inched over until she hung from the waist down. Lifted the sheets, curiously. So... There was a bar of chocolate under the bed. And an apple. Were they from Amy or were they from *her*? She'd noticed how her mother's barely suppressed grin was gradually paling to become a line of worry; did she want to back down and use Amy to do her dirty work? No, Joy couldn't believe it. Then they really were from Amy... Where did she get the money from to buy that big bar of chocolate? Joy knew how much it cost. Knew how much everything cost these days, especially the things she would most like to have, where on earth did she get the money from? And the apple, since when did Amy buy apples? Joy knew perfectly well that she did not, so she must have taken it from downstairs. She looked at the apple, at the chocolate under the bed, could smell the apple even, knew how the chocolate would taste, and almost, almost wanted to cry. But she would take nothing from Amy. Not from her, not from any of them! She pulled the articles out and tossed them under Amy's bed, who did Amy think she was, anyway, dishing out charity? She would have none of it. When Amy had turned up later with her tentative friendship smile on, Joy had taken no notice of her.

The following day, there was a piece of paper on her bed. 'Under the bed' above the arrow. Joy lifted the sheets. There she found a family-sized packet of crisps, which she tossed under her sister's bed and forced her growling insides to forget about.

On the third day, she entered the room. It smelled of cooking. A glance at the bed: no note on it. Her nose was not playing tricks on her. Yes, she knew what it was. She got on her knees, threw the sheets back, snatched the two objects hiding in tin foil. Stripped them: a breast of kentucky fried chicken and a triangle of pizza. Cheese and tomato. Onions. Mushrooms. Pepperoni. She slung them under Amy's bed, scrunched up the foil and slammed it onto Amy's pillow, there, in the hole where Amy's head had been, the hole into which she had most certainly been dribbling all night. As Joy had nowhere to go that day - she normally spent all day in the library or at the park, anywhere, as long as it was away from here, but it was way past closing-time now - there was only one option open to her; to stay in her room and try to cheat her nose. Then came a tomp tomp tomp tomp. Quickly, Joy gathered herself together before the door would fly open. In strode Amy, saw the tin foil on her bed, scrunched her face into the first signs of protest, decided to say nothing, picked the foil up and left. And yet, the following day the smell of food was constantly in Amy's nose whenever she entered the bedroom. She thought it strange. But then, many things were strange; this house was strange, the air here was strange, her whole family was bloody strange, so, so what? She thought nothing more of it until a few days later when she realised the room didn't simply smell, it stank. Joy wasn't giving anything away. She lay on her bed, disconnected. Cautiously, Amy had opened a few drawers, sniffed significantly at the air. Joy licked her finger and turned the page. Amy sat on her bed and wondered. Got up and opened the window.

"Stinks in here," she said, perplexed, but getting no response from her sister. She made to leave.

"When's the last time you cleared out under your bed?" Joy asked without bothering herself to look up.

The answer was, of course, that she didn't. Whatever ended up under that bed stayed there until the rats dragged it away or it got up and left out of sheer boredom. Amy got to her knees to lift the bedspread. In the thick mould of a dust which aimed to keep the colour of the carpet for itself like a secret, there, with the odd socks, the bangles she had long forgotten about, with the scraps of thread, her lost school book, a rubber and the pen she had had to buy back for a friend because she thought she had lost it, there, under her bed together with the bar of chocolate and the packet of crisps, was a softing furry apple, a dried-to-a-curl triangle of pizza and a leprous breast of chicken.

"I'm telling on you! I'm telling on you, I am!" is all Amy could bluster.

"Why don't you do just that. I don't know who the hell tell you I need any goddamn charity!"

"You swore! I'm telling on you that you swore too! I'm telling!"

"Amy, do me a favour will you?" Joy said sweetly.

Amy waited suspiciously, her hand on the knob.

"Piss off."

She knew exactly how much money she had but she opened her purse and had a look anyway. You never know, she might just have miscalculated somewhere along the line. Might have an extra few pennies, with luck a 50p. She hadn't.

The purse was a gift from her grandmother that weekend she had had to stay because she'd refused to go to the funeral. That weekend... Her grandma somehow seemed to feel that Joy deserved a present and had dug around in her many plastic bags until she had come up with the purse, an ugly brick of a thing with two change compartments and a side slot for notes. Not that Joy'd ever had any notes.

"Big gyal like a yu growin up nice as a shame. Time fi yu have yu own purse an put up yu own monni, yaa. Here, tek it."

Joy took the purse and said thank you, it was a nice purse, but she didn't have any money.

"Wat yu saying yu no have no monni? Yu no get no pakit monni?"

Joy said she did not.

"Dem don't give yu no monni? Why not?"

"Well, he used to give me pocket money. Not a lot. But he was always threatening to take it away if we didn't do what he told us to do. So one day I told him to stuff it, he's not blackmailing me with his money."

"Yu tell him fi stuff it?" Grandma's eyes twinkled.

"Well, not in so many words," Joy smirked.

"Amy an Rabert still deh get pakit monni?"

"Course they do, the dirty little crawlers. I'm not crawling for his money. I'd rather do without."

"Wuuiii!!" Grandma laughed. Sat on the bed, lifted her legs into the air. "Wuuiii!! Kuya! Did anybaddy see me trial!"
They amused themselves for a little while. Yes, Joy liked her grandma. She liked to have a good laugh, her grandma did, and even though they saw so little of each other, they got on well. Why was her mother so rotten when her own mum was so nice? She couldn't figure it out. She could only hope she wouldn't be the same. She thought about the young man she had met the night before who had stuck his tongue in her ear and let her know what he was after. What would her grandmother think if she ever found out? She wouldn't be laughing so much, that was for sure, and the secret made Joy feel somehow above her grandmother, whose little world was regular and dull.

"Wat a way di likkle pitni sparky!"

"Pitni? Just a minute ago you were just saying how grown up I was."
Grandma's face grew serious. "Yu deh grow up, but yu his still a pitni, yaa. Don't bother tink seh yu is a woman. Yu is still a pitni!" she sat pensively, looking at no-one, then back to reality and cheering up, "You wait there one minute."
Joy saw her disappear into her bedroom. She was overweight. You could hear her walking all over the house. Just like Amy. Tomp tomp tomp. Then she came back.

"Yu right not fi let him blackmail yu, but just you watch yu step, yu hear me? Don't get renk[41], or dem will knock yu off yu high horse, cut yu down to size, yu hear me?" she looked sternly at Joy.

"Yes, mama," Joy said quietly.

"Right, me gwine give you a likkle so'um put inna yu purse," she tossed the money on the bed and watched Joy's face light up at the four fifty-pence coins. "Put it away fore im come!" she ordered, smiling once again only when the money was out of sight. "Imagine, we married dis long long time an him still deh put up monni inna pan deh hide from me. Me deh wash him clothes and cook him food dis lang lang time an him deh put up monni deh hide fram me? Well, me done find out long time is where it deh, yaa, and when me feel like it, me tek some and gone!"

The way her grandmother slapped her hands together and wrenched her face made a little laugh bubble its way out of Joy, who thought precisely at this moment; she makes me laugh. I don't laugh so much...

"When him find out seh it gone, him si' down deh quiet an don' look at me. Him can't ask me if me tek him monni bicars him not s'pose fi have monni deh hide fram me, innit?"

Joy shook her head.

"Yes," grandma said thoughtfully, "Me old, but me not styupid, yaa. That day me mek any man mek a fool a me - huh! Den me know is time fi give up di ghost, amen. You si' down deh deh laugh," she eyed her grandchild critically, "If yu no listen to notting else, you listen to dis. Don't you tek no man who want to mek a fool a you, you hear? Never mind how him say him love you. And when yu grow up, don't you do none a dis rubbish joint account foolishniss. You have yu own account an keep yu monni seprit, yu hear me?" she was working herself up. "An don' let no man burden yu down wid no pack a children. Two or tree is more dan enough. Mek him burden yu down wid no pack a chilren mek yu can't work - is then him think him is master a di house and gwine start fi play up. Yu listening to me?" She snarled.

---

[41] *renk* = cheeky

"Calm down! I heard what you said."

"Don' just hear it, yu learn it, yu hear wat me saying to yu?" grandma ranted.

What the hell is she getting all worked up about? Joy wondered why her grandmother had turned so nasty all of a sudden. Like her mother, then, after all, and Joy wished she hadn't set eyes on the ugly old purse or the money she had been given to put in it.

"Me have to hurry up, yaa, or me gwine late fi church," she pulled the stocking off her head and plucked the curlers out on her way to the bathroom, dropping them into her nylon cap. A quarter of an hour later, grandma re-emerged all spruced up, her mouth set to a grumble though there was peace in her eyes.

Joy was still sitting on the bed, brooding.

"Wat a way di gyal quick fi puff up puff up, ee? Anybaddy tell yu a truth yu don' want hear and yu puff up gone to bed." She looked at herself in the mirror. "Well, and is how me look? Me can show me face?"

"Course you can," said Joy, submitting.

"Church me go, is white and black go deh. Me don' like di black church dem. People dem too unmannarsable. Anyhow me haffi go. Won' do to turn up late mek di ole white woman dem whisper, "typical!" Me did hear dem say it once, yu know, when a black sister come in late. And when dem see seh me did hear it, dem put on one friendly smile. Me just cut me eye[42] and listen to di preacher, yaa. One other time, one white woman talk how she shame her daughter go and get one pitni fi one black man. Me want know wat she got fi shame 'bout. Wish a black man wudda brok inna her house and breed her."

"Mama!"

"Wat yu deh *mama!* 'bout? Di woman is a walking hypocrite. Talk 'bout shame she shame when is jealous she jealous. Di whole lot a dem! How dem kooshy-kooshy and carry on wid di mix pitni dem, how dem sweet and how dem cute. You just let dem same pitni grow up, and see if dem don't sing annadda song. Me no have no time fi dem. But stop! Me deh stan an yap. Me gone."

---

[42]*cut me eye* = give them a nasty look

"You look nice. See you when you get back."

"Yes yes," she said, already on her way down the stairs. "Me not here."

Joy took the purse in her hand. Opened it. And closed it. Opened it. Let the money jingle. Closed it. It wasn't so ugly, after all.

She had two pounds thirty-five; three fifty pees, six ten pees, four five pees, one twopence and three one pees. And that was supposed to last for the whole weekend. Joy closed her eyes and sighed. She was tempted to have a look under Amy's bed for a few stray pennies. Caught herself almost beginning to bend at the knees... She snapped her purse to.

There were supermarkets. And there were supermarkets. Just like there was ugly and there was *h*ugly. There were always more women than men in the supermarkets. Joy could look at a woman; at her clothes, her shoes, the type of rings on her finger, and could tell you where she shopped. She'd done her homework, knew the little essentials. After her first trip to the shops with her first five pounds back then, Joy had carried her half empty plastic bag back home, sober to the world and its ways. There were those who simply loaded their trolleys as if there was no tomorrow, not even troubling themselves to look at the price. Those whose trolleys were filled with all the last-minute goods with their unmistakable *Half-Price!* in red stickered on. The young mothers who were frustrated and impatient, always throwing a look around them for their children, always snarling, "You put that back!" The old, some with buttons missing and stockings fallen down, shuffling along the aisles with their baskets and leaving behind them the rank smell of evaporated urine, they would check the items against the bill one by one because they couldn't keep up with the speed of the cashier's fingers and the digital till was so hard to read. Joy hooked the two middle fingers of her right hand through the handle of her Co-op bag, passed Tesco's, Sainsbury's, she moved out of the way for a couple from Marks & Spencer's where the plastic bags were loaded into the car and driven home.

She would treat herself to a take-away on Sunday. Why should she have to be huddling in her room over a can of cold baked beans and a few doughnuts bought half an hour before closing cos then they were half price? Why, when them downstairs were tucking into rice and peas and chicken, drinking pineapple juice with sweet milk and a dash of brandy? That Sunday dinner which would sneak up the stairs, under the gap beneath the bedroom door, sometimes she'd be so hungry… Once, Joy had gone down to the toilet and seen the kitchen and dining room door open. On purpose. That's when she started timing her meals with theirs. Well, they could stuff their rice and peas and chicken. Who wants to eat the same food every weekend, anyway? She was going to go out and get herself a Chinese.

40

Gertrude tiptoed back to her room, excited-to-bursting. Mrs Burke could say what she wanted, Gertrude and Winston were old enough to do what they liked. And they were doing it. Her mind on the whistling man on his way back to his cabin, she touched her ear, and instantly felt his hot breath steaming out over her. Rolled a nipple, and there were his teeth; biting, teasing. Cupped a breast, and he sucked hungrily on her and grunted like an animal. Felt her lips, and his manhood brushed her face, eased her mouth open, and entered.

"Me got a plan. Mek yu and me put we monni togedda an go a Hinglan."

"Hinglan? Is wha me want do a Hinglan?"

"Hinglan, man! Plenty plenty work a Hinglan. Plenty work mean whole heapa monni. Know a black woman is a sister in a hospital in Hinglan. Even di white people dem haffi do wat she tell dem..."

Gertrude's eyes searched his face for truths. "Yu too lie!"

"Tink is lie me deh tell? Me hear there is nuff nuff black nurse inna Hinglan. And yu no need no brown skin and long hair, neither."

"Is true?" she almost whispered.

"Twenty-four carat, man." He could feel her stiffening up for an orgasm, so he removed his fingers and wiped them discreetly on his leg. "Think about it, nuh?" he said, reaching down for his can of beer.

"Come, man," she pleaded. "Finish me up."

He let the warm beer in through his smile.

"Come, Winstan man, finish me up," Gertrude pleaded.

"Me fi finish yu up?" he tortured.

"Finish me up!" she ordered, reaching down and holding onto him firmly.

Well, Winston said, getting back to the story about his mama's hiding places for her money, di last place him madda cudda think of fi hide her money was inna her drawers, an when him farda couldn't find it, him tear off her clothes and di money drop outta her baggy. Him did pick up di money and say it can smell like fish or cabbage him still gwine spend it. "And dat b'lang to me too," him did say, and pull her down to di floor an jook her till she cry eye-water.

"Yu can cry eye-water?"
She rolled him onto his back and straddled him. "What mek yu no find out?"

She couldn't sleep. Either it was Winston grinding into her, or it was the vision of herself in a crisp blue uniform walking along disinfected halls, her clipboard tight against her chest as she hurried her way to a needy patient to administer some care. Was it true? She sprang from her bed, dug out her money-tin from its hiding place. Sat at the table. Lit a candle. Two-hundred and forty dollars. She split it and hid half in the hem of the curtain. From tomorrow she would try to save every single cent, even if she had to starve herself to do so. She had a plan. She was going to England. Gertrude stretched her arms wide and spun a full circle like she did when she was a child, then hopped into the bed. This was the happiest day of her life!

All day she had been waiting for an opportunity to go down to the kitchen and boil a kettle of water. Were they doing it on purpose, staying in the kitchen so she couldn't come down and eat? The gnawing in her sides robbed her of her peace. She could neither read nor sleep; had to distract it somehow, the hunger, the way one does a crying baby by clapping one's hands, by dangling some object before its protesting eyes, bulbs slid down her chin and... *gone*, crushed by a swift movement of the back of the hand, propelled by shame and anger. She snorted the liquid back and it seemed to go straight up to her head and jump out her eyes again, like children on a slide. A ring. A ring a roses. A pocket full a posies. A tish you. A tish you. We all fall - that is when she heard it, this something that came to her, held her close, unbuttoned its blouse and gave her the breast, saying, "Don't be ashamed." And her pride, it was forced to bow its head in acquiescence and this act alone caused the greatest pain.

It was dark when she woke up. Amy was snoring, so Joy knew it to be late. She retrieved her Pot-Noodle from the back of the wardrobe and tiptoed downstairs. Waiting for the kettle to boil – wouldn't take more than a minute or two - she removed the tin-foil cover and tried to break up the unappetising brown mass stuck to the bottom of the container. On a shelf above her head was that tacky souvenir Amy had brought back from a school outing to the seaside; a glass mug with *The World's Best Mum* tattooed on the front, but Joy knew that Amy had probably only bought it because it was cheap and that way she could spend the extra on other things for herself. She turned on the light to the dining room, where she hadn't been for such a long time now. It still smelled of the curry they had had for dinner. She went to the living room. The *lounge*, she smiled, where she felt like a stranger, looking at the chairs they sat in, the tv they watched... She turned the light out. Returned to the kitchen where the clock tocked a quarter past twelve. She burned her tongue wolving that Pot-Noodle down. At last, food in her belly. Flick - the light was off.

Amy had closed her eyes the minute she heard Joy's hand on the doorknob; closed her eyes and pulled the covers up way over her face. Why did she jump in her bed as if someone had frightened her? And why did she have to get up and turn on the light when she knew Amy was sleeping? She heard Joy get some paper. Was she writing, or something? Couldn't it wait until the morning? Joy hadn't written for ages, not since that letter and Amy had had a look, but she hadn't found any more shoeboxes even if her mother didn't believe her. What could she possibly have to write right now that couldn't wait till the morning? Then she heard Joy scrunch the paper up and start again. Scrunch the paper up and start again. Fa goodness' sake, Amy grumbled under the cover. Then the wardrobe was pulled from against the wall. Amy heard it dragging on the carpet. Heard Joy get something out. Those must be his letters! Re-activating the memory of the one she had read made Amy feel all prickly, she wasn't much younger than Joy, anyway. Only three years… The sound of paper ripping filled the room. Letter. After letter. After letter; scooped up and put in a plastic bag, where they rustled like leaves. Was that her crying? It frightened her. She wished she hadn't heard it, squeezed her eyes shut. Played dead. If only she'd had her own bedroom, she wouldn't've heard any of this. Joy was crying and that meant trouble. She knew what it meant, alright. Mother had won.

>A ring a ring a roses
>A pocket full a posies
>A tish you, a tish you
>We all fall -
>Down!

"Lard in heaven have mercy!" grandma clutched at her heart as she stumbled out of the room. Shouting downstairs. Robert and Amy were told to go. Go out and play until dinner ready. Stay in the front yard! Don't go off anywhere! Grandma turned on Gertrude.

What in heaven's name was going on in this house?
Gertrude said the girl too renk and think seh she is a woman. *Me is di only woman in dis house and me mean fi prove it*, only a sudden hot pain in her face sent her careering back to a chair and when she looked up, grandma's hand was raised to deliver a second blow.

"Is wat foolishniss yu talking inna me ears? She is yu *darta*!"

Mother held her cheek and looked the other way.

"Yu got no right! She is yu *darta*! Yu darta, yu hear me, yu *darta*!"

Gertrude, sensing that grandma was set on saying more, braced herself.

"An you listen to me - "
and as grandma's face fought to control the quivers, Winston bounced with his I'm-in-a-good-mood springstep in through the front door, said cheerfully, "Marning, Missis Simit!" until she threw him a look and he fell silent, waiting for a cue from his wife. Grandma spun back to Gertrude.

"No matter how a pitni renk don' nobaddy got di right..." and the quivers took over completely. "Lard in heaven have mercy." And the tears would not stop.

Winston eased his way out of the room, backwards. His toes whispered up the stairs as his thoughts grew bitter at the good mood they had stolen. Woman! He cursed behind his teeth.

Gertude watched him slink away, and there was hatred in her eyes.

"Don't yu know yu Scriptcha? Don't yu know 'bout Matthew 7:12? Come, say it to me!"

Gertrude looked at her hands. She hated shows.

Grandma stormed over to her and yanked her face up. "Say it to me!"

Gertrude kept her eyes down.

"Yu mean fi say yu don't know de word a di Lord, Gertie? Yu don't know the *word* a di *L-a-r-d*? Yu think you one own di child? Dat is not your child, yu hear wat me saying to yu? Is di child a de L-a-r-d! Is not a piece a property, is di child a di Lord, and Jesus said, Suffer di likkle children to come to me and forbid dem not, for of such is de kingdom of God! A-men!" She fell into the chair and wept. "Gertie, is what sarta *wotless* madda dat, mash up her own child? Yu seem to figget yu own experience, how yu own madda do yu and how she hurt yu up. How yu don't speak not one word to her from dat day to dis. Matthew 7:12. You look it up. You look it up, yu hear me."

Gertrude had never seen grandmother cry, even now she did not see for she kept her eyes fixed on the back of her hands. Only, her ears, how to close them? How to lock out that hurt battering at the door? She clenched her teeth, setting her full weight against the wood, letting her shoulder slip into the polished bowl it had moulded over the years, there, above the latch, somewhat to the right. The house was full. No room. No room for no more pain. Her ears were full, her throat, dry. Gertrude tried to swallow. How could she explain. How? This was not what she had wanted. She had not thought that it would have come to this. Things had a way of - but she couldn't explain.

She had heard the shouting. Now she could hear the slow heavy foot on the stairs.

"Joy?"
She sat with her back to the door, looking out of the window.
"Yes, mama?"
"Turn round and look wen me talking to yu!" grandma ordered.
She did as she was told.
But grandma could not look at her. She looked instead past Joy's bony shoulders out the window at the garden. "Come down and eat a likkle dinner."
Joy's eyes fixed themselves on the wasted hands in her lap. "I'm not hungry."
"Me not asking yu if yu hungry! Me telling yu fi come downstairs and eat a likkle dinner!"
"I don't feel like it," and to her outrage, beads of water formed in her eyes and threatened to fall.
"Child!" Grandma marched into the room and grabbed her by the wrist. Dragged Joy out of the room and she flew behind her grandma down the stairs like a fragile paper kite.
Rice and peas and chicken. Pineapple juice with sweet milk and a dash of brandy. Grandma slapped the plate on the table in front of Joy. Everyone stared into their own plate. This was the first time in a week that she had seen her mother. The first time in... it seemed to her, months... that she had sat down to a meal with her family.
"For what we are about to receive may de Lord make us truly grateful, amen." Grandma unclasped her hands and opened her eyes.
The family ate in silence.
"Joy, eat!"
"I'm not hungry."
"Me nay ask yu if yu hungry, me tell yu fi *eat*!"
Everyone was chewing slowly but the food would not go down. Joy picked up her knife and fork. So heavy, they seemed.
"By the way, happy birthday," Amy said without looking up from her plate.
"Yes! Happy birthday, Joy," grandma said as she scooped a spoon of rice and peas onto her plate.
"Happy birthday," the other three murmured.

The food stuck to the roof of her mouth. Her cheeks started twitching, uncontrollably, like her eyes did sometimes after she had washed her hair; took on a life of their own and she had no say in the matter.

Do you want to come and play? The see-through beads said they did and joined hands gleefully. Splish! Splish! They hit the rim of the plate and rolled into the gravy.

41

Weeds! They grew so quickly! Gertrude bent down to pull them out. Placed the flowers in their stand. Returned to the bench on the other side of the path. Not many there today. The weather, she supposed. On a nice day like this, people had other things to do. But she was there. She had come and pulled the weeds and placed new flowers. Winston refused to. Amy and Robert didn't like to. She knew grandma came more often but neither of them spoke about it.

She would have been seventeen today... Two years already... Gertrude had dropped an envelope in and the others each a handful of earth. Only she and Amy knew what was in it. The burden of the secret was destined to ruin all understanding between the two. Amy had found the paper on the bed. "You win." And one pound seventy-five; two fifty pees, five ten pees, four five pees, one twopence. And three one pees. Gertrude had broken out into a panic and searched the house. Then two policemen had come. A man and a woman. When Gertrude opened the door, they took off their hats. Mrs Simon? Mrs *Gertrude* Simon? They said they had come as quickly as they could. From the underground...

May we come in?

That was two years ago. Gertrude looked older, thinner now. She had been too fat in the first place. If only her hair hadn't fallen out... Amy was giving her grounds for worry. She was growing all sneaky and secretive. You couldn't ask her anything anymore. Gertrude wondered... no. She didn't want to know about it. The less said, the better. She looked about her, at the flowers, at the grass. At the stones. Hers was one of the better ones. Gertrude had chosen it. Winston had first seen it planted and said he would have chosen another one, how much she pay for it? Gertrude had shut him up with her eyes.

Bells chimed somewhere behind her off to the right. She looked at her watch. My goodness! It was midday already! She got to her feet. She would be late for work. Work, if that's what you could call it, and she held her bag against her breast, clipboard-fashion, dreaming. If they asked, she would say she had run late at the doctor's and scurry past them to her place on the conveyor belt. No time to go home and change. She would have to stick it out in these shoes unless the foreman gave her the go-ahead to go down to Stocks and sign out a pair of industrial shoes just for the day, which he wasn't likely to because he had taken a dislike to her from the very beginning and thought she thought herself better than the rest. She had earned herself the nickname the Coon of Sheba though she knew nothing of it, and wouldn't have cared. Who were they, anyway? They didn't know the first thing about her. Her talent. Her dreams. Her sacrifice. Her pain... She went over to the flowers once more, bent down, eased out a rose and pinned it to her cardigan; a red rose, smooth and powdery to the touch. A tight, juicy bud of a thing, straight of spine, de-thorned, its petals closed into a fist of potential. Still, it would not outlive the day. What with the heat. And it getting no water, poor little mite. She took one last look around her, then departed, the sun on her back as she headed for the main gates. Warming her, before its inevitable downhill. The weather, it was really far too nice.

Stand up sit down keep moving...

42

Martha Brae, October --, 19--

Dear Rose,

I'm sure everything in England is going fine for you. As soon as I open your letter and parcel, I sit down to write and tell you thank you, that Marlene and Leroy overjoy with the things you send them. You know me don't have a good head like you, and me is not someone love pen and paper, so I make it short. Marlene draw this little picture for you. She say you must make sure you keep it because when she come to England she is going to look and see if you still got it. The child cheeky as a shame.
You say everything is fine and I believe you, but me also hear bad story them from other people. I hear how black people can't go out at night and have to fear the skinhead them like the blacks in the fifties did afraid of the Teddy Boys. But because you don't go out so much you probably don't get to hear this. And other people talk how difficult it is to get a job or somewhere to live because the white people them prejudice and want to squash you up in a cooby like a chicken. I know you doing alright but I don't know if I could pick up myself go to a country where people look down at me. Is enough that them behave like that right here in Jamaica without you go abroad for the same treatment and get spit on even more. The black sometimes as bad as the white people them and ignorance spread out all over the world.
We talking about white. Me hear you have a white boyfriend. Is true or is not true? You don't have to hide it from me. Me hear him is one old old white man you meet at the bus-stop and him pay you fare everywhere you want to go in London. Him was one chaufur, or how you call it, and use to drive the big politician you see in the television up and down the country. Is true? Me also

hear him and Richard is best friend. Is how come you don't tell me the half of what happening over there, Rose? Is how come I have to find out everything second hand? People them asking me if me know this and if me know that, I must know because my good friend in England. I don't know what to say and I don't know what to believe when the people them talk. Don't you think it's time for you to put me in the picture?

It look like I am going to have another child next year. I don't need no doctor to tell me I'm nine weeks pregnant. I don't tell nobody - them will see for themselves in time. Glad him gone. Me did chase him out. Him too little and nasty. One more mouth to feed, I would like to know what the Lord have in mind for me? You know what it say in the Bible, to them who got shall be given and from them who don't have shall be taken away. Well at least that was a piece of clever thinking you did going to England. Now you move out of the one camp into the other while me still sitting right there as always with no way of getting out. Maybe me fix up myself with one a them Hinglanman[43] come back to J.A. and got a little something in him pocket. Who knows, such a nice girl like me (smile).

Well, this was just a thank you letter and to give you my little piece of news. Take care of yourself and don't forget that I'm waiting for explanations.

Your friend,

Junie.

---

[43] *Hinglanman* = Jamaican from England

43

Rose jumped out of her orange tailored suit into her day-to-day clothes. (Smile).

What a stir she had caused with that outfit today. The cleaning girls kept asking her who the lucky fellow was, but Rose had merely laughed and explained that she had a job interview to go to afterwards. When the first secretary, come in earlier to make some private calls at the company's expense, caught sight of what Rose had on under that apron, she merely sniffed, arched her eyebrows, then bickered about specks of dust that only her red-eye[44] could see.

And, of course, there was Jack. (Smile). She nay even like him, she told herself.

"Rose?" Miss Brown called out as Rose was making her way up the stairs at the end of the day's work; Rose, who should have attended her typing classes that evening, but the whole day had weighed upon her shoulders like an oppressive cold and robbed her of her concentration. It was all she could do to smile weakly at jokes where the others roared, and when it came to lunch-time, she just si' down look at di plate a food. An hour and a half peng-peng-penging on a typewriter? Not today. Dissipated as she was, she would only end up making silly mistakes and going home frustrated.

"Rose? Me got a visitor would like to have a word wid you..." mouthed Miss Brown, significantly. Her eyes kept darting back to her front door.

"Is who it is?"

"Richaad." She formed the name with her lips but couldn't bring herself to animate it with her voice. "Come, nuh?"

---

[44] *red-eye* = jealous and want what other people dem have

Long, long silence; long enough to take you time to climb all the way up to the cooby read Junie letter three time change you clothes come back.

"Is how him find out where me live?"

"Im come fi visit me an tell me seh him did see yu - what mek yu never tell me she yu did see him?"

"Me got *notting* to say to him. Notting!" she turned to continue up the stairs.

"Rose! Rose Thompson!" Miss Brown flew up the stairs after her. "But kuya! Yu seem to figget is whose house yu deh live in."

Rose span round. Retaliated. "Miss Brown…"
(You know when people speak slowly like that…?) The rage she sought to contain within her chest spat from her eyes.

"Seem to me *you* seem to forget seh me paying for the cupboard me deh live in."

"Oh, is a cupboard?" Miss Brown spluttered, not expecting any back-chat. "A cupboard? What mek yu no go straight and say is a shoebox!" Her bottom lip started to tremble. "And when it don't suit yu," she shouted up at Rose's back marching up the stairs paying her, Miss B., who had been so welcoming, so generous, no mind, "And when it don't suit yu," she shouted up again, stabbing her finger in Rose's direction, "what mek yu no go look someweh else? Well, as from tomorrow, you go look someweh else fi stay." She crossed her arms resolutely under her bosom. "Me no want no facety gyal inna me house deh cuss me down. You get up bright and early tomorrow marning go look somweh else fi stay, yu hear me?"

Rose no longer hear her. She already slam the door fling herself down on the bed grab up Junie letter rip it up.

44

"Wot's up, Rich, you walking around wiv a face like a bleedin' wet Sunday!" Had he already forgotten the fun they had had at Linford's and Lucy's? No, *juicy* Lucy's? That must've been the best curry he could ever expect to eat in his lifetime. He thought he was going to burst. The three men had played dominoes, had listened to records. Lucy just sat there laughing and kept on offering them food and drink; red stripe, and after dinner, all sorts of little crunchy snacks in their party-Susan. All so generous and natural, like. They seemed to laugh the whole evening, so why Richard was now moping around with a face like that was something that needed explaining.

"Hey, Rich!"

"Cho man, leff me alone." Richard brushed him aside. "Me no a no time fi yu right now." He strode out of the locker room on his way home.

"Ayup!" Jack blinked, "Who's rattled his cage, that's wot I'd like to know!"

Nobody laughed.

"Must be his time o' the month, wot you reckon, Bob?"

But Robert shrugged his shoulders, staying out of it. As you like, thought Jack, who wasn't having any of them spoiling his good mood. When he thought about the coming Sunday... his face transformed into a big smile. I can put up with anything, he sauntered over to his locker. Even you having your time of the month. But when he opened his locker door, a bunch of yellow bananas he hadn't put there, sheathed in white paper, tumbled past the bench and onto the floor. He removed the elastic band to read the attached note: *Lunch-time at the zoo*, it read. *Go and feed your ape friends*. Signed: *see no evil, hear no evil, speak no evil.*

Jack looked around but no-one seemed to have noticed. He put the bananas in his bag on his way upstairs to clock out. Smile.

"Hello love, I'm home." He hung his jacket up on his peg in the hallway.
"Hello love, I'm in the sitting-room."
Monica sat in front of the television, smoking.
They kissed.
Those days at Beverly's had done Monica good. She had regained a sense of herself. Bev had let her keep the dress, the sandals and the lipstick. For memory's sake. Anyhow, Monica knew now that she still had it in her; knew that a man would indeed look at her twice, and not necessarily her face only, either. That gave her the strength for another round of her marriage with Jack. If both were to put a little effort in, what a difference that would make; she fixed her skirt and put her feet up as soon as she heard his key in the lock.
Him: Where're the kids?
Her: Your mum's got em for the evening.
Him: Why's at?
Inner voice: She's past her prime. She really has let herself go. Doesn't do anything with her hair anymore. Doesn't make herself up. She's put on loads of weight…
Her: Oh, she wanted to and they wanted to. Gives us the chance to 'ave a little time on our own once in a while...
But Jack was looking at what was on telly. *Crossroads* was just finishing.
Her: Someone lost ten quid in the cinema last night. Ten bloody quid!
Him: You're joking! Anyone find it?
Her (smirking): I bet… *(picks a piece of fluff from her skirt. Flicks it to the floor.)*
Normally she was the one who had to do the listening when Jack came home worn out, he'd say, and tell her who had been larking around, or which foremen were getting on his wick. Nina and Ben liked to tell their stuff themselves, had already told her off once for pinching their news, so it meant that she didn't have so much to share when he came home from work. So today, she

baubled her bit of news in front of his eyes for as long as she could.

Her: I did... (*lets the words slip out as though they mean nothing.*)

Him (bolting up in his seat): You! You! You didn't... did you -

Her: What the bloody 'ell'd you've done?

Monica sat back and crossed her legs as though he really *was* making a lot of fuss about nothing, and watched a freckly-faced kid in yellow do silly things with his eyes cos he was so mad about Bird's™ custard.

Her: Course I bleedin' kept it! You hand it in, they only pocket it for themselves, anyway.

She sighed; all this talking was getting to be too much for her.

Him: Wooo! Monica! Ten quid! (*Reaching over to hug his wife*) You found ten bleedin' quid!

He still couldn't believe it.

Him: Give us a kiss!

Her (complying, tutting): You been real perky these last few days. Like the cat that's got the cream. Anyfing you're not telling me about?

She raised an eyebrow. But it was nice to have him hug her and kiss her spontaneously like that.

Him: Don't be so daft, who'd be foolish enough to want me?

Her: Well, thank you very much!

He got up and switched the telly over to BBC.

Him: Ten quid, I dunno...

Her: We got somefing nice for dinner; steak, chips and peas... Monica slid her feet down to the carpet and ran her fingers through her hair for something to do.

Her: N'after that I thought, well, I thought we might take a bath together n 'ave an early night...

Him: And the kids?

Her: Call your mum n tell 'er to keep em for the night...

Holding hands. So they missed the nature program in progress on the BBC, and didn't see the 'speeded-up' version of them rather luscious-looking tropical orchids bursting from their buds and palpitating into glorious, technicoloured life.

Monica lay on her back, her hair still wet, waiting, her Jack still in the bathroom combing his hair. His mind on Emily. What would it be like, this Sunday? Would she turn up? Course she'd turn up! She'd come nicely dressed like she was the other day, with her hair all styled and her fingernails painted and they'd walk up and down and laugh with each other. He could put on that fancy tie Rich had brought him. And his new second-hand jacket, the one she hadn't taken any notice of that last time. Where should he take her? He couldn't be going anywhere where anyone might recognise him, if Monica got wind of this there'd be hell to pay. Take her over to West London, to one of them fancy pubs? Buy her a glass of wine? Something medium-dry, and a little expensive? Maybe they could go for a walk through Hyde Park and he'd buy her an ice-cream, he knew what, he could take her to one of the London markets, that'd be nice. Loads of people brushing shoulders with each other, hunting for bargains. He might even splash out on a trip down the Thames, hey, he bet she hadn't done anything like that yet! He would get to take her by the elbow and lead her on board. I'll take a vodka and lime. And a glass of medium-dry for my lady friend, Jack grinned into the mirror. They might even go somewhere quiet and she might even let him put his hand up her skirt... no, Jack my boy, that'd spoil things. No point in rushing things, is there? A bird in the hand, and all that. Right? Yet the thought gave him an instant erection that propped itself up to meet his rather curious smile. Anyhow, Sunday was still two long days away... and there were other things he supposed he ought to get over and done with.

Right, Jack took a deep breath and stepped out of the bathroom. Time to face the wife.

"Well at long last!" Monica sighed, in her mauve négligé that stopped just before the knees, the one which she would only put on for special occasions like when she had to go to hospital. "I thought you'd escaped out the window and shinnied down the drainpipe!" She outed her cigarette.

"You can be really daft, you can!" he forced a laugh. What with all that food and that hot bath, all Jack really wanted was a good night's sleep but that was out of the question he guessed, wasn't it? And he had better jump to it, too, before his friend down there -

"Look what I got 'ere for you..."

He spread his legs in front of her. Closed his eyes and wished himself in some dark corner of Hyde Park with his fancy tie on...

Jack didn't always like it, but he seemed to want her to do it this time. Oh well, get on with it, girl, show a bit more interest, after all, it was her bright idea, wunnit? She found herself thinking of Beverly of all people. As if by magic, Monica wasn't Monica anymore, but Moni, in her black dress and gold sandals, sitting at the bar. Being driven back to Bev's place. She was Moni with that saucy smile as she watched him make himself comfy on the sofa and feel for his flies. Lipstick, Monica told herself as she dragged herself to the edge of the bed and pushed her hair out the way. It's just lipstick...

45

Whistling as he wound his way through the estate, Jack, in his faded T-shirt and his denim jacket, noticed what a mild night it was, warm even. He had had a smashing week. He would be seeing her tomorrow. He felt like a new man. He *was* a new man. That was all he had needed, really - a lucky break. Fed up to the back teeth with his grimy, soddy life, he was. A little peace. One person in the world who didn't piss you off, one person who thought you were something worth having. He lightfooted a flight of stairs, turned the corner…
Three ugly-looking youths in balaclavas. Arms folded across their chests, legs spread wide apart.
    Silence.
    "Erm, wotchya, mates."
    Silence.
He couldn't outrun these apes, that was for sure. Why the hell didn't they just mug him and piss off? He made as if to continue walking.
    All three step forward in unison.
    "Come on, mates. Wot you after?"
Through the slits of their eyes stream enough hatred for Jack to begin to feel well and truly uncomfortable.
    "If you think I'm afraid of you apes, you've got a next thing coming."
Boys trying to be men, he thought. That's precisely why he didn't want Ben growing up in these parts.
    "You're a dead man, nigger lover."
    Something in him went cold and sank.
Two of them grabbed him. Bashed him against the wall. The third, the gum-chewer, strutted over, taking his time.
    "You're a dead man, nigger lover…"
He threw his best punch below Jack's ribcage.

Jack let out a grunt as he collapsed to the floor, defenceless as they kicked his body around like an old tin can, aiming at his stomach, his groin, another at his back, the other at his head.

"Pick him up!"

A soggy squelch as his limp body makes contact with the stone, and a flash of silver as the ring-leader flicks open his pen-knife.

"Hey, leave it out!" one said, frightened.

"You shut the fuck up! Or you're next!"

This-wasn't-part-of-the-plan…

"Oh, Christ!" Jack closed his eyes…

He could hear their heavy boots thunder down the alleyways: Sieg heil! Sieg heil! Sieg heil! they chanted, one voice prominent above the others.

And then, there was something... like a woman screaming...

46

Rose had not slept at all at all at all well last night, in fact she hadn't had a moment's peace since she had agreed to meet him. She wished she hadn't, but then... She dressed slowly, putting on her things for church. For all she knew, he was probably married and got children. She wouldn't go! She would not go and that would be the end of it. She would have to find another route to get home or maybe try and find an evening cleaning job instead. What on earth would they have to say to each other? She would say she had a headache and leave. What if somebody saw them together? Well, let them look! Was she a pitni? Is fi who business?

"Cho man, him is a blasted nuisance!"
She busied out and locked her door, but opened it again immediately, impatiently, for she had forgotten her Bible. Rose slip the Scripture into her handbag. In her hurry, she knock over Marlene and Leroy. Pick them up brush them off put them back on her bedside table.

On a Sunday of all days. She locked the door and irritated her way out of the house into the mild, encouraging October morning.

The facts:

Emily Thompson had resolved to wait no longer than ten minutes. The weather had taken a turn, and her outfit was a touch out of place for the fat clouds ganging up to hurtle across the sky. Ten minutes, she had said. Nor had she had the foresight to take an umbrella with her. A sudden chill began to seep into her through her toes. Over an hour she ended up waiting, at the usual stop, before she stretch out her hand stop the next bus that come along as the first raindrops started blotting the pavement. She handed over her fare without a word, her eyes fixed on her ringless fingers.

We will all be merry and bright!

The truth:

from the shoebox…

Anon

Where is my place in this world?
A home,
a face
chiselled in a name,
indelible,
that I may claim for my own?

Borrowed,
begged, everything I have but my fear
to
leave
unnoticed, the
soles of my thoughts trampled by indifference,
the surface unrippled
by the tiptoes of my parting
breath,
mirror to the vacuity of the aspirations
whispered through fingers
so willing to take, to
give
so much;
gingered to paralysis by a search for beauty that
never ends in...

where is my stove?
Under a merciful slab of stone...

Ad Infinitum

If thy eye offend thee
Pluck it out

Or close it -

To the pain

Of my solitude...

Of my body's weeping
Wilting in the absence
Of compassion in warm skin

To clothe me

Wrapped up and whisked away

From a misery

I lack the
Strength
To rectify

Deny it -

Close those eyes

And carry on

Scrunch that pain

To a fistful of irrelevance

To a pinch of salt
Over the shoulder –

Twist! And

Gone...

Dispersed behind
In shards of glass

As I carry on –

An intermittent
Glance

At their twinkling

That once contained my happiness:

A redolent mess
Seasoning my resolve to

Carry on?

Zaubermann,
Whereto, once the magic has flown?

From Marlene with love…

Laughter

Laughter – what a funny sound,
In my head it goes round and round.
It makes me so happy,
When suddenly it gets snappy.
And it's gone!!!
Okay, I started fiddling
Soon I was giggling.
Quarter past,
How long is it going to last?
A bang, someone fell off the chair.
Somewhere else you can hear people say:
"It's not fair!"
Now, I was even more amused,
Funny words came out of my mouth, words I never used.
I laughed and laughed!
Thinking of a chocolate eating sheep
A short giggle and I fell asleep!

The whole truth:

"Leroy," Rose bent down to him, "me gwine leave yu likkle bit. Behave yusself and be good to yu sista, yu hear me?"

And nothing but the truth:

Cato: joins RAF when he is eighteen. He is sent to the Falklands, but after Margaret Thatcher had sorted out the Argentinians, so there was no real danger for him. Later, he works for the London Underground and buys a small house in Walthamstow. He never marries. He is saving up for his first trip back to Jamaica.

Goneril and Walter: return to Jamaica as pensioners. They lead silent, distal lives that breathe upon each other now and then. Walter contracts cancer of the prostate gland and returns to the UK for treatment, accompanied by his loving wife.

Tété: finishes school, comes to the UK in the 1950s. Works in a factory in SW14 till her retirement. When she have the fare and go to the airport to pick up her children, is two big smaddy deh tan up deh… She marries a Jamaican, unwilling to embark upon any further adventures with the English. If you ask her about her life she will say she satisfy.

Joy: follows the light.

Richard: marries an older woman and lives to regret the day. Jackass, no know seh a bird in di hand worth two in di bush.

Junie: fulfils her only wish to come and see England one time. She spends a month with Rose and returns home, happy. Rose grateful as a shame for their enduring friendship. Junie say: a two finger yu need fi pick up a flea.

Jack: leaves Monica in 1989. He is living with a Jamaican girl him call Princess, with whom he has a son, Linford Harley Dunbar. Jack and his new sweetheart do not intend to marry, but are saving up hard to buy a house.

Miss B: her name Pearl. She an Rose still fren.

Carmen: turn into a nice young lady. She is currently studying French at Warwick University.

Uncle Roy: the last I saw of Uncle Roy was just before him die. "Belief can kill and belief can cure. Well, I believe it's time to move on, for this life is not a conclusion." When I embraced him, unable to find the right words for a fitting adieu, he shrank back, unaccustomed to such a show of affection. Uncle Roy bequeathed me wise words on fidelity though he must have known that I knew of his thousand women. An old man of shaky voice, yet strength clung to his limbs like the babe to the mother's hem. Maybe he would be a different young man today. Not cause a woman so much pain. This first intimacy, this first philosophical ointment, although he had known me since my birth, and I will forever love him for it; for opening the wardrobe so that I may feel the fabric of his life brush my soul.

Uncle Roy took his last breath in 2004 at St Thomas' Hospital, tired of life without physical or mental mobility, and weighing a mere 42kg the day he passed on. In his will he had stipulated his wish to be cremated. Caused a scandal in the family. He who laughs last laughs best.

All the other characters are, to the best of my knowledge, in health and strength; they all lived happily ever after.

Apart from Sally. Sally pass on this long time now and sitting up there on her pearly cloud deh give Uncle Roy a piece of her mind.

Reader reviews

'Marvellous!' *Magda K., Warsaw, Poland*

'The most beautiful writing I have ever read.' *Christiane S., France*

'Joan Barbara Simon transforms something as mundane as two people meeting at the bus-stop (Rose and Jack) into a 'family fairy tale', a modern classic, in which she reveals her deep understanding and compassion for Mankind. Brilliant depiction of the British working class! Jack Dunbar, a white docklands worker with a soft spot for Jamaican lingo, mates, cooking and one particular Jamaican woman, the heroine, Rose. I still can't make up my mind whether I want to punch him in the face or buy him a beer. It's a pity he never gets to meet Uncle Roy, the protagonist's uncle-of-sorts, who knows a thing or two about food and women himself, although his greatest love seems to be for getting hold of the wrong end of British politics. Simon has been described as a wordsmith par excellence. Rightly so! Intelligent, humorous, tragic and sensual. Contemporary British literature at its best.' *Azma A., London, UK*

Joan Barbara Simon
Photo copyright © 2008, Pia Bursch

Teacher, lecturer, researcher, poetess, songwriter and novelist. Dr Joan Barbara Simon divides her time between researching chidren's plurilingual literacy development and writing fiction. Having obtained her first Ph.D. in educational studies, she hopes to complete a further doctoral thesis in creative writing in the near future.

Lightning Source UK Ltd.
Milton Keynes UK
UKHW011811311019
352661UK00001B/47/P

9 781906 558680